Tarra Khash: Hrossak!

TOR BOOKS BY BRIAN LUMLEY

THE NECROSCOPE® SERIES

THE TITUS CROW SERIES

THE PSYCHOMECH TRILOGY

OTHER NOVELS

SHORT STORY COLLECTIONS

Tarra Khash: Hrossak!

TALES OF THE PRIMAL LAND, VOLUME 2

BRIAN LUMLEY

A TOM DOHERTY ASSOCIATES BOOK
NEW YORK

TARRA KHASH: HROSSAK!

Copyright © 1991 by Brian Lumley

Previously published in 1991, by Headline Book Publishing, PLC

Map by Dave Kendall

A Tor Book
Published by Tom Doherty Associates, LLC
175 Fifth Avenue
New York, NY 10010

www.tor.com

ISBN 0-765-31075-9
EAN 978-0-765-31075-0

First Tor Edition: April 2006

Printed in the United States of America

0 9 8 7 6 5 4 3 2 1

FOR ANYONE WHO EVER DWELLED
IN AN IMAGINARY LAND

CONTENTS

ACKNOWLEDGMENTS

My thanks to Francesco Cova, and especially to Paul Ganley of Weirdbook Press. With the exception of "Told in the Desert," which first appeared in the Italian magazine, *Kadath*, all of the stories in this volume were first published in *Weirdbook* and one other Weirdbook Press publication.

THEEM'HDRA
The Primal Continent

The Chill Sea

Here Be
Monsters

Reef of Great Whales

Teeth of Yib

Mammoth
Plains

Greater Mar

Hjarpon
Settlement

Fjörds & Lochs

Ruined Keeps
of The
First Race

River Thand

Great Depths

Inner
Isles

Black
Isle

Unknown
Ocean

M
Of

Thandopolis

Great Roc Pass

N

Secondary Cone(Act

Volcano
Isle

Bhur-Esh

Scrublands

Wood & Grass Lands

Plains

Paps of Mam

Thinhla

S   Southern Ocean

Tarra Khash: Hrossak!

Treasure of the Scarlet Scorpion

I

IN THE COASTAL, tropical forests east of Thinhla, lost amid creeper-cursed and vine-entwined ruins of an ancient city—where orchids took root in crumbling courtyards and shifty-eyed chameleons swayed atop the slumping piles of primal ziggurats—there lay the toppled temple of Ahorra Izz, the scorpion-god, whose stone steps went down to caverns of forbidden treasure beyond all dreams of human avarice. Guarded to east and west by twin rivers no man had ever named, whose steamy banks crept with crocodiles and whose waters teemed with tiny, terrible flesh-eating fishes—and by jungles of hybrid vegetation voracious beyond any appeasement, whose spines and suckers were armed with potent poisons—the place would seem unassailable and the treasure of Ahorra Izz entirely safe from all outsiders . . . And yet—

At least one man had been there, had filled his pockets to brimming with brilliant red gems, and had survived to tell of that hellish hothouse of rotting ruins and vampire vegetation—but only at the expense of his freedom . . .

IT WAS FOUR long years now since Tarra Khash the Hrossak had stumbled half-dead into Thinhla. So thin as to be almost fleshless, full of a delirious fever, in his semiconscious nightmare he had gibbered and moaned of the treasure of the scarlet scorpion. And yet he was lucky, for if the scum of the city had found him in that condition—if his staggering feet had taken him into the city's stews or fleabitten flophouses—then Tarra Khash would certainly have vanished; swiftly and silently removed, food for the great fishes that follow the galleys and split the water dorsally in Thinhla's harbour. As it was, he collapsed outside the walled courtyard of a convent, where dwelled seventeen sweet sisters of mercy whose devotions were to Theem'hdra's benevolent gods and goddesses. And there they found him in the dawn: life all but ebbed from him, a scarlet fortune bursting from his pockets like clots of blood frozen in some cold and alien hell.

For three months they tended and nursed him, returning him to life and flushing from his system poisons which would surely have killed a lesser man; and as the fever went out of him so his strength flowed back, and soon he was able to frown and question and ask for his treasure, that scarlet wealth of rubies wherewith his pockets had been stuffed. And all of this time his presence in the convent remained a secret; because the sisters were what they were, no one questioned the fact that they now paid for certain of their provisions with tiny red rubies. No one, that is, except Nud Annoxin, Thinhla's fattest, richest and most loathsome jewel-merchant.

Such was Nud Annoxin's interest that he set a spy to

watch over the convent day and night; and when at long last Tarra Khash took his leave of the place and found himself a proper lodge in the city, then the secret watcher reported that occurrence to his fat and offensive master. Also the fact that Tarra Khash appeared to pay his way with rubies of a rare and flawless beauty . . .

Now the Hrossak was not a subtle man; little more than a barbarian, as were all the men of the steppes beyond the River Luhr, he was big, blunt, occasionally brutal, but above all, open as a book with its covers laid back. Another man endowed with Tarra's wealth might have tried to keep his secret hid, might have purchased a large property and employed hirelings to guard him and hoard both. But Hrossaks believed in living and few men of the steppes would willingly pen themselves, to which general rule Tarra was no exception. Now that his health was returned to him he began to live as he had lived before, and life to Tarra Khash could only be poured from a bottle, gnawed from a juicy bone, or found in the purple-sheeted bed of a bawdy-house belle. Which was why he was the perfect subject for the wiles of one such as Nud Annoxin . . .

WAKING UP LATE one hot morning, in his tavern bed above the waterfront, Tarra stuck his tousled head out of his high, small-paned window, smelled nets drying in the sun and the salt breeze off the Southern Ocean, and licked lips dehydrated by yestereve's alcoholic excesses. He remembered entertaining thoughts of a woman, and then of drinking to the idea until it became untenable, and finally of staggering back here under a reeling moon to climb corkscrew stairs to his horribly revolving bed. Now he laughed at such memories, then quickly groaned at the dull ache his laughter conjured up from the ghosts of his boozing.

Food, that was the answer! The Hrossak cursed himself for a fool. All of that drinking on an empty stomach. Well, he could remedy that: not the hangover but the emptiness, at least. A hearty breakfast would do the trick, washed down with a draught or three of good ale. Tarra grinned as he dressed and thought back on his life; but as his thoughts took form so his grin faded, and he grew remarkably philo-sophical for a Hrossak. There once was a time when he would drink for the hell of it, but since leaving the convent he seemed to drink only to forget . . . to forget the horrors he had known in the temple of Ahorra Izz!

And yet even now he could not be sure whether it had been real, or whether he had dreamed it all. He had cer-tainly *not* dreamed the treasure of the nether-caverns; no, for the pockets of his wide belt were even now full of perfect rubies large and small; but what of the rest of it? Tarra Khash shuddered as he sat down on his bed to roll up the sleeves of his shirt and the wide-cuffed bell-bottoms of his trousers, to peer yet again at the dozens of tiny white scars which marred the bronze tan of his calves and forearms . . . And suddenly his hunger abated somewhat as a renewed desire for strong liquor rose up in him like a tide.

Now naïve as the Hrossak was, he was not so dumb as to dwell on the seamy side of Thinhla without taking certain precautions—not while he was master of so much wealth. Eventually he intended to board a ship bound for Grypha, make his way up the Luhr and so back to the steppes; but for now he was satisfied to recuperate in his own way, to convalesce in a manner befitting his near-barbarian status, and Thinhla had more than enough amusements and diversions for a man of the Steppes of Hrossa.

As for his precautions: they were simple enough. This garret room, for instance: unassailable from the outside, it looked down precipitously upon the wharves. And its stout oaken door, double-barred and bolted—with a padlock whose single heavy key Tarra wore around his neck—would admit no one he wanted kept out. And so, no matter how drunk, he felt perfectly safe to sleep here; and awake— why!—who in his right mind would tackle a grinning Hrossak with arms like a bear and a wicked sabre sharp as a well-honed scythe?

As he left the tavern and made his way into the backstreet away from the wharves, Tarra came around a corner and bumped (by accident, apparently) into a fat, jolly-looking man who caught hold of his brawny arms to steady himself. This was Nud Annoxin—wearing a very false aspect—who had made a covert study of Tarra's habits and quite deliberately chosen this morning to place himself in the Hrossak's way. Now the fat man unhanded Tarra and bowed, as best his belly would allow, before introducing himself.

"Nud Annoxin," he informed, holding out a pudgy hand. "My pardon, sir, for almost tripping you; but dreaming of a hearty breakfast and a gallon of ale, I was not watching my way. I've just returned from a profitable business trip in the hinterland—but a dry affair and almost completely void of victuals—and now I hie me to my favourite eatery. You're a steppeman, I see. Perhaps you have an appetite?"

"Aye," Tarra grunted, "I'm a Hrossak—and a hunger on me, certainly—and something of a thirst to boot!"

"Then say no more," said Nud with a nudge and a wink. "Come, be my guest. I dwell not far from here; and no finer wine cellar in all Thinhla." And he took Tarra Khash by the elbow.

The Hrossak shook himself free and looked momentarily suspicious. "Your favourite eatery, you said."

"Most certainly!" cried Nud, standing back. "My own house, I meant, whose kitchen is that of a veritable king of gourmets!" He patted his stomach. "Can't you tell? But come, will you be my guest? And after we've eaten, perhaps my dancing girls may entertain . . . ?"

That last did the trick, for now the jewel-merchant had offered all three ingredients in the Hrossak's ideal brew of life. Tarra grinned and slapped Nud's meaty back, which made all of his flesh tremble like so much jelly, then bade him lead the way and gladly followed on behind.

FOUR LONG YEARS gone by, but the Hrossak remembered every detail of that first meeting as if it were yesterday. More clearly, in fact, for there had been precious little in between to dilute or dim the memory. Only this deep damp well of a cell and his nightly, self-imposed task of cutting hand- and footholds in its walls, which were too far round in the circle to climb as a chimney.

And yet Nud Annoxin had delivered all he promised—much more, to tell the truth. There had been food all through the fore and afternoon, and drink by the flagon—a deluge of drink—until Tarra's head swam in it like a fish in blinding, bubbly, sparkling shallows. And dancing girls (Annoxin's "daughters," the fat liar said, though Tarra had doubted it) and more food and wine. And Nud had grown merrier (or had seemed to), telling the story of his life to Tarra Khash; and oh!—they had become fast friends.

Until Tarra too told his tale: the story of how, wandering east of Grypha, he had paused to cast a line in the Bay of Monsters; and of the large fish he caught, and the greater Roc-bird that caught him and fish both; of the journey westward clutched in terrible, rib-cracking talons, until the Roc's nest of five hunger-crazed chicks big as lions was sighted atop a jungle-girt crag; then of stabbing his feathered captor, and of falling to the jungle's verdant floor cushioned by the carnivore's carcass; and finally of stumbling upon the lost city and the discovery of the temple of Ahorra Izz, its stone steps descending, the caverns of rubric-glowing riches . . . and—

And there the Hrossak came to his senses—or what was left of them—but far too late. Drugged, he lay supine upon Nud Annoxin's couch; and the fat merchant, sober as a judge, dragged from him the whole story in most minute detail; all the while forcing resistless potions down his throat, until the words poured from him and left him empty, unconscious, and doomed to dwell for the rest of his life in the deep, well-like dungeon wherein Nud's eunuchs then tossed him.

II

AS TO WHY Nud had not simply killed him: he was not happy that Tarra had told all. If the jungles were so dire and desperate, the swamps so full of foot-long leeches and the rivers a-leap with needle-tooth fishes, how then was the Hrossak come all these leagues to Thinhla? And all alone and unaided. Better to keep him in a deep dungeon and milk the whole truth from him bit by bit. For Nud was not satisfied with the rubies stolen from Tarra's belt; he wanted more—he wanted the entire treasure of the scarlet scorpion!

And so time passed, months growing into years, and Nud Annoxin going often to peer into the well-cell's deep throat, to coax and cajole Tarra Khash and drag from him bits of information, some of which even Tarra thought he had forgotten. But in the stillness of long nights, when only the cheeping of rats disturbed the silence, then the Hrossak chipped at the rotten mortar of his circular cell wall and slowly formed his life-ladder; and he swore a grim vengeance on the fat jewel-merchant, when at last his fingers should reach the rim and haul him up from hell . . .

"TARRA?" CAME NUD'S greasy voice one late afternoon, echoing in his captive's subterranean sinkhole and sending the rats scurrying. "Tarra, are you listening?"

"What else have I to do, fat dog?" And Tarra looked up to see Nud's rim-peering face high overhead.

"My friend, I have a flagon of fine wine, a fresh loaf of bread and a wedge of cheese. Aye, and a question, too."

"First the wine, the bread and the cheese," answered Tarra. "Then the question."

"And you'll answer truthfully?"

"As best I can, though for a fact I know that when you've done with me you'll simply let me rot down here."

A bucket was lowered with the aforementioned fare, while Nud tut-tutted and denied Tarra's charge, saying, "Come, come, old friend, let's not speak of tomorrow. Have I not promised that when my hirelings return with treasure and a well-marked map, that then I'll set you free? But until one or two such really do return, and until I have the map to hand and a portion of the treasure to prove it—"

"I stay where I am, eh?" said Tarra softly. "Well, it's my belief that when you have the route and a small sack of ruby-shards, then you'll send me down a flagon floating with poison. Either that or you'll block up this hole entirely." And then he gave himself up to the food and drink, for Nud had not fed him for a day or two.

Finally, when the chomping and swilling ceased and Nud heard only the Hrossak's low breathing, he called down: "Listen, and I shall tell you of my progress, which previously was far too slow . . ."

Now Tarra Khash had heard most of this before. He knew that Nud liked the sound of his own oily voice, and that he reiterated mainly for his own benefit, and so sighed as he resigned himself to the jewel-merchant's monologue. Anyway, he had nothing better to do, and it amused him in a grim sort of way (as much as he might be amused in this rat-infested hole) to learn of Annoxin's many trials and not so many tribulations.

"More than three years agone," the fat man began, resting elbows on rim and many chins in cup of flabby palms, "you told me your tale of the rogue Roc, of its death under your knife, of your fall to forest floor and subsequent discovery of ruins, temple and treasure. Since when, little by little, by one persuasion or another, you've remembered your route out of that place and other things important to my plan; and I, by use of certain hirelings—*many* hirelings, in fact, and well paid to boot—have attempted to retrace your steps.

"I asked you, you'll recall, how you crossed the nameless river and where. And you replied near its mouth, where the water was salt from the Southern Ocean; for the terror-fish are of a fresh-water species and not much given to swimming in brine, likewise the crocodiles."

"All true," replied Tarra, stifling a sigh. "Including the curved, giant palm-leaf plank I used for boat."

"I was coming to that," said Nud, annoyed, "but let it pass." He paused for a moment before once more taking up the tale.

"Well, I sent out three men and they crossed the river at place and in manner prescribed—and one came back to tell of the death of his mates from fever, himself expiring within a day and a night. Now you, too, were taken by fever but survived. How? Your strong Hrossak blood, I supposed. Should I next employ Hrossaks? And where to find such, for you're a rare breed west of the steppes.

"What say Yhemnis? Ah! Now there was a thought. Yhemnis: black as pitch, born and bred in jungled Yhem, whose blood must taste singularly sour on the tongue of the fever-fly, for he rarely sips it. And so I found me four frizzies, bent them to my will, gave them directions and sent them forth. But what if they should fail to return? How should I know what became of them? And how might I follow their progress?"

"How indeed?" the sunken Hrossak sighed.

"Why!—by enlisting the aid of Thinhla's master-mage, Hatr-ad of Hreen Castle!" Nud enthused. "For in his shew-stone he could surely see afar, through river mist and jungle leaf alike. Aye, and expensive the hire of his talents, I might add—but worth it, I expect, in the long run . . .

"Now then, it had also occurred to me to put it to you, you'll further recall, how come the vampire vines, noxious orchids and poisonous plants in general had failed to fetch you down. And after some small starvation you had answered that when you fell with Roc through jungle roof, your crash was brake by bush whose thickly clustered black berries besmeared you head to toe in their smelly juices—"

"—Whereafter none of the viler vegetation bothered me at all," Tarra quickly finished.

"Just so," Nud sniffed, a trifle miffed. "And so I instructed my blacks that when they came to the place of lethiferous leafage, there they must seep themselves in the fruit of the black berry bush before proceeding farther. Which they did, for Hatr-ad saw it in his sphere. After which he saw them no more . . ."

"The swamps," Tarra knowingly nodded.

"Indeed, the swamps," purred Nud, "whose sucking depths you'd omitted to mention, or mentioned merely in passing, placing more emphasis on their inhabitants— leeches who'd sluice a man dry in a trice. And so it went, the perils and protections, banes and balms; and all extracted most tortuously—and *expensively*—from caged and crafty Hrossak. Oh, you gave up the tale in outline most willingly— and at our very first meeting at that—since when, in respect of fine detail, a more reticent rascal I've yet to discover. But for all that, still your days are numbered, Tarra Khash."

Tarra's ears pricked up at that and his mind began to race. Nud's voice was far too soft and his threat had sounded imminent, and still a few handholds to scrape before rim be breached and vengeance wreaked. Tarra's mouth grew a little dry and he damped it from the flagon before carefully choosing his next words, which were these:

"So, my end draws nigh, hey? You sound most sure of yourself, Nud, who came with a question which yet remains unasked. And when you do ask it should I answer, whose fate would seem hung upon that very thread?"

"This time," answered Nud, "the answer is not imperative. Your words may save a future life or two, no more. And certainly not mine, for I shall never journey in yonder jungles, be sure."

"Then ask away," said Tarra, mind alert as he sought a way to extend his life, at least until he could snuff out Nud Annoxin's.

"Let me first tell you how far we have come," answered Nud. "Seven sorties now I have sent against the river, jungle, swamps and hideous herbage, and six of them disappeared forever from the world of men. Ah!—but of the seventh party—one survives! And he, too, has visited the temple of Ahorra Izz. Moreover, he went down into the subterranean sepulchre and returned therefrom to the upper world! Hatr-ad saw it in his shewstone, though some dire magic kept him from penetrating the caverns themselves. Four descended and one climbed back, pockets abrim with scarlet fire; and even now that one retraces his steps, returning to his grateful master with well-marked map and fortune in gems . . .

"Very well, my question is this: what of the other three? What is it lurks beneath the scorpion-god's shattered temple, which blots out three and allows a fourth to live?"

After a long moment, weighing his words most carefully, finally Tarra Khash answered, "Two things I experienced in those shadow-cursed caverns. One of which was real, for I shall carry the scars forever . . . the other of which—"

"Yes?" pressed Nud Annoxin.

"—Of which I will not speak. Not yet."

Now it was Nud's turn to sigh. "I can starve it out of you," he softly threatened.

"That will take some little time," Tarra answered, "for before ever I speak again—even of the first temple-hidden terror—I shall have from you a further flagon, loaf and cheese-wedge." And with that he fell silent.

Up above, Nud ranted and raved a while, threatened, pleaded in the end, then sent for the Hrossak's specified victuals. And only when he had those things in his great hands did Tarra tell of the first terror.

"Scorpions," he said.

"Scorpions?" (Suspicion and surprise, and the vision of a fat face frowning in confusion, causing Tarra to smile a very little).

"Certainly! In the treasure-caves of a scorpion-god, what else would you expect?"

"The scars you spoke of!" Nud now gasped. "I saw them on your calves and forearms when you were stretched helpless on my couch: white pinches against the tanned leather of your limbs!"

"Scorpions," confirmed Tarra Khash. "Scarlet scorpions, and lethally venomous. The caverns are acrawl with them!"

"Liar!" cried Nud in another moment. "A hundred stings you suffered, according to those scars, and yet you live? How so?"

"I am immune!" whispered the other. "The grey cousin of the scarlet scorpion is not unknown on the steppes, where as a child I was stung nigh to death. I was legend as a lad, renowned for the number of stings I'd taken, which should have killed but merely sickened; until in the end I took no ill at all but won many a bet by courting the scorpion's barb. Immune, Nud, aye—and the minions of Ahorra Izz killed me not, though for a fact my scars declare their determination! And there's this lad, you say, escaped arachnid's ire when three for sure succumbed? Perhaps he too is immune. Valuable, that one, Nud Annoxin."

"Immune!" and now Nud slapped fat thigh, "You think so? The dear lad!"

"Perhaps," Tarra grunted, "and perhaps not. For there was that other thing I saw—or think I saw—in the ruby caves . . . but of that I will not speak. Not now."

"Speak!" cried Nud in sudden rage. "Speak now, I command it!"

"No," the answer echoed from below, and in deep gloom the Hrossak shook his head. "Since your sole surviving hireling is three-quarters way home by now, you'd best ask it of him. *If* he makes it. But if you really cannot wait . . . why, then you must starve me!" And he chuckled, albeit grimly, as he hugged his wine, bread and cheese—small but precious provender—to his bosom . . .

III

THAT NIGHT (TARRA could tell it was night from the descent of darkness most utter; also from the silence which settled over and reigned in the vast and high-walled house of Nud Annoxin), the Hrossak climbed his prison's funnel to the topmost extent of his hand and footholds, and working longer and harder than ever before he probed and picked and gouged, with only his horny fingers as tools, until faint stirrings were heard overhead and the grey half-dark which was day seeped down once more into his cylinder dungeon. Then, fearing that Nud's eunuchs might find him where he clung like webless spider to wall and discover his four-year secret, he climbed down again to the bottom, curled up in nitrous damp and at once fell asleep.

Now Tarra Khash was not normally much of a one for dreaming (his sleep was usually much too shallow, from which he would rise up in a trice) but on this occasion he slept like a dead man. It was the sleep of exhaustion, of the culmination of four years of contained loathing and revenge lusted after, and it was a sleep well deserved. For Tarra knew that in the next night he would finally breach the wall, then that he would find the fat man in his bed and let out his life in a stream scarlet to match any flood of red-glowing jewels.

And so he dreamed, but not of escape, not of vengeance. No, he dreamed of his visit to that forbidden, jungle-drowned fane of Ahorra Izz, and of what had transpired—or what he had *thought* transpired—in those vasty vaults beneath. It could of course have been, probably had been, the fever. But—

There had been the stone steps leading down, festoons of smoky cobwebs like the ropes of some death-ship's reek-shrouded rigging, great piles of dust centuries sifted and vaulted ceilings furred over with the myriad clustered forms of *Cynonycteris*, the bat of the mastabas, whose glittering eyes were sinister scintillant. And at each landing stood a carven stone scorpion, once scarlet, whose ancient paint had fallen like flakes of rust; and each successive idol larger than last, until at lowest level the likeness of Ahorra Izz stood half as tall again as Tarra Khash, with massive rubies for eyes and a curved, high-swaying, scythe-like sting of a silver metal whose secret was surely lost to time immemorial.

In his dream Tarra paused and stared up at the ruby eyes of the idol, and at the great sting which formed, even as he watched, a pearly liquid globe, big as his fist, to fall with a splash from wicked tip to dusty, flagged floor. In the genuine arachnid this droplet would be venom, but in its massive like-ness of hard stone and unknown metal . . . surely moisture seeped from the high ceiling? What else, possibly? Which-ever, Tarra paused not but passed on; and with his head feverishly aswim, finally he came to red-glowing cavern. Al-most volcanic, that inner glow; and now the Hrossak saw what appeared to be an actual crater brimming with fiery lava—and walls all aglow with a moving warmth as of coals under a bellows—and all without slightest trace of heat!

Only then, dreaming, did he know the source of the ruddy light—just as he once had known it in reality. For the crater-like depression of the floor was in fact a huge and sunken bowl—and the contents of the bowl were myriad rubies, ranging in size from pin-head to pigeon's eggs! And all around the walls dusty, inward leaning mir-rors of bronze, reflecting and heightening that Tartarean rubescence.

At that point Tarra's sleeping figure moaned most piteously at the bottom of his prison pit. For even dreaming he knew what would next occur, as indeed it *had* occurred four years ago—with one small difference. *This* time, alerted by a sudden and gigantic scuttling, knowing what he must see entering the treasure cave behind him, Tarra lifted feverish eyes to that mirror which faced the cave's entrance, and saw—

Yes, certainly, Ahorra Izz the scorpion-god!

But more, he saw himself—or should have. Except that the man who gazed back from burning bronze was *not* Tarra Khash! Another, this other—a stranger. And now the Hrossak remembered all of his previous visit to that cursed cavern: how that great stone statue come to life stood over him—scarlet and quivering with rage—its mighty stinger poised, adrip with pearly poison. And how in that moment he had felt upon his naked forearms, upon his legs from knees down where breeches hung in tatters, a hundred tiny stabs from scarlet miniatures of monster, and knew the cavern crawled with scorpion horde. Then—

"They harm ye not, my little ones," had come the clacking voice from morbid, mandible mouth. "Your flesh puffs not, but merely twitches at their barbs; your blood drinks their venom with a rare thirst! Who be ye?" And the massive stinger had poised itself above Tarra's broad back.

"Tarra Khash," answered the Hrossak, turning to face the monster-god, Ahorra Izz himself, where he blocked the entrance. "A man of the steppes, whose friends the grey scorpions are. And many the playful sting I've known, which never harmed me, nor I your scorpion minions."

"Is it so?" had come the horridly clacked question.

"Indeed," Tarra had answered, deliriously snatching up a handful of livid, living death. "See?" and he grinned as a half-dozen stingers stabbed and stabbed again. "It is our game, you see, in no degree malicious."

"Who sent ye?" the demon then had clacked, his poised and needlessly poisonous scythe visibly retracting somewhat, relaxing.

"No one but fate," cried Tarra, swaying with fever and unaccustomed dose of venom both. "Perhaps to let you know you still have worshipper amongst men—one, at least!"

The monster had nodded once, slowly, and his faceted jewel eyes had regarded the Hrossak strangely. Then: "Others have been here, Tarra Khash. Once in a hundred years, perhaps, one such will come, and sometimes two. Strayed wanderers and seekers after treasure, wizard-sent thieves, savages cast out from heathen tribes. But never a worshipper, until now. As for the others: their bones are dust. And now I am tired of visitors who wake me from my slumbers immemorial. Know ye this, Tarra Khash, that I may take whichever form I wish. E'en yours if I so desired. And from this day on if ever I be waked, then walk me forth for sure to seek him out who sent the wakener. As for ye—"

"Aye, kill me," the reeling Hrossak had then prompted. "For if you don't the fever surely will, or deadly jungle."

Ahorra Izz shook his jewelled head. "Not I. Lay ye down and sleep, Tarra Khash, and when ye rise up eat of the food which ye shall find and drink of the sweet water. Then take what ye will of this ruby hoard and get ye gone . . ."

Then the Hrossak, falling to his knees and sending rubies flying, had offered up a loud cry—of thanks perhaps, perhaps a fevered shriek—a prayer?—and toppled sideways cushioned by the gems. And knew no more.

This had happened, and now, dreaming, Tarra Khash *knew* it had happened. But in his dream he was someone else, some other. And now the conversation went like this:

"They harm ye not, my littles ones, whose stings pierce not the leather which ye wear. *My* sting, however, will pierce mail and split the wearer to the bone! What say ye?"

And Tarra, who was *not* Tarra, fell upon his padded knees and babbled and screamed.

"Cease now or die at once!" clacked Ahorra Izz, and the screaming turned to sobbing and fitful, spastic grovelling.

"Who sent ye?"

"Nud Annoxin," came the sobbing cry. "The fat jewel-merchant of Thinhla. He sent me. Spare me, spare me!"

"And did he also send the three whose unprotected ankles felt of my minions' stings?"

"Aye, aye, 'twas Nud. Nud Annoxin sent us!"

"Man," said the monster in another moment, "die!" And his stinger flashed forth and shattered skull through helmet, ripped breast through fine mail and leather, sliced trunk to groin through steely belt, leather breeks and all; and so Nud's hireling fell in two directions.

Then Ahorra Izz looked down on what had been a man and his arachnid form shimmered as if seen through smoke; his outline changed, shrank; he became—

—The selfsame man whose halves now lay on blood splashed hoard! And this the dreaming Tarra Khash saw from two different angles, through bulging, separated eyes which glazed even as he started awake with horrified cry upon his well-cell's slimy floor . . .

THAT HAD BEEN at noon. At noon, too, had Hatr-ad espied in his shewstone the hooded hireling striding the plain at the edge of the coastal forest and heading straight for Thinhla. And Hatr-ad's beady eyes had brightened as he recognised the man's mode of dress and his shape, and he nodded eagerly and licked thin lips greedily at sight of the small but fat sacklet at the man's belt. But then, when Thinhla's mage (a mean magician, known better for dark than kinder magicks) might have winged a bat messenger on its way to the house of Nud Annoxin—just at that moment when he made as if to turn from his shewstone—something about the rapid approach of this lone survivor of all Nud's expeditions arrested his attention, striking him at odds.

High in his turreted tower at Hreen Castle, the pallid mage frowned and gazed again down hooked nose into the swirling depths of his sphere, causing with his concentration swiftly gathering mists to draw back again from the conjured scene. Indeed, there was something odd about this survivor of Nud's quest. Several things, most odd . . . His preternatural speed for one, who should by rights be exhausted from jungle-trekkings, river-crossings, avoidances of perilous plants and such. And yet he came on apace, his long, tireless, almost mechanical stridings most eerie to watch. Why, at this rate he would be here in Thinhla before the midnight hour!

Hatr-ad remembered Nud speaking of this one: who rubbed himself with ointments against insect bites and took with him upon the quest an assortment of protections against every possible eventuality lethal. Aye, a professional he, and rightful survivor. And the miles flying beneath ceaselessly striding legs, and noon sun striking hot on him; for which reason, doubtless, he had put up his hood against its furnace glare.

Hatr-ad frowned harder yet, his concentration growing as he drew the striding figure closer, closer, until the shewstone was filled with cowled head, until he could peer into the shadows beneath that cowl—at glowing ruby coals that burned for eyes in a face mottled grey and vacuous as that of a dead man! The strider *was* a dead man!

Then, before the mage could make another move, his ears seemed to ring to a clacking, imperious command, cold as northern snows. *"Begone, watcher! Get ye gone from me—lest I seek ye out also, e'en as I seek Nud Annoxin!"*

At which Hatr-ad shrank back at once from his sphere and let its misty drapes fall. And shaking in every limb he

descended from his aerie and set about renewing the mag-
ickal protections about Hreen Castle. He put his familiar
demons atop the battlements, and he locked himself in a
deep and secret room for the remainder of that day and two
more . . . None of which was ever brought to the attention
of Nud Annoxin.

AT THE ELEVENTH hour a striding stranger approached the
east gate and entered into the torch-flickered shadow of its
arch. The guard commander might normally have stopped
him, and indeed had approached him so to do; but there
was that about the cowled stranger which forbade any real
interference, and in passing his cold hand pressed into that
of the sergeant something hard and glittery in the dark,
which later proved to be a priceless ruby; so that the question of the stranger's entry into Thinhla did not arise.

And at the gate of Nud Annoxin's high-walled house a
similar scene, where eunuchs who had been ordered to
keep watch for the lone quester's return now found themselves recipients of riches. And into Nud's house the
stranger strode, all unannounced, to the very door of the
jewel-merchant's private chamber . . . where he rapped
with deathly knuckles upon heavy oaken panels.

EVER SINCE THE first hour of utter dark, Tarra Khash had
worked on the high walls of his prison. Stuck like a fly to
curving surface, he frantically clawed at crumbling mortar; a
nameless urgency drove him constantly to take risks. Such
was the violence of his attack upon the wall that on several
occasions he nearly shook himself loose from his precarious

position, which would almost certainly be a fatal occurrence. But finally, somewhere between the eleventh and
twelfth hour, he was able to thrust an arm upward until
bloodied fingers found the rim.

After that—

A matter of moments to haul himself to freedom, seconds
to let his senses soak up the faint feelings of the night, minutes to discover a room with jewelled ceremonial swords
upon its walls and to take one . . . and at last, silent as a
shadow, he crouched with murderous intent before the
door of Nud's own room—which stood open! Even as he
paused in momentary indecision, Tarra's foot touched
something fallen to the floor. A pouch or sacklet, of the sort
used for jewels or nuggets—except that the contents of this
one were already fleeing its loosened neck: scarlet scorpions, their stingers rampant and deadly!

The scorpions alone would not have sufficed to stop
Tarra, but there was more. A dim light within the room
threw shadows into the corridor. The Hrossak saw the shadows and in the next moment heard voices, one being
Nud's—babbling, disbelieving, gasping for breath—the
other . . .

Oh, Tarra Khash recognised the other! Its clacking notes
were unmistakable; and the Hrossak's scalp crawled as he
drew back with silent snarl from the open door. Then: one
shadow expanding, elongating, changing; and the other, fat
and human still, falling into a kneeling position, hands
raised in supplication. The Hrossak paused no longer but
turned to flee. He went, knowing now the source of that
earlier urgency, knowing also that he was too late, that
Ahorra Izz himself had beaten him to the prey.

Confirming his thoughts, as he vaulted a low balcony out

into the spacious gardens, he heard a mighty swish as of a giant's scythe and a great tearing of flesh—and Nud's rising scream cut gurglingly off at zenith. Then, horror riding upon his ragged back, Tarra was climbing the wall. No thoughts of gems or thievery this night. Only of flight. He had the jewelled sword and that was enough. He wanted nothing more. Not from this house.

Not from the cursed and fear-crazed house of Nud Annoxin . . .

Isles of the Suhm-yi

I

ASTONISHED, THE BRONZE-SKINNED man in leather breach-clout and sandals, with jewelled ceremonial sword in its long curved sheath strapped to his broad, well-muscled back, kneeled beside the dead but still-warm corpse of Lula Arn. The steppeman knew her not, this daughter of the Inner Isles, knew nothing at all of the Suhm-yi other than vaguely-remembered campfire whispers, myths and legends. The Suhm-yi, aye, "the Rarely Seen"—but now the Hrossak saw that indeed the myths did not lie, that the Inner Isles of the crater sea were in fact peopled by a race of . . . well, by beings other than men. Indeed, by beings *un*human, for the dead body, whose golden eyes he now closed against the sun's glare, was not—despite its obvious femininity, its beauty—a human corpse. She was, or had been, Suhm-yi, and this tiny jewel of an island must have been her home.

A great anger stirred in the bronzed breast of Tarra Khash. His nostrils flared. And men called his brothers of the steppes savages! But the black-hearted band responsible for this . . . they were the real barbarians. Northmen, and their stink lingering yet over this lovely, alien body they'd ravaged and robbed of life.

The girl had been tall, fine-limbed and comb-headed; though her silver-grey, brutalized flesh was dull now in death, in life its sheen must have been quite wonderful. There was an elfin, ethereal something about her hard to define. It made Tarra Khash sorry he had never spoken to her; he felt sure her tongue would have been music to his ears, whose usual fare was the guttural oaths of polyglot taverns, or the hot, sultry whispers of the whorehouse. Well, he couldn't speak to her, not now—odds were they wouldn't have had anything to talk about anyway—but he knew who to speak to *about* her.

A certain long-maned, boastful brute of a Northman, Kon Athar, born of the cold fjords and lochs far north of the River Thand. Oh, yes, Kon and his gang of wandering cutthroats were responsible for this. One more reason why Tarra Khash would take the greatest possible pleasure in slitting that bull barbarian's throat ear to ear. One reason among several. Tarra knew of two others at least . . .

IT WAS SIX months now since the Hrossak had fled Thinhla on the Southern Ocean, heading north-west with a caravan bound for Thandopolis. Or perhaps "fled" is too strong a word; instead let's say "removed himself from," for in fact Tarra Khash had rarely fled anything in all his young life. But his adventures before, and in Thinhla, had been terrific, and their culmination had been one from which most men might reasonably flee. Tarra's long years in that seaport city, prisoned at the bottom of a deep, dried-out well, had been literally years of living death. Except he had not died.

And since then—certainly since reaching Thandopolis— Tarra Khash had lived as only a true Hrossak can. His years of deprivation had neither reduced him in spirit nor detracted from his zest for life; rather had they sharpened his appetite for all the good things so long denied him.

Rich when first he'd made his ill-omened entry into Thinhla—loaded down with rubies from the jungle temple of Ahorra Izz, scarlet God of Scorpions—Tarra had been a ragged beggar when he left. All save his ceremonial sword, stolen from the house of the fat jeweller Nud Annoxin, who no longer had need of it . . . or of anything else for that matter. And a single fine stone, prised from the hilt of that wand of death, had paid the Hrossak's way in sophisticate city, so that his five-month stay in Thandopolis had been both curative and pleasurable. To eat red meat and drink good, sweet wine; to bathe in clean waters and breathe the balmy air of freedom; and above all to sleep in silken sheets (and rarely alone) and thus soften those callouses hard come-by in Nud Annoxin's deep well-cell: these things had returned him fully to health and former heartiness.

Alas, a hale and hearty Hrossak has ever been *genius loci* for all the demons of mischief, and Tarra Khash no exception.

An irate taverner, his plump daughter well seduced and by now doubtless plumper still, had sufficed to bring about Tarra's speedy departure. It had been that or kill the taverner (or worse still wed the girl, and three-quarters of Theem'hdra still unvisited, still unseen) which hadn't left

horny Hrossak a deal of choice. And so, following the lonely
Thand east toward its source, finally he'd met up with a pair
of prospectors working the winding riverbanks.

Gold was a lure he couldn't resist, not after they'd shown
him the prize nuggets already wrested from river's rush; and
working with the pair, Ilke Phant and Bogga Tull of
Thandopolis, Tarra had soon packed away a pouch or two of
nuggets and dust of his own. And as the days stretched into
weeks they'd all three panned their way through the
foothills of the Great Circle Range, into the scarps and gulleys of the mountains themselves. Then—

—Enter Kon Athar and his bully-boys.

They came at night, and city lads and Hrossak alike fast
asleep and dreaming of riches untold, exhausted from
their hard day's work. And Kon and his five, coming out
of the darkness and shadows, creeping like dogs, their
white teeth aglint in guttering firelight, their swords upraised . . .

Bogga's death-scream had roused Tarra up, and Ilke's last
throaty rattle had certified the danger. Then . . . the feel of
his weapon's jewelled hilt in hard bronze fist, and the snick-
ering of the steely blade as it cleared its sheath in a *hiss* of
slicing motion—but too late! Tarra hadn't even glimpsed the
hulking coward whose blow cracked his skull and buffeted
him head over heels down the riverbank and into the darkly
swirling Thand. But before the blackness closed over him he
heard an oath and a hoarse laugh, and a voice that cried:
"Missed that one, Kon Athar! But the river'll do for him, be
sure . . ."

Thus it was the waters bore him away from scene of
slaughter, casting him up at last—half-drowned, half-
frozen—on a shingly shore where the river broadened out,

a full mile from the erstwhile camp he'd made with two firm friends.

And what of Ilke and Bogga now . . . ?

II

THE MORNING SUN had warmed him to life, soaked and stiff and fingering gently the gash beneath tangled brown locks and the chicken's egg fresh-laid on tender scalp. But no sooner on his feet, and a fish from the river raw in his belly for breakfast, than Tarra gritted his straight strong teeth and headed upstream once more, his aching head and body full of red revenge. He knew who'd struck him down, knew also that Kon Athar's name—and the names of those he ran with—were a curse on the lips of decent folk from Thinhla to Hjarpon Settlement. Aye, and the barbarians would know Tarra's name, too, before he was finished with them. This he had promised himself.

And so to last night's camp and the sad, sickening sight waiting there. A sight which brought up half-digested fish from Tarra's gut for all that his sort were not much known for puking at murder, mutilation and such; for it's a hard world in the steppes east of the Luhr. And no gold to be found, not even the twin gold teeth which used to flash in Bogga's laughing mouth. And the corpses stripped naked, for even their clothes had value. And Ilke's little finger missing from his left hand, where a wide golden ring had fitted too tight and glittered too bright.

As for Tarra's own gold: his pouches were lost in the river, the dust and nuggets returned whence they came.

And so he'd buried his friends there, beneath a jutting

ledge, and blocked them in with boulders from the river's rim, and stood a while over them, head bowed, till certain they acknowledged his tribute. Then down to the river again, this time following the trail of last night's tumble; and sure enough his sword was there, half-buried in sliding grit and pebbles. In the dark the Northmen had not seen the jewelled hilt where it protruded close to river's edge. But they'd see it soon enough, that sword—by their own black god Yibb they would!

AFTER A LITTLE while he picked up their trail. Following their tracks was no hard task; they'd little enough to fear, that band, or so they must have thought. And follow it Tarra did, all they way to the great waterfall where the Thand flowed out of the crater sea; and up the side of the falls, too, to stand in the spray-wreathed saddle and gaze inwards upon that vasty lake whose bed was once the throat of creation's mightiest volcano.

And with the melt of spring finished and the sun beating down upon him and making rainbows, the Hrossak had marvelled at Nature's rawness and felt the blood racing in his veins. And the beat of his heart had quickened as he saw, far out on the deep blue bosom of that mountain-girt sea, the single rude sail of a roughly fashioned raft, and the tiny figures of the six who plied oars and paddles to speed their vessel away from the suck of the great falls.

A burly raft at least, be sure, for six big lads like these . . . but none such required for one man alone. Then Tarra had clambered down from saddle to shore, finding him a tree washed up from which he stripped all but two strong branches, and to these lengthwise made fast a stouter branch, so building himself a catamaran such as used by fishers on the lakes of his steppes. And using his jacket and breeks for sail, and fashioning a paddle which would also serve for rudder, he soon set off in hot pursuit of the greater vessel and the six who sailed her. From which time on, for all of a dozen days and nights, the Hrossak had lived on fish; until at last he'd come upon the Inner Isles.

The first of these was so tiny as to be little more than a rock; but it had trees with great nuts and others with fruits, and from the crest of its single peak—

Open now to Tarra's gaze the Inner Isles in all their jewel-bright beauty, reaching away like a string of emeralds cast upon a blue, blue mirror. And somewhere out there a raft and six; and now the Hrossak believing he knew why they'd come this way, those reavers. For if they'd heard the same rumours he'd heard—why, it was obvious!

These were the isles of the Suhm-yi, a mysterious race legended to have gained unlimited access to a magnificent cache of rare gems, with which its members would deck themselves head to toe till they glowed with the sheen of rainbows. If that were true, then these islands were ripe for the sack. Indeed now that he thought of it, Tarra could hardly see why they hadn't been sacked before! Of course the rumours also had it that the crater sea was aswim with monsters (not that Tarra had seen a one), and wasn't there something else tickling the back of his mind? About the Suhm-yi themselves having weird powers, which made them favoured of the gods? Well, perhaps, but the Hrossak wasn't much for chasing misty memories.

And all through that long day Tarra had paddled and sailed between the islands, finding nothing at all upon the first three save trees and birds and dwarfy pigs. But on the fourth . . .

It had been bigger, that fourth isle, all of a mile or more long. Landing, the Hrossak had seen smoke rising thick and black from some spot beyond a spine of low hills. Though crater sea were mainly tideless, still he dragged his makeshift craft out of the water a little way before climbing the wooded, flower-decked slope at the trot; and having chosen what seemed the easiest route—a worn way, where often feet had passed before—he saw that indeed others had made the climb, and most recently. No more than three or four hours ago.

Cresting the spine of hills the Hrossak had moved more slowly, carefully, soon coming upon a wedge of rock like a lookout rising from a tangle of trees and flowering shrubs. And to its summit ladders of lashed bamboo, and at its base an oddly-structured house—or what remained of a house.

Half-lost in vines and orchids, that dwelling, but gutted now with fire and burning still. The place had loamy gardens and a deep well, low walls of cemented conches and verandas seemingly unsupported . . . all wreathed in smoke and asmoulder now. And the frame of its roof, collapsing in ruin even as Tarra Khash looked on, showed a strange but pleasing skill in design and structure unknown to human builders in all the length and breadth of Theem'hdra; so that he knew he watched the fall of a house of the Suhm-yi. And the smoke rising thick and black as the day wore to its close, and the island deserted and still. No bird sang; no wild piglet squealed, not now; even the gentle wash of waves seemed hushed where they foamed a little upon the isle's far shore.

Now Tarra's movements had grown more cautious yet, his eyes bleak as they reconstructed scenes unseen save in his imagination. He saw the Northmen climbing the path to the crest, coming across the house at base of lookout rock. He saw them close on the house, swords drawn. Then . . . a figure, fleeing, male or female he knew not. His eyes were on the path leading through shrubs and doubtless down to the beach below, just as the path behind had led him up from the shore where his boat was beached. And upon that path flying footprints, dainty and four-toed, almost obscured by more obvious scuffs. And while one had stayed to loot and fire the house, five others had followed their prey, just as Tarra Khash now followed.

And going with him as he descended through shrubs, the island's silence like a shroud, so that despite the glare of the late afternoon sun the way seemed full of shadows and gloom. But Tarra's eyes missing nothing, and his mind building upon what he saw. Here a scattering of shingle and sand, where a flying, frightened figure stumbled and sprawled, and a spot of blood upon a stone, where rested for a moment a grazed knee; then the leaping footprints once more, but not so widely spaced as those of a man. Female, this unseen, fleeing creature.

Now the beach where the footprints ran in sand—hither and thither and to and fro and back, frantic—and nowhere else to run. And the heavier prints of booted feet closing, and Hrossak's heart beating to a crescendo in his chest. Behind a low dune the prints converged, and there he had found the body of Lula Arn. Not decked with jewels, no, but he could well see how that silvery skin of hers must flash in life, like mother of pearl in the sea or gemstones under the sun, and he could well imagine the source of the legend. Here, now, the legend itself, brutalized and dead . . .

III

TARRA KHASH STOOD up.

He had kneeled there for some little time beside the dune, unaware of the sun's slow sinking as his thoughts had wandered. But now, as shadows lengthened, he grew aware not only of evening's creep but also of a slender canoe, beached some small distance down the strand. The canoe had not been there before, of that he was sure. And yet . . . he had heard nothing.

He stood stock still, squinted his eyes, saw etched the small shadows cast by prints leading from craft to green cover of thickly grown shrubbery. And he felt eyes upon him where he stood, a perfect target. Did they have the use of weapons, the Suhm-yi? Tarra knew not; but if they did, and if this one wished him dead, then were he already dead. He let tense muscles relax, controlled the creep of gooseflesh, stooped and carefully, tenderly lifted up the corpse in his bronze Hrossak arms.

And up the path to gutted house he carried her, to the garden where he dug a narrow grave. Orchids to cover her, to keep the uncaring earth from her silvery flesh, and a cairn of stones above in the manner of the steppes, though Tarra was sure no wild beast here would trouble her grave. And always upon him in the twilight the weight of eyes, the knowledge that death lurked close as an arrow's *hiss*. For aye, the Suhm-yi knew the use of weapons.

Hearing nothing, still the Hrossak knew he was not alone, that another stood with him now in the quiet, shadowed garden. He raised up his bowed head, gazed steadily into eyes golden as his were brown . . . stared also at the slender arrow nocked, whose barbed head centered on his chest.

A movement in the surrounding shrubbery!

So swift the Hrossak's eye could barely follow, a flash of silver-grey as bowman fell into a crouch, pivoted, let fly his deadly shaft—and a piglet squealing once! The silent watcher (for surely this could be none other) seemed to melt into shadowy greenery, returning in but a moment with skewered piglet, handing meat and arrow both to Tarra Khash, then standing back from him.

Hungry? the Hrossak was that all right, and he'd had his fill of fish!

He set up a spit well away from the grave and cairn, brought driftwood up from the beach (for he would not use timbers from the house), kindled a small fire and hunkered down, his mouth watering as the pork began to roast. And later, having eaten, he returned to the grave where the Suhm-yi male sat; and there they sat apart and yet together, all through the night . . .

IN THE CHILL of morning Tarra woke with a start, jerking his head erect from where it had lolled. His limbs were stiff from sitting but the sun was already beginning to warm them, with golden disc fresh-risen from scarlet crater sea. The house white ashes now, bringing back memories to sleep-fuddled mind of all gone before. And no sign of the Suhm-yi male, but a small mound of fresh fruit close to hand, breakfast for a yawning Hrossak.

While Tarra ate, Amyr Arn came, standing before him with questioning look in his huge, golden eyes.

"Good morning," said the Hrossak, unsmiling. "And I thank you for the fruit." The Suhm-yi made no answer but stared intently.

Tarra cocked his tousled head. "Is there something? Can't you speak? Or is it that my tongue's so wildly different from yours?" He shrugged. "Ah, well—" and made to climb to his feet. But in a moment the Suhm-yi's hand lay four-fingered upon his shoulder, and in another Amyr Arn sat cross-legged, facing him.

Tarra waited, and in a while said, "There's much to be done. I have to be up and about. I follow the Northmen, who are in my debt just as they are in yours. I mustn't tarry here . . ." And again he made to rise. This time Amyr Arn offered no resistance but also came to his feet, saying:

"You follow them who did this?"

Tarra nodded. "For revenge!" almost before realising he'd been spoken to in his own tongue. "But . . . you know the language of the steppes! Who taught you?"

"You are my teacher, bronze one. As you speak, so I learn. The Suhm-yi have a way with tongues."

The Hrossak was astonished, then suspicious. "You'd make a fool of me? What creature is it, however strange, learns another's language so quickly—and so well?"

"It is an art of the Suhm-yi," the other seemed to shrug, his tone of voice silver as his skin. "Part is learned from the lips, the rest from the mind that works them."

"You read minds, too?" Tarra shook his head. "And you a naked savage!"

"I read feelings, emotions," the un-man did not appear insulted. "You felt right, bronze one, and your emotions were real and warm. Otherwise—" again the shrug,"—it would not have gone well for you last night. Not in that moment when you laid hands upon my Lula."

Tarra stared at his naked, comb-headed host and nodded. "I sorrowed, aye. They owe me a deal of sorrow, that half-dozen, and not a little gold to boot. But you have lost much more." He frowned. "So you would have killed me last night? And yet the Northmen are not dead."

"I was fishing," said the other, the silver notes of his voice a fraction tarnished now, "else were they surely dead—or I myself dead—even though our olden laws decry vengeance as a great evil. But . . . I was not here. I did not see them until they were well out to sea, and even then they did not see me. But when I returned here . . . then I found you. And I found Lula."

Tarra nodded again, sighed and sadly shook his head. But after a moment he ventured a smile. "How are you called, man of the Inner Isles?"

"My name is Amyr Arn. And yours?"

"Tarra Khash, a Hrossak. A man of the steppes, far from home."

"And I am Suhm-yi." Amyr turned to face the cairn, golden eyes unblinking, but clouding a little, Tarra thought. He bowed his combed head. "She was my mate."

After a while the Hrossak said, "But you're young, Amyr Arn. I know not your ways, but time is a great healer for all men and creatures. There'll be other maids of the Suhm-yi for you."

Amyr shook his crested head. "No, not even if I wished it. We were the last. I *am* the last."

"The last? Of your race? I don't understand."

"It was a plague, came from the south-east in a cloud of

red dust, blown on winds which never blew before. And all the isles of the Suhm-yi east of here covered in a red ash, and all the Suhm-yi themselves dead in a day and a night—save Lula and I, who saw the cloud but suffered not its red rain of ashes. And now she too is no more."

"So you really are the last of your race!" Tarra said, adding, "And indeed your loss is greater than mine . . ."

DOWN ON THE beach Amyr Arn looked at Tarra's crude craft and shook his head. "You sailed the crater sea on that? But no, you can't hope to hunt them down with vessel such as this! And with this sail—why, they must surely see you coming! I endorse your enterprise—even though vengeance is not the way of the Suhm-yi—but I cannot give a deal of credit to your chances. You will expend all of your strength in paddling and sailing your craft. In my canoe, however . . ."

"You'll not go with me?" Tarra found himself constantly taken by surprise by the strange being. "But surely you'll want your share of—"

"No," the Suhm-yi shook his head. "Have I not made myself clear? Vengeance was never our way. Last night was different. Last night I might easily have killed even you, my friend. And if I had come upon them about their evil business . . ."

"I understand," said Tarra gruffly, but he really didn't. Was life really so cheap to Amyr Arn? And the life of his one love—*the* one love in all these Inner Isles, this entire world—at that? Well, so be it. Some men are lusty fighters born, and some are not. And anyway, Amyr Arn was not even a man. Not human, at any rate. Who was Tarra Khash to query the ways of strange, unhuman beings?

The other knew his thoughts. "There are . . . things I must do," he said. "Anyway, I shall be with you, in spirit at least. What will you take with you?"

Tarra shrugged. "Sweet water and a little meat. A couple of yellow fruits and a great nut." And he shrugged again.

"And in your memory a picture of me, Tarra Khash," implored the other, "last of the Suhm-yi. Remember me all your days, as I shall remember you. And who knows, perhaps we shall meet again, though I doubt it."

And one hour later, the Hrossak set out in Amyr's canoe . . .

IV

NOW, WITH ALL the Inner Isles in sight, (at least the nearest of them, and the rest clustered close, so that from one island one could usually see the next) Tarra quickly learned the skills necessary to send Amyr's canoe skimming low over the calm waters of the crater sea; rapidly closing the gap, he suspected, between himself and the Northmen he pursued.

Two small islands he saw with smoke rising, and knew that this could only be the work of the six. And quickly ensuring that the reaver band had departed, he spent the night upon the second of these jewelled islets, rising early with the dawn. But having breakfasted and climbed to the island's tallest place, there he stood at a loss and gazed out upon the crater sea. No fires or smoke to be seen, and nowhere in sight the crude craft of the Northmen or its sail. Then the thought came to him that, discovering the islands empty of human (or of Suhm-yi) life, perhaps the barbarians had given up their pointless arson. One sets fire to another's property to do him harm, cause him grief; but if he is already dead, what profit then in burning his house? And surely by now the Northmen had seen, as Tarra had seen them, Suhm-yi skeletons sprawled where the plague of red ash had taken them?

All very well, but those columns of black smoke rising to the blue skies had been as signal fires to Tarra Khash, leading him on in the wake of those reavers with whom his score lay still unsettled. He frowned and considered the problem. Now what would *he* do, and which route take through these Inner Isles, if *he* were reaver seeking gold and gemstones?

Away eastward, central in a scattering of smaller islets, stood perhaps the largest of all the isles of the Suhm-yi, whose mass must be almost as great as all the others put together. Surely the reasoning of the barbarians would not differ so widely from Tarra's own? Surely they, too, would now realize that if aught were here worth the pillaging, then were that something most likely found upon the greatest landmass, doubtless the principal isle of the Suhm-yi?

Very well, there must he go, and hopefully collect a debt in his own and in Amyr Arn's account. Aye, and with luck and justice settle the business once and for all . . .

MEANWHILE, AMYR ARN had not been idle.

In a second, older canoe dragged out from mossy berth in tangled undergrowth and bathed in crater sea's soft brine to swell dried-out hull and fill fine cracks, the last of the Suhm-yi had sculled tirelessly a day and a night. Now he prepared to beach his craft upon a strand forbidden of yore, where only the naked feet of High Priests of the Suhm-yi had previously trodden, and only then in great reverence.

For the isle was Holy of Holies, and in aspect alone would suffice to send away the merely curious. No jewel of the crater sea, Na-dom, but a gaunt crag whose single fang reared from the deeps like some sea-beast's talon, which beckoned not but forbade intrusion. And no green thing growing thereon, where neither lizard crawled nor bird nested; and the rock itself black as if painted over with pitch. And Na-dom stood well off from the other Inner Isles, for which reason the gods of the Suhm-yi had, since time immemorial, been given to visit there; or rather, they had allowed themselves to be called thereto.

And because of the spire's ominous aspect, and insomuch that Amyr stood in awe of the place, he had indeed approached most reverently, plying his paddle soft as the fall of feathers and bowing his head as he beached his canoe in the tiny bight where a huge and ocean-hollowed cave gloomed like some slumbering ogre's mouth in the base of the rock. There, after long moments, finally Amyr lifted his head and gazed with wide golden eyes upon the cave and crag. And where the first gaped like an untended wound, the second towered skyward, a bleak look-out whose sides seemed precipitous beneath summit unattainable.

But . . . Amyr was not entirely unfamiliar with Na-dom, Isle of the Gods. True, he had never before set foot thereon, and even now felt that his presence was probably an abomination in the eyes of the olden gods, but he was not totally ignorant. Long years gone, when Amyr was very, very young, his own father had been High Priest. And that wise and honorable elder of the Suhm-yi had been close indeed to his only son. Their minds had been almost as one, so that Amyr had gleaned from his father something of the nature of the ocean-girt rock.

And as the old one had grown older still and passed on the sigil of High Priesthood to a younger priest, so his tongue had loosened a little and occasionally he would whisper in his sleep of Na-dom's cave and the steps therein, which formed a narrow way to soaring summit. Amyr had paid little attention then, but now he remembered all.

Aye, but he knew that while the powers of the gods were strange and far-reaching, they were often loath to answer the invocations even of their most elderly and practised priests—and how then the pitiful pleadings of an uninitiated youth?

Weary from his paddling and fatigued from fasting—for he had not eaten nor even thought of food for himself since the murder of his mate—Amyr now sighed, dragged his canoe from the shallows, entered the yawning cave and sought the rock-hewn steps. And indeed he found the way narrow, the stone slippery and the chimney steep, so that he must needs sling his bow over one shoulder and so keep his hands for balancing and for grasping the rough walls.

And tall that crag, so that it seemed a half-hour at least that Amyr toiled upwards; and gloomy, for only a little light filtered down from above and hardly anything from below, except in his ears the sullen hush of wavelets in the shingle-strewn bight.

Now, about the gods:

As stated, Amyr knew that they did not dwell upon the roof of this rock, but might, in auspicious circumstances, be called down to light upon it—normally through the medium of a priest of the Suhm-yi. And he also knew that Gleeth, the blind God of the Moon, was high-ranking amongst the gods of the Suhm-yi. It might just be that he could call up Gleeth himself to his aid—or rather, to the aid of Tarra Khash—but he doubted it. Gleeth was after all very old and very nearly deaf; he heeded calls rarely; and blind, he could not see to perform any but perfunctory services. So Amyr had heard it whispered. But . . . Gleeth *was* advisor to the gods, and the Elder of their Council, and so would make a useful ally. *If* he could be roused up from his centuried slumbers. The occasion was auspicious, however, for tonight would be his night, when a full and golden moon would be riding the skies over the Inner Isles.

And at last Amyr Arn came to the roof of the rock, and there sat him down to rest a while from his labours. On his way he had passed many lesser caves leading off from the winding stairway, and had allowed his eyes briefly to gaze upon the contents thereof; so that now he knew the legended treasures of the Suhm-yi were on no account mere legend. For indeed Na-dom was a treasure-house, whose lesser caves were caches for rubies, opals, diamonds, gold, ivories and jade and pearls galore; and now the last of the Suhm-yi could see why men of the outer world—the world beyond the rim of the crater sea—might desire to come here. Especially such men as Kon Athar and his brutes.

But the thought of those murderers roused him up and strengthened his resolve, and he set about his supplications there and then, repeatedly beseeching Gleeth that he hear him and come in answer to his call. And so he kneeled and mumbled and muttered (if that term be at all applicable to the silver tones of the Suhm-yi) all the long day, directing his will upon the solitary spire of weather-fretted rock rising like a finger up from the flat summit's table, whose stem was pierced by a perfectly oval hole like the eye of some petrified Cyclops; and slowly the sun sank down over the sea and the shadows lengthened, at first imperceptibly, then ever more rapidly . . .

V

WEARY AS AMYR Arn himself, Tarra Khash had reached the shallows of the principal isle of the Suhm-yi in that hour immediately after noon when the sun stands seemingly immobile in the sky and the air shimmers with his burning rays; when the sea lies still and calm and blue, almost seeming to *hiss*, but silently; and small silver fishes leap from dazzling water to fly a little way, as if deliberately breaking the stillness and reminding the world of its vasty reel and rush through the cosmos of space and time.

The beach was broad and white, with little of cover for Tarra and his canoe, and the crater sea a great unblemished blue expanse upon which burly Hrossak and slender craft both must surely stand out sore as a gap in otherwise perfect teeth, or mote in a bright eye; but of options he had none. And surely were the six here, for their raft stood drawn up and beached above the narrow wash of wavelets, alerting the Hrossak to their prior advent. Aye, and if Kon Athar had set a lookout, then were Tarra Khash observed. Well, so be it . . .

But the northern reavers had set no lookout, and so Tarra's own coming had gone unobserved and his presence here unknown (for the nonce), while some way inland Kon Athar and his five made their hulking, shambling way down the main thoroughfare of a deserted Suhm-yi city.

It was a straight and dusty street of finely-fretted stone,

where several of the principal buildings went even so high as four storeys, showing architectural skills prodigious and awesome in the eyes of any average, untutored Northman. Except that Kon Athar and company were never much awed by anything of skill or beauty, unless it were perhaps skill in fighting or beauty in a well-proportioned and comely woman. And even then, the first they would pervert with cowardice or cheating, and the second bring down to beastliness, so that all was destroyed by them.

And there, in a walled square of paths and trees, before the open portals of a large and impressively ornate stone edifice, the barbarians found a fountain where water spurted still, there pausing to slake their thirst and reckon their course from this point on. One of them, Kon's right-hand man—a bulky, black-maned brute named Bejam Thad, whose name alone was ill-omen and whose cowardly blow, on the night of the murder of Bogga Tull and Ilke Phant, had plunged Tarra Khash only half-conscious into nighted, swirly Thand waters—now spoke up:

"I'm thinking, Kon," he growled, "we've come far enough—and for little enough. Naught here worth the sweat of reavers born, in these isles of silence and dust and skeleton corpses. And for a fact no treasure such as lured us here in the first place!" His tone, while in no wise threatening, was sullen beyond a doubt . . . Perhaps too sullen.

Kon Athar glanced at Bejam Thad and the corner of his slack mouth twitched a little. Kon was gross even for one of his breeding. His eyes were black and his grimy, matted mane of hair yellow, which was a rare colour for Northmen and so set him apart. It swept wild down his back like the mane of a lion. But dull the yellow now as he stripped off his goatskin jacket and plunged it unceremoniously into the font's pool, instantly fouling the water with clouds of dirt and dust and pungent sweat. Naked from the waist up, Kon's muscles rippled like coiling serpents. And his eyes glinted narrowly as he answered:

"Is it so, Bejam?" From hot conduit throat and cavern lungs such soft and gently spoken words. But Bejam Thad no fool:

"Kon, we're like brothers, you and me. Brothers can talk—say what's in their minds . . ."

The other nodded. "And they can fight, too," he replied, dragging soaking jacket from font and wringing it in gnarly hands that squeezed out every last drop of water in a trice. "I *had* a brother, Bejam, remember? He was my twin—and I killed him."

Bejam Thad paled. "But we've been more than brothers. Why, I love you!"

"And I you," Kon slapped his back, grinning mirthlessly. "But 'ware—'twixt love and hate stretches a skin thin as fjord ice in the melt." He hung his jacket over his shoulder. "Tread wary, for the water's swift and cold beneath." Then his oh-so-soft voice took on more of its accustomed grittiness. "Any odds, why d'you say we're doing so badly? There've been wenches to stick, not so? And booze—though precious little since Thandopolis, I'll grant you that. And I admit that the Suhm-yi wine we found wasn't agreeable. But as for loot—we had rich pickings from those oafs on the Thand, didn't we? Why, you never saw so much gold in your life, not in one place! And what of the finger-and ear-rings lifted from those skinny, stinking Suhm-yi corpses? A small fortune there."

"Aye, not bad, I suppose," the other yielded with a shrug, "though a bit played out now. But . . . a queer gang, these

Suhm-yi. Four-fingered, four-toed? How's *that* for queer? And their skins—" he wrinkled his nose.

One of the others, little more than a lad, spoke up: "You didn't complain so loud when you had that Suhm-yi bitch bucking under you like a wild pony! Though damn! you yelped a bit with her nails in your back!"

Bejam glared at him. "Wipe your snots, pup—while you've still a nose to wipe!"

"What killed 'em, you think?" asked a fourth reaver, his words cutting through Bejam's heat. This one was tall as a pole and twice as thin, but tough for all that; and he had the sword's-reach of a giant to boot. "The Suhm-yi, I mean . . ."

His question was directed at Kon Athar, who pursed his lips and considered it before answering: "I've thought about it. That island where we found the female, for instance. It was well away from the main group—which was why she lived while the rest died. At least, that's how I see it."

"Eh?" Bejam grunted. "How do you mean?"

Kon raised sun-bleached blond eyebrows. "This damned red dust," he said. "Did you notice any of it on the island of the female?"

"Why, no, come to think of it," Bejam frowned.

"Think?" Kon's eyebrows climbed higher. "You?" His tone was heavy with sarcasm. "Self-praise indeed!"

"Well what in the seven hells . . . ?" Bejam burst out, tired now of game and thinking both, "Dust is dust!"

Kon grinned broadly. "Aye—but this dust was death! Volcanic, I'd guess, and poisonous." He laughed harshly as his men began hastily dusting themselves down. "Not now, you buffoons, but poisonous in its falling! Clogging the air and turning to red brick in Suhm-yi lungs—and stinking of sulphur and the reek of hell's own chimneys—which is all volcanoes are, of course."

"Poisoned, aye!" the smallest reaver whispered, scowling at the red dust where it lay thickly blown in gutters and corners. "Breath of devils, belched from inner earth!"

"But it did our work for us," Kon Athar reminded. "We'd be hard-put by now if these isles were a-crawl with Suhm-yi." He glanced about, scowling. "Where's young Bandr Toz?"

The reaver he referred to was that same youth who had lipped Bejam Thad. The latter now issued a scowl to match Kon's own, saying:

"A yappy, scampering pup, that one—forever sniffing where he shouldn't. I saw him a second ago on his way in through yon doorway. Perhaps he felt, and feared, my need to give him a good clout!"

"Bejam," said their leader, sighing mightily, "you're a big brave lad and no error—but you forget now and then that we've a clouter elect right here in our midst. Bandr's a pup, aye, and yappy as all pups are, but one day he'll make a very fine hound indeed. By which time you'll be old bones and good for nothing much except sitting by the fire and slurping soup. Now kill him if you must and be done with it, but don't clout him. Not so he'll remember, anyway."

"Kon!" came Bandr's cry from where he suddenly appeared in gloom of door, excitement shrilling his voice almost to cry of wench. "Their history, here—all here! Pictures on the walls, carvings—and they tell it all!"

"History? What's he gabbling?" Bejam scowled again.

"Tell all of what?" Kon Athar called back, stretching himself up from rim of font.

"Why, of the Suhm-yi!" the youth shrilled louder still. "Of them, of their gods . . . *and of their treasure!*"

VI

TARRA KHASH, WHEN he set his mind to it, was a man of reason. He had his rages, as most men do—his passions and his thunders—but never those blind passions and thunders renowned of the Northmen. Which possibly explained why, despite all his adventuring, he was still sound of mind and limb in a world where magic and monsters were frequent hazards, where life was cheap and swords kept ever sharp and ready.

In short he had a keen mind to match his brawny bronze back and arms, and at times when danger threatened—for instance, in the shape of a large fistful of coarse-maned reavers from the north—he was given to using that mind with a cold and calculating dexterity. How easy it would have been to let hot blood surge, to go roaring inland with flashing sword and foaming lips . . . and to die there in some dust-blown, alien street. And lie where he fell and rot under countless suns, until even his bones were dust in the wind, and never a grave or a marker to tell the world that this had been Tarra Khash, a Hrossak.

But why wear himself out in the seeking of enemies who, in the fullness of time, must surely return to this very spot, this pebbly strand where their raft lay beached just above the narrow tidemark? Let them be the tired ones when, returning to the beach, they would face the might of full-rested Hrossak. It was as simple as that . . .

No, not quite so simple.

Surprise, too, would be on Tarra's side. Aye, and what a hot, red and raw surprise it would be! Tarra smiled grimly, smacked his lips in anticipation, sharpened his wits. Time was now of the essence: time to work, time to rest, time to strike. First the work.

He carried his canoe up the beach, following the broad swath of scattered sand and pebbles tossed aside by booted reaver feet; but where the earth turned stony he veered off to find storage for his slender craft in a clump of boulders. Then, at a spot not far from Kon Athar's trail, he found himself shade from a sun already slipping fast from its zenith, ate of his provisions and made to rest himself; but before that, on impulse, he made one further excursion and climbed to the crest of the coastal ridge. Inland the terrain was mainly flat to the foot of a distant mountain range, but keen Hrossak eyes minutely scanned the land between.

There were cities out there, shining white in the sun—the strange cities and towns of the Suhm-yi, all ghostly and ashimmer now, and empty of life save somewhere the shambling shapes of barbarian intruders. And apart from them, and from Tarra himself, the entire island seemed a place of strangely dreaming ghosts, of moaning dust-devils and destinies unattained.

Tarra returned to his cover and stretched himself out. Never had he felt so alone, not in all his life, not even at the bottom of Nud Annoxin's well-cell, and for all that he was far from cold, still he shivered as the shadows slowly stretched themselves out, straight black fingers crawling on the rocks and shingle and stunted yellow grass.

It took some little time before Tarra slept, and when at last he did the sun was falling faster and the shadows creeping apace. And visible now, far out over the sea, a milk-

misty hemisphere like the domed head of some aquatic be-
hemoth rising from the deeps—the moon, eager to be up
and abroad in the night skies of Theem'hdra . . .

FOR LONG HOURS Amyr Arn had crooned the moon-runes of
Gleeth, blind God of the Moon, his supplications going up
from the rock of Na-dom first into the evening, then the
twilight, finally the night. And Gleeth had seemed lured by
the Suhm-yi's summons, for slowly but surely his celestial
course had crept him through the heavens until even now
he began to pass behind that uppermost pinnacle of Na-
dom, that pierced rock-finger whose empty socket was oval
as an eye. And the moon itself the orb which would fit that
socket perfectly, when at last the transit was at its full.

Never had Amyr Arn seen so full a moon, nor ever a
moon so beautiful . . . unless it were when his and Lula's
love was new, when all the world had seemed beautiful beyond compare.

*Oh, Lula! Lula! Last maid of the Suhm-yi. Gone, gone now and
all promise gone with you. A race no more. Perished the Suhm-yi . . .*

Amyr got to his feet. Cramped and cold he shivered as he
gazed at the golden orb in the sky, whose rim was even
now obscured by flank of spindly needle rock. Ah, such a
moon! For in those primal days the craters were not so
many and the mountains of the moon less high, and its ball
so perfectly a ball.

"Gleeth! Gleeth!" cried Amyr Arn, unmindful now of the
proper conjurations. He threw up his arms to the dark sky,
as if to fasten upon the golden orb itself, and cried of his grief, his
rage, his love, his hate. He told all the tale: of the coming of
the red dust, the death of the Suhm-yi, the tiny island para-

dise where only two had been saved, untouched by the terror-dust blown on strange winds from stranger lands. Cried of the rape and murder of Lula, of the blood-quest of a brawny, brassy Hrossak, whose fierce pride and lust for vengeance had taken him where Amyr himself was forbidden to go.

"Forbidden, aye!" he cried, striking at the needle rock with clenched fist. "Forbidden by god-given laws—which you know well enow, Old Gleeth, for you were the god who gave them. They came down from the moon, those laws, and by them since time immemorial have all the Suhm-yi faithfully abided. And so I am forbidden to strike mine enemy, who has so sorely stricken me. Which is why I am here now, to crave justice. If I may not smite him and them who worked this evil upon the last of the Suhm-yi, then give your aid, I beseech it, to one who may—to the Hrossak, Tarra Khash. Do you hear me, Gleeth? Ah, wake up, old God of the Moon!"

And now the golden disc of the moon showing a quarter-sphere through the oval orbit of the rock; and the rock itself like a thin, one-eyed menhir looking out the corner of its eye, but looking at nothing; and Amyr beginning to despair that all his prayers had gone unheard, would remain unanswered. "Gleeth! Ah, Gleeth!" he cried again. "Will you not at least answer me?—if only to deny me! I know you are blind, or very nearly so, and almost deaf from the unending songs of the stars, but are you also dumb?"

Half-way into the oval orbit now, and more like an eye than ever, finally the moon—or Gleeth, the soul and spirit of the moon—gave ear to Amyr's impassioned plea . . . and answered it! Thin and reedy that ghost-voice, that god-voice, wavering and indistinct in Amyr's ears or mind:

"Who . . . who calls me up from . . . from my centuried slumbers? And . . . and why?"

"What?" Amyr was astonished. "Have you not heard me? For hours I have called upon you! Have I not told you of the doom of the Suhm-yi, who were ever your most faithful worshippers? And did I not—"

"Yes, yes . . . all of that . . . I know, I know!" Gleeth was irritable now, not quite awake and sour in his drowsiness. *"But . . . who are you? A priestling? . . . A Suhm-yi priestling?"*

"No!" cried Amyr in his despair. "My father was a priest— a High Priest—but I have never held such office."

"Not . . . not a priest?" Gleeth began to lose interest. *"Ah! . . . Not . . . not a priest, after all . . ."* His voice, mental or physical, was fading.

"I am the last of the Suhm-yi!" Amyr howled. *"The last,* d'you hear? And before I hurl myself down from Na-dom's peak, I ask this one boon for all my race."

". . . Last? . . . Na-dom? . . . Boon? . . ." The voice faded away, drowned out by the moaning of a small night-wind come to investigate the shouting.

Amyr threw himself down on Na'dom's dome and clawed at the rock until his four-fingered hands bled. A waste, all a waste. He had failed. Last of the Suhm-yi, and a failure. Better if he had gone with Tarra Khash; better to die in defiance of god-given laws than to die utterly ignored of the gods.

And the face of the moon, blandly golden, blindly serene, standing central in the eye of the needle rock . . .

VII

TARRA KHASH HAD heard them coming a mile away. Awakened by voices blown to him on cool night breezes, he had kissed his curved ceremonial sword—sharp as a razor for all its fancy jewelled hilt—and moved lithely into the shadow of a boulder where the trail narrowed and the reavers could pass only one at a time. And as their coarse, hated northern accents grew louder, along with the scuff of booted feet and slither and clatter of pebbles, so he waited, ready to pounce upon the six.

Bejam Thad led the bunch, or rather strode at its head. Kon Athar never went first, not in the night, not even on this dead Suhm-yi island. He did not fear the night, Kon, but who could say what might or might not lie ahead? And anyway, it pleased Bejam Thad to play at being leader. Better to have him in front than behind on a night such as this, for surely the time would come when he would tire of playing and seek to lead in earnest. They were all the same, the Thads, Kon knew: treacherous! And so he brought up the rear.

Which meant that he did not even see Bejam's death but merely heard a double *hiss* in the moon-silvered darkness—the first being that of Tarra's scimitar cleaving the night in a bright, curving flash, the second the rush of air from Bejam's collapsing lungs, whistling from his severed neck.

Then Bejam's blocky headless body tumbling, and the second and third reavers in line crying out their astonishment and rage, colliding as they drew their own blades; and a figure in the full moonlight stepping forward over Bejam's body, grim and menacing as he sought to pick a target in the confusion.

The second barbarian fared no better than Bejam. He'd cleared his weapon sure enough, but stumbled as he moved forward over the body of his erstwhile comrade. Tarra had moved back a pace, but seeing the man trip he lunged forward with the point of his curved sword, which passed clean through the other's chest, ribs, spine and all.

Bandr Toz was next, whom Bejam Thad had thought a pup; but youth has its advantages, not the least being speed of thought and reflex.

Bandr snatched at the vibrating, transfixed frame of the man in front even as he died and would have fallen, hurling the upright corpse forward upon Tarra Khash. Tarra was unable to withdraw his blade, for his second victim seemed to follow him as he backed off. Indeed—despite the fact that it even now chattered a death-rattle direct into Tarra's face—the glaring, dead thing impaled upon his blade seemed intent upon knocking him from his feet! And fall Tarra did, thus losing his advantage but at least regaining command of his weapon as it jerked free of the rolling reaver's ribcage.

In the time it took Tarra to spring to his feet, however, the remaining four were through the gap. Bandr Toz, following up his ploy with a forward rush, was almost immediately upon the Hrossak, his sword splitting the air towards Tarra's head. Tarra ducked, felt steel tug at his hair, took both hands to scimitar's hilt and spun his body like a top in the manner of a steppe dervish. The first six inches of his weapon's blade entered Bandr's flesh at his side and left it at his navel, not killing him immediately but good as. Bandr went down coughing blood, cursing the Hrossak through scarlet-foaming lips.

"Three down and three to go!" roared Tarra. "And who's next of you craven dogs?"

The three closed in on him a little, while Bandr Toz writhed and cursed where he lay coiled in moonlight. "A murdering Hrossak!" Kon Athar panted, spitting his accusation as Bandr shuddered and moved no more. "But who . . . ? Why . . . ?"

Tarra knew there was little time left for lengthy words. They were still dazed, these Northmen, but that wouldn't last. He backed away a little, feigning a stumble and falling to a crouch, then coming upright with a fistful of sand and pebbles.

"A Hrossak, aye," he answered Kon, "but no murderer. I leave that to dogs such as you—night-crawlers who'd kill men in their sleep for a fistful of gold!"

The tallest of the three—that thin and gangling giant with arms long as an ape's—was closest to Tarra and inching closer. Now he gasped his recognition. "This must be the one Bejam knocked into the river!" And with those words he sprang.

His reach was amazing—and his aim deadly! Tarra turned and felt the other's blade like a fire where it singed his ribs— but at the same time he hurled his handful of dirt straight into the thin giant's snarling face. The other cried out, staggered—then shuddered mightily as Tarra's scarlet steel chopped him crosswise ear to breast. And as the thin man crumpled, so the Hrossak shouldered him to one side.

"And two to go!" he cried, still backing away. "Two more dogs, before Bogga Tull and Ilke Phant may rest in peace."

"Rush him!" cried Kon.

He and the smallest reaver sprang together, but Tarra had moved so that the fallen giant lay in the way. Kon saw his ploy and leaped over the corpse; the small reaver was not so wily. Tripping, he flew forward—full on to Tarra's point. The steel popped through his throat, punching out in a dark spray from the back of his neck—but in the next moment Kon's own blade, a massive straight-edged broadsword, came crashing down and shivered Tarra's scimitar into shards before he could draw it back from the choking reaver's throat. And as the small man died, so Tarra turned and ran for the beach, Kon Athar laughing as he stalked him down the sand and pebbles trail, under a full and apparently merciless moon.

Tarra still carried the jewelled hilt of his broken scimitar. At ocean's rim he hacked at the lashings of Kon's raft, kicked its members flying hither and thither. But the Hrossak was weakening and he knew it.

Blood seeped from the gash along his ribs, action and effort and flight had near-drained him; weaponless, he stood little or no chance against the brutish, hulking Northman. Oh, he could still stab him, but long before he got close enough for that, Kon Athar's mighty sword would have halved him.

Kon knew this too, and leaned upon his sword and grinned when he came upon Tarra and saw what he had done to the raft. "That can be mended," he rumbled low in his throat, "but you will be quite beyond repair."

Tarra stood panting, holding his wound, incapable of further effort and unwilling to flee. "Do your worst, baseborn scum of frozen fjords," he answered. "Woman-killer!"

That stung. "Woman-killer?" the reaver roared. "I've killed only men, Hrossak—a good fifty of them—in my time."

"And a woman," Tarra insisted, "whose body I found on a tiny jewel island, ravaged and murdered!"

Kon Athar started, frowned, then laughed. "A woman? Nay, lad, a creature! Suhm-yi, that one."

"A woman for all that, dog!" Tarra cursed.

Tired of talking, Kon scowled and shrugged. "Have it your own way. Me, I've a raft to repair, treasure to find and steal, and so can't linger here." Two-handed, he weighed his great sword, advancing upon the Hrossak.

"Treasure?" the other hastily questioned, clinging to life, hoping to hold his adversary back for a second or two. "What treasure? Where? Here?"

"No," Kon shook his head, sending matted mane flying. "Not on this island. But there's a holy place where their priests made offerings to the moon, to stupid old Gleeth. There go I."

" 'Ware, barbarian," said Tarra Khash. "Gleeth may be a little deaf and somewhat blind, but he's in no wise stupid. Why, the Hrossaks themselves give praise to Gleeth!"

"Aye," Kon nodded, coming close (but not so close Tarra could stab him) and lifting his sword on high, "and look where it's got you, eh?"

Behind Kon the moon stood full and round in the sky, a golden halo around his dark, evil head—a halo split by the upraised blade of his sword. "If you're a true believer, Hrossak," he grunted, "then call on your gods now, for it's farewell to all this."

And Tarra really *did* believe: he believed he was about to die. But . . . not yet! Not without one last . . .

He hurled the hilt of his sword like a knife, saw Kon twist aside as the broken blade tangled in his jacket. And the barbarian laughed deep in his throat, lifting his sword higher yet as he stepped in for the kill . . .

VIII

TWICE THIS NIGHT Old Gleeth had heard his name impugned, once by a worthy creature and once by a creature worthless, and now he was fully risen from a rarely-broken slumber of ages. And Gleeth remembered what Amyr Arn had told him, and his thoughts were now quicksilver, even as the moon is silver on wintry nights.

"Amyr Arn!" came that voice in the mind of the huddled Suhm-yi male, high on the rock of Na-dom. *"Quick, take up your bow, while still there's time!"* And no way infirm that voice now: neither infirm nor wandering but full of an awesome strength; the strength of the moon itself, which moves whole oceans on the merest whim, and balances the lunar orb above the world, bright beacon on the darkling land.

"What?" Amyr Arn came to his feet, took his bow and nocked an arrow. And eager now this revenant, last of the Suhm-yi. "Have you finally hearkened, Old Gleeth? Do you give me my boon?"

"Indeed! Be quick and take it. Draw back your bowstring, let fly your shaft!"

"But—" Amyr gazed all about into the empty night. "Where?"

"Through the hole in the rock, where else? Directly into mine eye. Sight as you understand it was never mine, Amyr Arn, and your arrow cannot harm me. But I am not so blind I can't see right from wrong. Aye, and deaf I am, but not so deaf I may ignore the outraged cries of the murdered dead!"

Amyr aimed, let fly his shaft—and through the hole in the rock sped that avenging arrow . . . and disappeared!

But before it passed from this place, this time, into some other—before Amyr saw its blurred form flicker from existence—he saw something else. A blink, yes! The blink of a great blind eye, into which, without pause, his arrow had sped upon an unthinkable journey . . .

TARRA KHASH SAW that same blink—that split-second open-ing and shutting of the moon's eye behind Kon Athar's head—but he did not see the arrow which, materializing out of the moon's face, sped to its mark in the barbarian's spine. He *did* see Kon's blade tremble on high, when by now it should be rushing down in a deadly arc, and he did see the barbarian's eyes flash open in astonishment and hear his breath rush out in a great gasp. Then it was as much as he could do to get out of the way as the Northman toppled.

After that—

Time only to find the feathered shaft buried in Kon's back, to staunch the flow of blood from his own ravaged ribs, and gather up the jewelled hilt of his scimitar. Time only to lift the small pouches of gold from Kon's pockets, and to drag his canoe painfully down to the sea. And only when he was well out on the moonlit bosom of the deep, time to begin breathing as normal and let his risen hackles settle down and his nerves stop jumping.

Then he was away as fast as his rapidly stiffening wound would let him paddle, and never a backward glance. For Tarra Khash had had his fill of these isles of the Suhm-yi. What were they, after all, but isles of shadows and ghosts . . . and magick?

Magick, aye, for how else might one explain Amyr Arn's arrow in Kon's back, and Amyr himself nowhere to be seen? Then Tarra remembered something he *thought* he had seen: the blink of the moon's great golden eye, which seem-ingly spat out an arrow to strike a man dead.

And lifting his face up to the night sky, the Hrossak

yelled: "All praise to you, Old Gleeth! A steppeman gives his thanks . . ."

And as the gooseflesh crept again on his arms and back he paddled a little harder, following the moon's path across the silent crater sea . . .

Told in the Desert

FOOTSORE, WEARY, AND black now, rather than his native bronze—his hide crisped by the inescapable sun and corrugated by weeks of wind-blown grit—a lean and ragged Hrossak staggered under a waning moon across seemingly endless drifts of sand. Lost, hungry and athirst, he knew the end was near. Dawn would bring the sun, freed once more from Cthon's nets to rise above the rim of the world and let down his golden, shimmering curtain of heat. The desert would become a furnace, a sea of dunes to trap and reflect the heat inwards, baking human flesh like that of a pig on a spit. After the many adventures Tarra Khash had known, it seemed somehow improper that he should now die here in so mundane a fashion, but that appeared to be the way of it.

Better, perhaps, to take the hilt of his jewelled ceremonial scimitar—only the hilt, with perhaps an inch or two of sharp blade remaining, for the weapon had been shattered in a grim and grisly fight—and slit his wrists and stretch out upon the sand, there to sleep his last long sleep and dream his last short dream. But . . . hope springs eternal.

Where he was, Tarra Khash knew not. Only that he headed east, and that six months had passed since he crossed the crater sea and climbed the Great Circle range of mountains which girt that land-locked ocean about. Since when he had wandered, finding water where he might, until there was no more water left to find and Death stalked him over this wasteland of yellow sand and sun-bleached stone, white now in the crisp light of stars and moon.

And so blunted by privation his once-sharp mind, and so weary his bones, that it took long and long for the fact to dawn that while his bleeding feet ploughed in sand, nathless he wandered in the drift-drowned streets of some ruined, crumbling and forgotten metropolis, some city of sand—lost in the desert no less than Tarra Khash himself. And indeed, he thought himself delirious when, approaching what had been the city's heart along a once-great thoroughfare, he saw, where mighty avenues of sand cojoined, a single silken tent and the glow of some strange nomad's fire.

But mirages were ever attendant unto the blazing sun Tarra knew, and never spawned of the moon (though certainly odd things happened when the moon was full!), and fever dreams (to which he was no stranger) were rarely accompanied by aromatic wafts from roasting, richly-spiced meats. And staggering closer he rubbed at grit- and night-inflamed eyes, seeing beside the tent a carpet spread with cushions, upon which reclined two figures, one being clad in raiment of silver while the other wore cloth of gold. So that again the thought occurred: *perhaps it is only a dream* . . .

Overcome by a sudden bout of dizziness, he fell to his knees and felt sand sting where desiccated skin split open, and gave a little cry from lips parched and puffed . . . at which the figure in gold came upright in a trice. Tarra saw, reached out, shuffled forward on tortured knees, fell at last and rolled over on to his back. And there he lay, gazing up at a sea of stars bright as jewels, where a horned moon sailed low on the rim of his vision—to be eclipsed in a moment by a figure bending over him and a face which gazed into his face.

And a voice rich as deep red wine, saying: "Woman, bring a little water, and help me draw this stricken creature into the light from the fire." A strange voice, aye, deep and strong but somehow gentle; and yet one which Tarra guessed had been hard and cold as glacial ice in its time. But not tonight.

He felt hands tug at him and could do little to help; but in another moment sweet water touched his lips and the dried-up pores of his mouth cracked open in spontaneous rejoicing. He drank, coughed, drank again . . . and cool life began to course in veins quenched of Death's destroying flame. And now at last they could help him to his feet, and guide him stumbling to their fire . . .

FOR WHAT SEEMED a very long time Tarra ate of smoking, tender meats and drank of light, refreshing wines, until he was almost ready to believe that he had in fact died and departed Theem'hdra for some Hrossak heaven of which steppe theology was totally and inexcusably ignorant. Or perhaps the gods of the desert, mistaking him for a nomad, had accepted him into a nomad heaven. Well, if so, it was taking them an inordinately long time to discover their error and cast him out.

Finally, with many an appreciative belch (a custom of theirs, he fancied or hoped) he fell back and rested himself from his feasting. And now, too, he offered his most heartfelt thanks for the life-saving repast and tossed down the jewelled hilt of his broken sword in payment. His golden-robed host—surely a lord of sorts, who sat cross-legged and watching Tarra, as he had watched since his arrival—took up the hilt and admired its gems, but shook his head and handed it back.

"No, my friend," he said in that curious voice of his, "you owe me nothing. Your company on this night of nights is more than ample repayment."

"Then," said Tarra, who had small sacks of gold tied about his waist, "at least let me pay for a little water—just a little—in which to bathe myself. Poor company I'll make, stinking of sweat and dirt and desert, and sitting here sore in my every quarter!"

"Man," said his host, smiling a strange smile, "I do not own the oasis yonder," and he nodded into the shadows beyond his tiny tasselled tent. "Its presence is providential, a boon to all travellers in this parched land."

"Oasis?" Tarra came creakingly to his feet, staring unbelieving into the dead city's central place. There beyond the tent, where certainly in the city's heyday a fountain might have spouted, tall palms made dark, stirless silhouettes against skies whose brilliant jewel stars were mirrored at their feet in deep dark waters. Tarra blinked fevered eyes and looked again. Why, now that he saw it, he could almost *smell* the water! Passing strange that he had not noticed the palms before. Or perhaps he really had stood upon Death's darkling threshold, his senses dull as the body that housed them.

But certainly the oasis was there, and so: "Will you excuse a Hrossak sore in need of bathing?" he mumbled, scarce glancing at his lordly host but gaping at the palm-fringed pool. And drawn more surely than moth to flame, he crossed to that blessed basin and gradually, gaspingly, stepped down deeper and deeper into cool depths of laving liquid; until he floated there as in the most delicious dream, his cracked skin soothed and anointed and soaking up water like a sponge. And like oiled hinges, Tarra's joints came un-stuck and his coarse hide turned back to skin, however blackened, and at last he drifted to the bank where he sat and washed away all the aches and pains of his body and the sloth of his fatigued mind. So that while he cleansed himself he pondered something of the strangeness of his situation.

Clear-minded for the first time in—how long?—he con-sidered all. This wasteland was doubtless the ill-omened and Nameless Desert, wherein legends whispered of just such a sundered, smothered city. Nothing strange in that . . . but an oasis? Now maps were scarce in Theem'hdra, but Tarra had always had an interest in such and had studied them minutely whenever the occasion arose. But no map he ever saw had shown a water-hole here. And the place in such ut-ter abandon. Why, the pool was more a small lake, doubt-less sprung from some deep well! Possibly the olden collapse of the city had been due to a gradual blockage or drying-up of ancient natural springs, which had now replenished or opened themselves up once more. In which case nomads would eventually find it, name it, and life would flourish here again.

But . . . the Nameless Desert? Hundreds of miles to Chlangi the Doomed across the Mountains of Lohmi, and farther yet to Eyphra on the River Marl. And so . . . whence came the lord and lady here?—how, and why? Where were their yaks, their beasts of burden? Nowhere in sight, at least. And where the servants of the pair, whose eminence was obvious? Perhaps camped elsewhere, thus ensuring the pri-vacy of their master and mistress.

But . . . no footprints in the sand save Tarra's own, no distant glow of campfires, no evidence at all to support the theory that his benefactors were escorted and protected by a retinue of servitors. Most odd . . .

The Hrossak finished his ablutions and looked back beyond the tent to where the two sat together, silent in the guttering firelight and the gleam of stars and crescent moon. They leaned a little toward each other, and there was a sadness in the scene. Had they been young lovers, then even now were they safe in the tent, naked as babes and twining in silken sheets, hot in each other's arms. But they were in those years when lust has given way to a truer love, when the companionship and trust of years has blossomed into a greater understanding and a fondness beyond the youthful fascination of mere flesh. A oneness.

They were fortunate, Tarra thought, beyond measure fortunate. In that they had each other. And he felt the stirring of a certain loneliness deep inside, for he had no one . . .

What?—he checked himself, snorting. *What . . . ?* He snorted again.

A man alone, aye, and better that way by far. What?—a wandering, unfettered Hrossak—lonely? Ridiculous the very thought! But he felt an ache in himself for all that. Funny to think that one who just an hour ago had stumbled doggedly from Death's relentless pursuit should now seemingly begin to despair the futility of living! And yet again Tarra Khash snorted. The futility of life? Hah! It was only the chill of the pool which caused him to shudder, nothing more, as he made to put on his ragged breech-clout.

"Hold," said that rich strong voice close at hand, breaking into his thoughts and causing Tarra to start under the palms. He had not heard the approach of his host—wondered, indeed, how anyone could have managed it in the mere moments elapsed since he had peered curiously across the sand-sunken thoroughfare, past the tent, to where the two had sat upon their fine carpet—but here he was, and handing the Hrossak garments of sheeny silk at that.

"Be at your ease in decent raiment, Tarra Khash, soft against your roughened skin. Keep them as long as you may."

Tarra was overawed. "But these clothes . . . I mean, I can't . . ."

"Not that there's aught amiss with a breech-clout—in the right place and at the right time. But not, I fear, in the Nameless Desert's sundered city; not at night, when the chill of the desert tends to bite. Now dress and join us at the fire and tell us your tale."

"My tale?" Tarra looked vacant; but with a smile the man had already turned away, a shadow beneath the palms. "My tale . . ." the Hrossak mumbled again, then called out loud, "Aye, why not? I've a tale to tell for sure! If it will . . . amuse . . ." But he was talking to himself. He shrugged, put on baggy silken breeks and shirt, and made for the low-guttering fire.

NOW TARRA KNEW that by rights he should sleep. That way the good wine, the food, the water in which he'd swum and cleansed himself, would all work on him to their best effect and he'd rise up a new man, fit once more to face whatever lay ahead. But at the same time he knew he stood in the debt of the man in gold and the woman in silver: sore in debt. Without their intervention—had he not stumbled upon them in the night—then Tarra Khash had been one dead Hrossak for sure. Fit only for the morrow's vultures.

And sure enough he had a tale to tell. And who better to tell it to than a man who knew his name without ever being told it?

So . . . tell it he did, cross-legged in the glow of the fire, upon which his host tossed a knotted, sun-bleached tree root to bring it sparking and crackling awake. He told of all of his wanderings:

Of the tribal feud which had driven him from the steppes in the first place, swearing to return one day and right a great wrong—of his adventures in the coastal forests far to the south, and in the subterranean vaults of Ahorra Izz, the god of scarlet scorpions—of his sorry sojourn at the house of Nud Annoxin in Thinhla, and his feverish flight therefrom—of his doings in Thandopolis (but not all of them, for the gentle lady's sake) and his subsequent panning for gold in the foothills of the Great Circle Range—of the murder of two new-found friends at the hands of fjord-bred barbarians, and of the sudden demise of those same dogs at his own hands, with the help of Gleeth, blind old God of the Moon—and finally of his journey from the Inner Isles of the Suhm-yi to this place, this wilderness of sand with its lost city and life-giving oasis.

"And that," he finally concluded, "is that. Here I found the two of you, and was restored. There is no more, the tale is told."

His host nodded. "Indeed. A fine tale. And well told. It has given us pleasure." His lady agreed, saying:

"The gods favour you, Hrossak, for your goodness. They would not let a good man die but guided you here. And now you grow weary and would doubtless sleep. There is a blanket in the tent. Go there, cover yourself, sleep well. And please, no protestations. Tonight my husband and I sit beneath the stars. Tonight we have no need of sleep. Tomorrow, perhaps . . ."

Tarra looked at her for long moments, looked also at his host. He was tired, true, but . . .

"Hrossaks," he said at last, "are not generally known for their curiosity. By token of which I am unusual. In any case, it is an old custom in the steppes, about the campfires, to answer one tale with another. It could be said, I suppose, that I presume upon your already unrepayable generosity, and yet—"

"You would have a story?" his host smiled a slow sad smile, and nodded. "I know of that custom. Very well—but understand, it is merely a story, a fable, a trivial thing. Your tale was a chronicle of your life, your adventures. A tale of blood and swords, of monstrous men and beasts. A wild, surging, passionate thing. Mine will be a tale of lovers parted and sorrow turned to red revenge. By comparison, a sad thing."

"A tale is a tale," said Tarra Khash, "and I would hear it."

"So be it," said his host. And this is the tale he told.

ONCE UPON A time, oh, many, many years ago, before even Mylakhrion, that mightiest of wizards, was grown to maturity—indeed in an age when Mylakhrion was the merest apprentice in the tutelage of Khrissa's ice-mages—there dwelled here in the Nameless Desert, which was then a fabled, far-flung forest, a magician of no mean prowess whom we shall call Dramah, because that was not his name. But he was a good man as wizards go, and none went in fear either of Dramah or of his sorceries, which were white magicks as opposed to black. Aye, and he had the girl of his young dreams for wife, and they had lived together long and long, and happy, in each other's arms.

Now in those days there was a king of these parts, a man of many great strengths and some great weaknesses, one of which being his gluttony. Gylrath was his name, Gylrath the Great; but a joke whispered among his people was that his name referred not alone to deeds but more properly to the size of his belly! Be that as it may—his gluttony and all—still he was king. And his wizard advised him, read runes and omens and auguries for him, cast protective spells about his palace and lands, and so on and so forth. So that the king, Gylrath, might be thought more than satisfied with the works of his wizard. And so he might have been, except . . .

The king had gout, and Dramah . . . well, he was a wizard, *not* a physician. And as the king's condition worsened, so that worthy mage found himself more and more the butt of his sire's bad temper. And particularly galling the fact that the cure was in the king's own hands. All Gylrath need do was control his eating and drinking, and his temperance would do the rest; his grossly swollen left foot would shrink commensurate with his diminished intake of rich, rare foods.

Unfortunately, for all that the wizard could do nothing about King Gylrath's condition, he had at one time in an unguarded moment mentioned to his monarch a certain legended panacea, all of whose exotic ingredients were in his possession save one. This one missing agent was the crushed root of the green and poisonous swamp orchid of Shadarabar across the Straits of Yhem, where seldom a white man, even a wizard, had ever dared set foot. Many Yhemni tribes were known as cannibals, their forests and

swamps full of malignant monsters, hybrid beasts and carrion birds, where crept vile vegetation and injurious insects.

But it seemed the king had taken no note of his wizard's
words on that subject . . . until a morning dawned when
Gylrath's pain was very great, when finally recalling the slip
of that good mage's tongue, he demanded that a quest for
the green orchid of Shadarabar commence at once, and that
once found the root of the flower be brought back with all
dispatch to his palace, and that there the panacea be prepared and a cure affected.

Now the king's wizard was a learned astrologer, and he
read in his own stars a terrible calamity should he under-
take this quest on behalf of the king; and so he pleaded with
Gylrath that the journey be postponed until the auspices
stood more in favour. Gylrath would have none of it, order-
ing that the mage be on his way at once, lest his lands and
lordly house be taken from him and he himself cast out to
seek service with some other monarch. And the good mage
read the king's signs, seeing that they, too, were less than
favourable, and told this also to Gylrath. Whereupon the
king waxed wroth indeed, stating that it seemed his magician sought only to deny him a cure for his ailing foot, and
warning him that it were best he got about his wizardly du-
ties without more ado.

And being good and loyal—even to a master such as Gylrath, and for all that the king himself was wrongheaded and
wilful—Dramah sighed and said a fond farewell to his wife,
took up his runebook and soared southward upon a carpet
endowed by his magick with the power of flight. And thus
his search commenced.

Alas, because of its poisonous qualities, the green orchid

was much sought after by the blacks of Yhem for use upon the points of their blow-darts, spears and arrows; and even in jungled Shadarabar itself, that darkest of Yhemni strongholds, the species was fast nearing extinction.

And through six long fruitless months of searching, Dramah grew ever more dismayed. Because of the thickness of jungle growth, the density of swamp's lethiferous leafage, he was in the main at a loss with regard to using his flying carpet, and going afoot into these boggy, hothouse places was fraught with peril.

But go he must, and uncomplainingly, for other than Gylrath's disagreeable nature—which might well abate upon production of the sought for panacea—Dramah's life was good and he had all he could desire of splendid things. Aye, and the great forest a beautiful place to live, where nowhere were seen the blistering drifted dunes which today are all that remain of that forgotten demesne.

And so the months grew into a year, and Dramah longed for home and gradually sickened from the fevers of the swamps and the foulness of their vapours. The insects stung him and drank of his blood, likewise great leeches which inhabited the sullen waters; and on more than one occasion only his magick saved the sorcerer from certain death. But as the mage weakened so the efficacy of his spells suffered, and toward the end of his search he spent much of his time racked upon a Yhemni pallet in a smoky village of savages, who revered him because he was a wizard.

And tossing in just such a fever—one which lasted for twenty days and nights—Dramah did not see the visiting Yhemni chief who took a fancy to his carpet and bore it away with him, never knowing its thaumaturgical properties. So that when at last Dramah awakened and raised himself up from his fevers, it was only to be plunged into deepest despair by discovery of his great loss.

But at last he found the green orchid and procured its root, and tried to be firm in his conviction that the worst was behind him and that the disasters foreseen in his stars now lay in his wake, all overcome and receding. And so he prepared for his return to the Nameless Desert, which was in those bygone days a great and green forest.

Alas, the worst was not yet.

Because of the loss of his carpet, Dramah must now employ lesser marvels to speed him on his journey; and to this end he unwrapped from oiled skins that great runebook containing all of his spells and enchantments. There was a spell there for the conjuring of boots which walked with the speed of a running yak, and another to turn miles into half-miles and legs into stilts. And . . .

Worms had eaten of the oiled skins! Dramah could not believe his eyes, his ill-fortune. The skins were in holes and a rot born of the swamps had found its way into the bundle. Aye, and the illuminated pages of the runebook all in tatters, with neither sigil nor cypher visible in the mould, so that all fell into smoking dust from Dramah's trembling fingers!

And a year and a quarter elapsed since last he had seen his beloved wife, and still a journey of months ahead, of privations and agonies and fever dreams. But locked in Dramah's head countless smaller spells and thaumaturgies, protection against the perils of the way, which should at least give him advantage over any merely mundane traveller.

And so he set out.

Long the jungle trails to Shad, and wide the Straits of Yhem—where Dramah's chartered Yhemni ship was tossed by storm and whirled in resistless maelstrom—and dense the mainland's coastal forests before fever-weary eyes lighted upon the grass-lands and steppes of Hrossa. And many the dark dream sent to torment the mage through endless nights of tossing and turning, while his skin burned and sweated and the poisons of the swamps coursed in his veins.

Dreams of dark omen, of nightmare portent. And Dramah, because his knowledge of oneiromancy was great, read in these dreams DOOMS and DAMNATIONS, so that he smoked of the Zha-weed and called upon the ghosts of his very ancestors for their aid and advice. And in this that long-suffering sorcerer knew he risked great disfavour, for ghosts are loth to be disturbed and Dramah's forebears had been mighty wizards all.

Nathless they heard his pleas, saw his plight, came to him one by one in the turmoil of his dreams.

And he said to the first of them: "I know you not, only that I am of your blood, your line. Grant me a boon."

"What is it?" asked the shade.

"Give me that which will speed me home."

"I cannot," the revenant shook its hooded head. "But I may tell you this . . ." And he told Dramah how armies might be whelmed at the utterance of a word, so that the dreaming mage knew that this one had been a great warrior wizard. And that thunderous Word of Power lodged itself firmly in the tortured mage's mind.

Then, upon another night, came a second spirit, and this one's voice was a whisper of reeds in the wind. "How may I help you, Dramah, son of the sons of my sons?"

"O ancestor mine," said Dramah, "I seek transportation to my house, which is far and far away, to the loving wife who awaits me there. Make the miles between dwindle; give me wings; speed my feet homeward."

"No," the spirit shook its mummied head, its worm-fretted lips quivering, "that is beyond me. But I do not come empty-handed." And from skeletal fingers Dramah accepted a vial of amber fluid, whose purpose his long-dead ancestor explained in whispered detail, so that Dramah knew him for a powerful alchemist.

And in time yet a third night visitor came, of whom Dramah implored the same boon, and who likewise denied him but offered instead a strange spell. "A whistle?" Dramah's perplexion was plain. "Of what use a whistle?"

"There are whistles and whistles, child of my children's children," said the mist-shrouded visitant, "and in my day I was acclaimed the greatest whistler of them all." And he whistled a weird tune which entered Dramah's mind and stayed there, so that he might never forget it.

Finally, upon a night when the mage had crossed the River Luhr and the Great Eastern Peaks lay upon his right hand—indeed when the mighty forested domain of Gylrath lay only weeks and days distant—there came a cereclothed ghost who gifted to him a rune awesome and awful; of which Dramah made careful note, then put at once to the back of his mind. For this latest lich had been a necromancer, knowing all the secrets of Death and the lands beyond; and Dramah considered it an event of great ill-omen that this had been his final visitor.

Now, as the footsore sorcerer covered the last of those miles of his journey, so the fevers left him and his strength returned. And though his mien was changed forever (grey now his hair and faded his once-bright eyes) in spirit he remained the same . . . at least until he came to the forest's edge.

Came there—and found the forest burning!

And all about in the fire and reek, the huts of woodsmen and the mean cottages of the king's gamekeepers in flames, and the men themselves slain and their women murdered or carried off. And in a daze Dramah came to his own house, whose great garden walls had kept the blaze at bay, and entering found an old and faithful retainer who told him all that had passed while he was away: how a barbarian warlord had arisen amongst the tribes of Lohmi, and how that warrior had banded all the tribes together and brought them down out of the mountains to war with Gylrath. How even now the king lay ensieged in his great walled city at forest's heart, while barbarians scoured the land about for women to ravage and goods to plunder.

But when Dramah asked for his wife, then his ancient servant bowed his head and fell silent and spake no more. And divining the truth, Dramah went to Gylrath's city; even to that besieged city whose name has never since been spoken, word and legend of which were long-since stricken from all books and charts. And there he saw the barbarian horde ringing the walls about, and when they would come upon him spoke that Word of Power given him by a certain dead ancestor.

And lo!—the army out of Lohmi was whelmed, turned to sere dust in a moment and blown away on the wings of a demon wind.

Now the city's defenders, all that were left of Gylrath's troops, looked down from the walls and saw Dramah alone where barbarian hordes had laid in siege. But they knew him not, this ragged wizard whose doomful mien could in no wise be that of the Dramah they had known, long gone upon a king's mission into the south. And when he called up to them to open the gates, then they took up their bows and would have slain him; except he whistled a peculiar note, then several more, weaving them into a tune. And lo!—the city's walls trembled and split assunder, and tumbled down as if riven by lightnings and earthquakes.

And the survivors of the crashing walls cowered back and offered no interference as Dramah went to the palace and came before his monarch where Gylrath lay sick abed. Sick, aye—sick with terrors and tremblings and fear for his own skin. And the king was surrounded by his ladies and courtiers, and by platters of succulent meats, dishes of fruit and flagons of wine, with which he comforted himself.

When Gylrath saw Dramah he rose up at first astonished, then outraged. And unmindful of the mage's strange air and the ominous alterations in his bearing and aspect, Glyrath blustered and roared until he foamed at the mouth, saying:

"Where have you been, dog of a wizard? Sent out upon a child's errand and only now returned, these many months later! Speak!" For as yet the king knew nothing of the whelming of the barbarian horde, nor of the sundering of the city's walls. And in his great fear of the mountain warriors he was nigh distraught, for at any moment his defences might be breached and the enemy loosed upon the palace and Gylrath himself.

"Good news, Gylrath," Dramah bowed low, his face unchanging. "For I have returned with the root of the green orchid."

"What?" the king's amaze was vast. "*What?* A flower's root? Man, mine enemies are upon me! What use such petty potions now?"

Still the wizard's visage remained calm and strange, and seeing this many courtiers and ladies gradually backed away and made quietly from the king's chambers. "The barbarians are no more, O King," said Dramah. "I blew them away, dust upon the wind."

Gylrath's mouth fell open. "Is it so?"

"It is so, sire," said the mage.

Now the king commanded a runner go see if it was so, and the man returned saying it was. But he also whispered to Gylrath of the matter of the utterly sundered walls. Enraged once more the king pointed an accusing finger at Dramah, saying: "And what of the city's walls and my defenders?"

"They would not let me in. Indeed, they would have slain me, who only desired to serve his king," said the mage. And still unchanged the sad, vacant expression upon his face, the monotony of his voice.

"Then I shall slay *them*!" cried Gylrath, "Those of them that remain—to a man."

"And yet you did not slay the barbarians who took my belongings for their own and ravaged my wife unto death," said Dramah; and now there was a strange yellow fire burning in his eyes.

"I had my lands to protect, my city, my palace!" the king protested. "How then might I be expected to protect the lodge of a wizard at the very edge of the forest?"

"How indeed?" Dramah nodded his understanding, his voice sinking to a whisper, the fires in his eyes blazing brighter.

"But I sent out my generals with all their troops, who fought bravely—or so I'm told."

Now Dramah lifted his eyebrows. "You were not with them, O King?"

"What? You would expect me to fight? With a foot like mine?"

Dramah smiled a mirthless smile—seeing which, several more courtiers and ladies left the king's chamber. "Well, my liege," the wizard finally answered, "at least the cure for that is at hand. Your great foot shall soon be shrunken down, highness, and all your miseries at an end."

"Then get about it at once!" Gylrath commanded, for he was the king and all his enemies destroyed, and so his fear was forgotten.

And Dramah prepared his potion thus and thus (which should be prepared so and so). And he made this sign high and wide (which should be low and narrow). And he spoke the right words in the wrong order, until at last an ointment steamed in a bowl, which with dispatch the mage applied to Gylrath's great blue and lobsterish foot.

At once—upon the instant—the king uttered an "Oh!" and an "Ah!" and settled back sighing upon his silken cushions, closing his eyes in the abrupt and delicious relaxation of his pain. And as his grotesquely distorted foot commenced to shrink, so Gylrath reached out his hand and took up a bunch of grapes, munching until their juices ran down his jowls; for a sudden thirst was on him. And after the grapes he quaffed down a great goblet of wine at a single draft.

And more courtiers and ladies fled the room, for the fires behind Dramah's eyes were grown fierce now and feral. Only the king himself seemed blind to the sorcerer's silent passion, for he had eyes only for the wonder of his rapidly shrinking foot—and for the platters of food surrounding him where he lay. And, "Look! Look!" he cried in his delight. "See what my most worthy mage has done!" And he reached for a slab of steaming meat; for now he felt of a great hunger, as if he had not eaten in days.

Down went the bloated member, its poisonous hues fading fast and all the puffiness going out of heel and toes; until in a trice the king's foot was returned to normal shape and size, and all pain vanished along with throbbing flesh.

But hand in hand with the rapid reduction of his foot came a sharp increase in Gylrath's already overactive appetite, so that he could scarce speak for the viands and fruits and wines with which he stuffed and swilled his mouth; and still no alarm in the king, merely delight at the cure Dramah had wrought upon his no longer distended member.

Ah!—but while Gylrath himself was blind to the strangeness here—to a sudden and dramatic change in the very atmosphere of the palace, which now seemed charged with an hideous expectation—not so his court flunkies. Only a handful of these remained now, and when Gylrath gave his first sharp cry of pain, they too departed in less than decorous haste.

And now Dramah's eyes were balefires and his face a skull fixed in what might have been a mirthless grin. And when the king cried out again Dramah's jaw fell open and he bayed and boomed and laughed a laugh harsh and throaty as the rattle of Yhemni crotala; and his back and sides jerked and heaved with his laughter, which was quite mad and loud so as to utterly drown out the king's shrieking.

For the shrinking of Gylrath's foot had not stopped upon its attaining the correct dimensions but continued without abate, and now the skin covering that offending member was white as driven snow and slack as a eunuch's foreskin. And not only the king's foot but all of his limbs, shrinking away and whitening while his skin lay in pallid folds about his once-great neck and arms and thighs. Indeed all of his person, shrinking away . . . with the exception of his belly.

Gylrath's belly, to the contrary, came rising up, splitting his satin breeks, shiny as a ripe apple and spherical as the full moon! And still he crammed his screaming mouth with food and slopped wine into his contorted, quivering jaws. Too late he saw how he had wronged his mage; too late he recognized the monstrous magick wrought upon him. And now Dramah stopped laughing, glared once upon the white and swollen spider-thing which gobbled and gibbered upon the bed, swelling huge amidst white and billowing expanses of defunct skin, then turned and with never a backward glance strode from the chamber, a man demented.

And a white foam flecked the corners of the sorcerer's mouth, and whoever saw it covered his eyes and fled him at once. So that he stalked through the palace like a spectre, and only Gylrath's choking, slobbering screams to accompany him.

And where Dramah walked, there he scattered amber droplets from a vial given him in a certain dream; and fine marble fell to sand all about him, and statues of onyx crumbled away, until the palace was a sagging ruin. And still the shrill, agonized wails of the ensorcelled Gylrath continued—but only for a little while.

For as Dramah made away from the palace of the king—now a tottering pile which spilled sand from its every portal—there came a final shriek which gibbered quickly into silence, preceding briefly the sound of a rending too terrible to describe . . .

Then Dramah left the city, scattering droplets along his way, and all who saw him knew the place was cursed, took up belongings and fled. And in a day and a night the entire area of the city was a desert; the sand rapidly spreading outward like a blight, consuming all that remained of what had been a great and wondrous forest. Aye, and even today the blight spreads, though much more slowly now.

Well, for many a weary day Dramah wandered and raved in his madness, until rising up one morning he knew what he had done and wept. And remembering his wife, dead now and gone forever from the world, he wept again long and loud and unashamed.

Gone forever, unless . . .

For at last Dramah had remembered the rune given him by the fourth dream-lich, and now he knew what he must do.

Putting aside all other things he made his preparations; and a joy was in him as the correct season approached, bringing with it an auspicious quarter of the moon; and the stars turned in their inalienable orbits and became positioned aright. Then, at the precise minute of the hour, he offered up a last prayer for all wizards past and wizards yet to be, and in no small trepidation said the words of the rune; upon which, in the merest blink of an eye, Dramah became one with the sands of this vast and Nameless Desert.

Gone—gone like the good wife of his young dreams—but not gone forever!

For the magic of the rune was this: that in giving up his own worldly life he had engineered the return of his dear wife from the world of shades; so that he might be with her again, full-bodied and -minded, but for only one night out of any year, which night would be upon the anniversary of the utterance of the rune. And this was the boon his necromantic ancestor, who had known all the secrets of life and death and the lands beyond, had given Dramah in a dream.

And now the tale is told . . .

THE FIRE HAD guttered down to red embers and Tarra could no longer hold off his weariness. His eyelids drooped and his head nodded where he had slumped down upon the carpet in his fine silks; and Shoosh, Goddess of the Still Slumbers, called him gently to her arms and would not be denied. Nor was his fatigue entirely natural, for his limbs were leaden now and answered not at all the commands of his will. It was as if he were drugged, or perhaps hypnotized. Aye, and certainly his host's voice had been hypnotic in its timbre. But . . . still there was a question Tarra Khash would ask, if only his trembling lips would obey him.

They would not, but no matter: it seemed his host had read his mind.

Through shuttering eyes the Hrossak regarded the pair where they sat opposite, now in each other's arms, and they smiled at him. And the man in gold said:

"What? You think that I . . . ?" And he gave a little chuckle. His voice was teasing when he continued: "No, no, Tarra Khash, not I. I merely came here to fathom the mystery of the tale, that is all. To discover if a myth might not in fact be reality. For indeed this is the night, and this is the place. But . . ." and he shrugged. "Dramah and his lady came not, only a Hrossak lost and athirst—and very, very weary. So sleep, Tarra Khash, and do not let the question trouble you. May your dreams be pleasant, and all the gods of the steppes be with you."

To which, by way of reply, Tarra sighed and began to snore . . .

DAWN'S LIGHT AND chill roused him up, before the sun was full-risen. He felt well and restored and good for a thousand miles. Which was as well, for he might have all of that and more to go.

Of the oasis, the tent, the carpet and his breeks and jacket of silk—nothing, no trace. But he found his breech-clout tossed down in the sand.

Aye, and something else:

Two low mounds of sand in human outline, flowing one into the other. One flecked with gold, the other with silver . . .

Curse of the Golden Guardians

I

THIN TO THE point of emaciation and burned almost black by a pitiless sun, Tarra Khash came out of the Nameless Desert into dawn-grey, forbidding foothills which, however inarticulate, nevertheless spoke jeeringly of a once exact sense of direction addled by privation and dune blindness. For those misted peaks beyond the foothills could only be the southern tip of the Mountains of Lohmi, which meant that the Hrossak had been travelling a little north of due east, and not as he had intended, south-east toward his beloved and long-forsaken steppes.

Another might have cursed at sight of those distantly looming spires of rock in the pale morning light, but Tarra Khash was a true Hrossak for all his wanderlust, and not much given to bemoaning his fate. Better to save his breath and use the time taking stock and planning afresh. Indeed, it could well prove providential that he had stumbled this way instead of that, for here at least there was water, and an abundance of it if his ears played him not false. Surely that was the thunder of a cataract he heard? Aye, and just as surely his desiccated nostrils seemed to suck at air suddenly moist and sweet as the breath of his own mother, as opposed to the desert's arid, acrid exhalations.

Water, yes!—and Tarra licked his parched lips.

Moreover, where there's water there are beasts to drink it, fish to swim in it, and frogs to croak in the rushes at its rim; and birds to prey upon frogs and fishes both. But even as thoughts such as these brought a grin to haggard Hrossak features, others, following hard and fast upon their heels, fetched on a frown. What he envisioned was nothing less than an oasis, and never a one-such without its lawful (or often as not *un*lawful) masters and protectors. Mountain men, perhaps, well known for their brute natures; or polyglot nomads from the desert, settled here in what to them must surely be a land of plenty.

Or . . . or perhaps he made too much of a mere sound, a touch of moisture in the morning air. For after all he *had* ventured here by chance; perchance he was the first such to venture here. Still, better safe than sorry.

Tarra had several small sacks of gold tethered to a thong about his waist. Other than these he wore a loincloth and carried a scabbard slung diagonally across his back, in which was fixed the jewelled hilt of a curved ceremonial sword; but just the hilt and a few inches of blade, for the rest had been shivered to shards in battle. Tarra kept the broken sword not for its value as a weapon but for the jewels in its hilt, which were worth a small fortune and therefore held high barter value. A man could buy his life many times over with those gemstones. Moreover, anyone seeing that hilt stuck in its scabbard would picture an entire sword there, and a Hrossak with a scimitar has always been a force to be reckoned with.

Jewels and gold both, however, might well prove too much of a temptation, for which reason Tarra now removed the sacklets from their thong and buried them beside an oddly carved rock. That was better; few men would risk their necks for a sweaty breech-clout, and scarcer still one who'd attempt the removal of a man's personal weapon!

And so Tarra climbed rocks and escarpments toward sound of rushing water and taste of spray, and along the way ate a lizard he killed with a rock, until after half a mile an oft-glimpsed glimmer and sparkle was grown to a shining spout of water descending from a high, sheer cliff. By then, too, the sun was up, and the way grown with grasses however coarse and bushes of thorn, then flowers and a scattering of trees with small fruits, and some with carobs and others with nuts. Here a small bird sang, and there the coarse grasses rustled, and somewhere a wild piglet squealed as it rooted in soil now loamy. A place of plenty indeed, and as yet no signs of Man or of his works, unless—

—Unless that was firesmoke Tarra's eager nostrils now suspicioned, and a moment later more than suspicioned: the tangy reek of a wood fire, and the mouthwatering aroma of pork with its juices dripping and sputtering on smoking, red-glowing embers.

By all that was good!—sweet pork for breakfast, and a pool of clear water to draw the sting from sandpapered skin and soothe the stiffness from creaking joints. Tarra went more swiftly now, lured on irresistibly; and yet he went with caution, until at last he reached the rim of a great bowl-like depression in a wide terrace of rock beneath beetling cliffs. And there, lying flat upon his belly, he slowly craned forth his neck until the cataract-carved pool below, and its sandy margins, lay visible in every aspect to his desert-weary eyes. And a sight for sore eyes it was:

The pool was round as a young girl's navel, and its waters clear and sparkly as her blue eyes. Fish there were in small shoals that Tarra could plainly see, and reeds along one curve of bank, giving way to a species of wide, low-hanging willow which grew in a clump where the rock was cleft. And there sat one who looked like an old man half-in, half-out of the sweet green shade, at his feet a fire whose smoke rose near-vertical to the sky, except where gusts of spume from the waterfall caused it to eddy.

Even as Tarra watched, the old man (if such he was) baited a hook and tossed it on a line into the pool, where fish at once came speeding to investigate. The Hrossak glanced back over one shoulder, then the other. Nothing back there: the foothills and mountains on one hand, the shimmering desert on the other. And between the two this hidden pool, or rather this lake, for certainly the basin was a big one. He relaxed; he scanned the scene again; his mouth watered at the delicious, drifting odour of roasting meat. Down below a fish took the hook, was hauled in a frenzy of flexing body and flash of scales dripping from the water. It joined several more where they glittered silver in a shallow hole close to where the old man sat. He baited his hook again, turned the spit, swigged from a wineskin. Tarra could stand no more.

Here the descent would be too steep; he would break a leg or even his neck; but over there, close to where the waterfall plunged and turned the lake to milk, were rounded terraces or ledges like steps cut in the rock, and projecting boulders for handholds. No problem . . .

He wriggled back from the rim, stood up, loped around

the edge of the bowl toward the waterfall. Almost there he stopped, used his broken sword's scant inches of blade to cut a bow, strung it with the thong from his middle. Two straight, slender stems for flightless arrows—crude but effective at short range—and he was ready. Except . . .

It is never a wise move to come upon a man suddenly, when he may well be shocked into precipitious and possibly violent reaction. Tarra went to the head of the water-carved steps, leaned casually upon a great boulder and called down: "Halloo, there!"

The basin took up his call, adding it to the thunder of plummeting waters: "Halloo, there—*halloo, halloo, halloo— there, there, there!"*

Down below, the lone fisherman scrambled to his feet, saw Tarra Khash making his way down slippery terraces of stone toward him. Tarra waved and, however uncertainly, the man by the pool waved back. "Welcome!" he called up in a tremulous croak. "Welcome, stranger . . ."

Tarra was half-way down. He paused, yelled: "Be at your ease, friend. I smelled your meat and it aroused a small hunger in me, that's all. I'll not beg from you, though, but merely borrow your hook, if I may, and catch a bite of my own."

"No need, no need at all," the other croaked at once, seemingly reassured. "There's more than enough here for both of us. A suckling pig and a skin of wine . . . which way have you come? It's a strange place for wanderers, and that's no lie!"

Tarra was down. Stepping forward he said, "Across the Nameless Desert—which is just a smidgeon dusty this time of year!" He gave his head a shake and dust formed a drifting cloud about his shoulders. "See?"

"Sit, sit!" the other invited, fully at his ease now. "You'll be hungry as well as thirsty. Come, take a bite to eat and a swig of sweet wine."

"I say gladly to both!" answered Tarra Khash. "But right now, the sweetest thing I can imagine is a dip in these crystal waters. What? I could drink the lake dry! It'll take but a moment." He tossed his makeshift bow and arrows down, stepped to pool's rim. The scabbard and hilt of sword stayed where they were, strapped firmly to his back.

"Careful, son!" the oldster cautioned, his voice like dry dice rattling in a cup—but the Hrossak was already mid-dive, his body knifing deep in cool, cleansing waters. "Careful!" came the warning again as his head broke the surface. The old man fairly danced at the pool's rim. "Don't swim out too far. The water whirls toward the middle and will drag you down quick as that!" he snapped his fingers.

Tarra laughed, swilled out his gritty mouth, turned on his back and spouted like a whale. But the oldster was right: already he could feel the tug of a strong current. He headed for the shelf, called: "Peace! I've no lust for swimming, which seems to me a fruitless exercise at best. No, but the dust was so thick on me I grew weary from carrying it around—*Ho!*" And he hauled himself from the water.

A moment later, seated on opposite sides of the fire, each silently appraised the other. The old man—a civilized man by his looks, what Tarra could see of them; possibly out of Klühn, though what such as he could want here the Hrossak found hard to guess—was blocky turning stout, short of stature and broken of voice. He wore loose brown robes that flowed in the nomad fashion, cowled to keep the sun from his head. Beneath that cowl rheumy grey eyes gazed out from behind a veil of straggling white hair; they were deep-set in a face much seamed and weathered. His hands were gnarled, too, and his calves and feet withered and grey where he shuffled his open leather sandals to scuff at the pebbles. Oh, he was a grandfather, little doubt, and yet—

Tarra found himself distracted as the other teased a smoking chunk of pork as big as his fist from the spit and passed it over the fire on a sharp stick. "Eat," he growled. "The Nameless Desert is no friend to an empty belly."

Feeling the sun steaming the water from his back, Tarra wolfed at the meat, gazed out over the lake, dangled a toe languidly in its waters. And while he munched on crisp crackling and tore at soft flesh, so the other studied him.

A Hrossak, plainly, who beneath his blisters and cracked skin would be bronze as the great gongs in the temples of Khrissa's ice-priests. Not much known for guile, these men of the steppes, which was to say that they were generally a trustworthy lot. Indeed, it was of olden repute in Klühn that if a Hrossak befriends you he's your friend for life. On the other hand, best not to cross one. Not unless you could be sure of getting away with it . . .

The old man checked Tarra over most minutely:

Standing, he'd be a tall one, this Hrossak, and despite his current leanness his muscles rippled beneath sun- and sand-tortured skin. Hair a shiny, tousled brown (now that dust and dirt were washed away) and eyes of a brown so deep that it was almost black; long arms and legs, and shoulders broad as those of any maned and murderous northern barbarian; strong white teeth set in a wide, ofttimes laughing mouth—aye, he was a handsome specimen, this steppeman—but doubtless as big a fool as any. Or if not yet a fool, then shortly.

"Hadj Dyzm," he informed now, "sole survivor of a caravan out of Eyphra. We had almost made it through a mountain pass and were headed for Chlangi—our planned watering place, you understand—on our way to Klühn. Mountain scum ambushed us in the eastern foothills. I played dead, as did two others . . ." (Tarra, still munching, glanced quickly about and to the rear, his keen eyes missing nothing.) Dyzm nodded: "Oh, yes, there *were* three of us, myself and two young bucks. But . . ." He paused, seemed to withdraw a little and catch at his breath. Tarra could almost taste him biting his lip. Well, he wouldn't pry. The old man could keep his secrets. Anyway, it was easier to change the subject:

"Khash," he said. "Tarra, to my friends. I'm heading for Hrossa—or should be! Now—I suppose I'll rest up here for a day or two, then get on my way again. Go with me if you will, or is your aim still set on Chlangi the Doomed?"

The other shrugged. "Undecided. Chlangi is a place of brigands, I'm told, and your Hrossa is likewise somewhat . . . wild?"

"You'd be safe enough with me, and there's sea trade with Klühn—though not much, I'll admit. Again, I've been away for many a year; relations may well have improved. One thing's certain: if a man can pay his way, then he's welcome in Hrossa."

"Pay my way!" the other laughed gratingly. "Oh, I can do that all right. I could even pay you—to be my protection on the way to Chlangi—if you were of a mind." He dipped into his robes and came out with several nuggets of gold, each big as a man's thumb.

Tarra blinked. "Then you're a rich merchant, Hadj Dyzm, or at any rate a man of means! Well, I wish I could be of assistance. But no, I believe it's Hrossa for me. I'll think it over, though."

Dyzm nodded. "Fair enough!" he barked in that strange rough voice. "And in my turn I shall give some thought to your own kind offer. But let me say this: of all my treasure—of the veritable *lumps* of gold which are mine—those nuggets I have shown you are the merest motes. For your help I would pay you ten, nay twenty times what you have seen!"

" 'Ware, man!" Tarra cautioned. "Men have been killed for a toothful! Speak not of lumps—at least not so carelessly!" It was a true statement and a sobering thought.

They sat in silence then, eating their fill for a long while, until the pork was finished and the wineskin empty. By then, too, the sun was riding high in a sky so blue it hurt, and Tarra was weary nigh unto death.

"I'm for sleeping," he finally said. "I'll be happy to find you here when I awaken, Hadj Dyzm, and if you are gone I'll not forget you. Peace."

Then he climbed to a shady ledge almost certainly inaccessible to the oldster, and with a single half-speculative glance at Dyzm where he sat in the shade of the willows below, and another out across the glittery pool, he settled himself down to sleep . . .

II

TARRA KHASH WAS not much given to dreaming, but now he dreamed. Nor was his dream typical, for he was not a greedy man; and yet he dreamed of gold.

Gold, and a great deal of it. Heaps of it, ruddily reflecting the flickering light of a torch held high in Tarra's trembling fist. Trembling, aye, for the dream was not a pleasurable thing but a nightmare, and the treasure cave where the dreaming Hrossak waded ankle deep in bright dust not merely a cave but—

—*A tomb!*

The tomb of Tarra Khash! And as behind him its great stone slab of a door pivoted, shutting him in forever—

—Tarra came awake in a moment, jerking bolt upright with hoarse cry and banging his head on jutting rim of rock whose bulk had kept the sun from him. But now . . . the sun already three parts down the sky and shadows stretching; and already the chill of evening in the air, where overhead kites wheeled against a blue degrees darker, their keen eyes alert for carrion; and the great pool grey now where it lay in the shade of the basin, and the spray from the cataract a veil of milk drifting above the fall.

Tarra lay down again, fingering his skull. He shivered, not so much from chilly flesh as a chill of the spirit. A dream such as *that* one were surely ill-omened, whose portent should not be ignored. Tarra touched his bump again and winced, then grinned however ruefully. What? A Hrossak full-grown and troubled by a dream? Terrors enough in this primal land without conjuring more from surfeit of swine-flesh!

"Ho!" came a gritty, coughing shout from below. "Did you call me? I was sleeping."

Tarra cloaked himself in his wits and sat up—this time more carefully. "I wondered if you were still there," he called down. "I couldn't see you in the shade of your tree, and the fire appears to be dead."

"What?" Hadj Dyzm came from cover, stretched and yawned. He poked for a moment at dull embers, then snorted a denial. "No, not dead but sleeping like us. There . . ." and he propped a dry branch over hot ashes. By the time Tarra had climbed stiffly down, smoke was already curling.

"Fish for supper," said Dyzm. "If I may depend on you to see to it, I'll go tend my beasts."

"Beasts?" Tarra was surprised. "Beasts of burden? Here?" He stared hard at the other in the dying light. "You said nothing of this before. Things take a turn for the better!"

"Listen," said Dyzm. "While you slept I thought things over. I've a tale to tell and a proposition to make. I'll do both when I get back. Now, will you see to the fish?"

"Certainly!" the Hrossak answered, kneeling to blow a tiny flame to life. "Beasts of burden, hey? And now maybe I'll reconsider your offer—my protection, I mean, en route for Chlangi—for it's a shorter way far to the so-called Doomed City by yak, than it is to the steppes on foot! And truth to tell, my feet are sore weary of—" But Hadj Dyzm was no longer there. Humped up a little and wheezing, he had made his way carefully upward, from one rock terrace to the next higher; and he needed his wind for breathing, not chatting to a suddenly gossipy Hrossak.

Tarra, however, chattered only for effect: chiefly to hide his hurried reappraisal of this "stranded merchant." Stranded, indeed! How so? With beasts of burden at his command? There were deep waters here for sure, and not alone in this crystal pool!

Using his broken blade the Hrossak quickly gutted the fishes, spitted them together on a green stick and set it over the stinging smoke, then checked on Dyzm's progress up the side of the bowl. And . . . he could climb surprisingly well, this old man! Already he was at the rim, just disappearing over the top. Tarra let him get right out of sight, then sprang to his feet and raced up the terraces. At the top he followed Dyzm's trail beneath the cliffs to where the water came down in a near-solid sheet from above, its shining tongue lunging sheer down the slippery face of the rock. No need for stealth here, where the thunder of the fall deadened all else to silence.

Then he spotted the oldster, but—

On the other side of the fall? Now how had he managed to get across? And so speedily! The old fellow was full of surprises, and doubtless there were more to come; Tarra must try to anticipate them.

He watched from the shelter of a leaning rock, his gaze half-obscured by rising spray from the lake. Dyzm's animals were not yaks but two pairs of small camels, which he now tended in the pale evening light. Tethered to a tree in the lee of the cliff, three of them had saddles and small bags, the other was decked more properly as a pack animal. Dyzm put down a large bundle of green branches and coarse grasses collected along the way and the camels at once commenced to feed. While they did so, the old man checked their saddle bags. And furtive, old Hadj Dyzm, as he went about his checking, with many a glance over his brown-robed shoulders, which seemed a little less humped now and, oddly, less venerable. But perhaps that was only an effect of the misty light . . .

Keeping low and melding with the lengthening shadows, Tarra retraced his steps to the bowl, down the terraces to the lake, and was just in time to keep the fishes from ruin as the fire's flames blazed higher. So that a short while later, when

Dyzm returned, supper was ready and the fire crackled a bright yellow welcome, its light reflecting in the water along with night's first stars.

Seeing that all was well, Dyzm handed Tarra a blanket he'd brought back with him from his camel-tending; Tarra threw it gratefully across his shoulders, drawing it to him like a robe. Hunching down, they ate in silence; and then, with the last rays of the sun glancing off the western rim of the bowl, the old man shoved a little more wood on the fire and began to talk:

"Tarra Khash, I like you and believe that you're a trustworthy man. Most steppe men are, individually. Oh, it's true I know little enough about you, but we've eaten together and talked a little, and you've given me no cause to suspect thay you're anything but a right-minded, fair-dealing, strong-limbed and hardy Hrossak. Which are all the qualifications you need to be my partner. Hear me out.

"If you hadn't come on the scene when you did—indeed, only half an hour later—then I'd have been long gone from here and even now on my way to Klühn via Chlangi, and to all the many hells with trail brigands and bandits! And fifty-fifty I would make it unscathed, for I'm a survivor, d'you see? Not that I'd normally complain, even if I didn't make it: a man has a life to live and when it's done it's done. Being a Hrossak, you'd agree with that, I know.

"Ah! But that's a poor man's philosophy, Tarra Khash—the philosophy of defeat. For a poor man has nothing to lose, and what's life itself but a burdensome, lingering thing? When a man becomes rich, however, his viewpoint changes. And the richer he becomes, the greater the change. Which tells you this: that since coming here I have grown rich. So rich that I am no longer willing to risk a fifty-fifty chance of hying myself to Chlangi all in one piece. Aye, for what's wealth if you're not alive to enjoy it?

"Wait!—let me say on. Now, I can see your first question writ clear across your face. It is this: how, by what means, have I, Hadj Dyzm, a poor man all my life, suddenly grown wealthy? Well, this much I'll tell you—" He brought out a weighty saddle bag from beneath his robe, spread the hem of Tarra's blanket over the smooth rock, tipped out contents of bag.

Tarra's jaw dropped and his eyes opened wide, reflecting the glow and glitter and gleam of the heap of gold and jade and jewels which now lay scintillant in the fire's flickering. And: "By all that's . . . !" he gasped, stretching forth a hand. But before his fingers could touch, Dyzm grasped them in his own wrinkled paw.

"Hold!" he cautioned again. "Wait! You have not heard all. This is but a twelfth part of it. Eleven more bags there are, where this one came from. Aye, and an hundred, a thousand times more where *they* came from!"

"Treasure trove!" Tarra hissed. "You've found a cache!"

"*Shh!*" said Dyzm sharply. "A cache? A hoard? Treasure long lost and buried in the desert's drifting sands?" Slowly he shook his head. "Nay, lad, more than that. I have discovered the tombs of a line of ancient kings, who in their time were wont to take with them to the grave all the treasures gathered up in all the days of their long, long lives!" And chuckling hoarsely, he patted Tarra's knee through the blanket.

The tombs of kings! Treasures beyond avarice! Tarra's head whirled with the sudden greed, the poisonous *lust* he felt pulsing in his veins—until a cooling breeze blew upon his brain from dark recesses of memory. In his mind's eye he saw a huge slab of stone pivoting to block a portal, heard the shuddering reverberations as that massive door slammed immovably into place, felt the weight of a million tons of rock and sand pressing down on him, keeping him from the blessed air and light.

He drew back his hand and stopped licking his lips. His eyes narrowed and he stared hard at Hadj Dyzm.

The oldster gave a harsh, hoarse chuckle. "That's a rare restraint you show, lad. Don't you want to touch it?"

"Aye," Tarra nodded. "Touch it? I'd like to wash my face in it!—but not until you've told me where it comes from."

"Ho-ho!" cried Dyzm. "What? But we haven't settled terms yet!"

Again Tarra nodded. "Well since you're so good at it, let's hear what you've to say. What are your terms?"

Dyzm stroked his gnarly chin. "The way I see it, with you along—especially in Chlangi—my chances for survival go up from fifty-fifty to, oh, say three out of four?"

"Go on."

"So let's settle for that. For your protection I'll pay you one fourth part of all I've got."

Tarra sat back, frowned. "That doesn't sound much of a partnership to me."

Dyzm chortled, low and throaty. "Lad, these are early days. After all, we can only take so much with us—*this* time!"

Tarra began to understand. "As I prove myself—that is, as you continue to survive, which with my protection you will—so my percentage will improve; is that it?"

"Exactly! We'll return—trip after trip until the vaults are emptied—by which time you'll be earning a full half-share and there'll be men enough in our employ to keep all the brigands in Theem'hdra at bay!"

"But where are these vaults you speak of?" Tarra asked, and got exactly the answer he'd expected:

"Man, if I told you that at this juncture . . . why, what need of me would you have then? Anyway, the vaults are impossible to find; I myself found them only by dint of sheerest accident. Aye, and I have sealed up the hole again, so that it's now doubly impossible."

Tarra grinned, however mirthlessly. "It would seem," he said, "for all your high opinion of Hrossaks, that this one is only trustworthy up to a point!"

"If there's one thing I've learned in life," Dyzm answered, "it's this: that *all* men are trustworthy—up to a point." He pointed at the fortune nestling in the corner of Tarra's blanket, tossed down the saddle bag. "But keep them," he said. "Why not? And take them up with you to your ledge to sleep the night, where a poor old lad with a pot belly and bandy legs can't reach you and choke your life out in the dark. But don't talk to me of trust and mistrust, Tarra Khash . . ."

Tarra reddened but said nothing. Truth to tell, old Dyzm's arrow had struck home: the Hrossak *had* taken his precautions before sleeping, and he'd done a fair bit of suspicioning, too. (Only thank goodness the old fox hadn't seen him following him, else were there a real tongue-lashing in the offing!)

At any rate Tarra said no more, nor old Dyzm, and after sitting awhile in silence they each began to make their arrangements for the night. The Hrossak found himself a smooth hollow in the stone close by—but far enough away from spouting water to be bone dry, and still retaining the sun's heat—and there curled up in his blanket. Hadj Dyzm retired yawning to an arbor in the willows, rustling about a bit amongst the branches until settled. Only then, before sleeping, was there more talk, and brief at that:

"When do you want my answer?" Tarra softly called in the night.

"Tomorrow at latest—else by noon I move on alone. But for goodwill, if that's what you seek, keep that saddle bag anyway—if only to remind you of a once-in-a-lifetime chance missed. You have a molehill; you could have a mountain."

And on that they settled down, except . . . neither one slept.

III

FOR TARRA IT was like this: the old man had seemingly dealt with him fairly, and yet still something—many things, perhaps—bothered him. The yellowish texture of Dyzm's wrinkled skin, for instance; though why simple signs of age and infirmity should bother Tarra he couldn't imagine. And the old boy's voice, croaking like Khrissan crotala. A disease, maybe? His name, too: for "Hadj Dyzm" as name were more likely found attached to a man of cold Khrissa or Eyphra, and men of those parts rarely stray. They are rigidly cold, such men, brittle as the ice which winters down on them from the Great Ice Barrier and across the Chill Sea. And merchants they scarcely ever are, who by their natures are self-sufficient. And yet this one, at his time of life, alleged a longing for Klühn, city of sophisticates, warm in the winter and the temperate currents of the Eastern Ocean even as

Khrissa in mid-summer. Or perhaps, weary of ice and frozen wastes, Dyzm would simply see out his life there, dotage-indulgent of luxuries and soft sea strands?

But what of the two who'd fled beleaguered caravan with him? Old Dyzm had mentioned precious little of them, and had seemed to regret even that! Anyway, if he were so enamoured of Klühn (via Chlangi) why come this way—around the southern tip of Lohmi's mountains, in precisely the wrong direction—in the first place?

Lastly, why show Tarra *any* of his treasure? Why not simply make him a decent offer for his assistance in crossing unscathed the badlands twixt here and Chlangi, and thence to Klühn? Surely that were wisest . . .

These were the thoughts which kept Tarra awake, but Hadj Dyzm's were something else. For where the Hrossak's were vague, curious, inquiring things, Dyzm's were cunning-sharp and dire indeed. At any rate, he had not long settled before stirring, however furtively, and rising up in the night like a hunched blot on rocks white in the moonlight. Then, pausing only to listen to Tarra's deep breathing and so ensure he slept, (which still he did not, and which Dyzm knew well enough) the old man made his way up the terraces and quickly became one with the shadows.

Tarra watched him go through slitted eyes, then replaced his sword-stump in its scabbard, rose up and followed silently behind. And no hesitation this time, no feeling of guilt or question of "trust" to bother his mind. No, for his thoughts on Hadj Dyzm had commenced to come together, and the puzzle was beginning to take on form. How the last pieces of that puzzle would fall into place, Tarra could not yet say, but he had an idea that his immediate future—perhaps his entire future—might well depend upon it.

Straight to the waterfall went Hadj Dyzm's shadow in the night, with that of Hrossak fleeting not too far behind; so that this time Tarra saw the old man pass *behind* that shining spout of water, his back to the cliff, feet shuffling along a projecting ledge, and so out of sight. Tarra waited for long moments, but no sign of the oldster emerging from the other side. The Hrossak scratched impatiently at an itch on his shoulder, scuffed his feet and adjusted the scabbard across his back. Still no sign of Hadj.

Taking jewelled hilt of sword with its precious inches of steel in hand, finally Tarra ventured on to the ledge and behind the fall—and saw at once whereto the wily old tomb-looter had disappeared. Behind the fall, hollowed by water's rush through untold centuries, a moist cavern reached back into forbidding gloom. But deep within was light, where a flickering torch sputtered in a bracket fixed to the wall. Tarra went to the torch and found others prepared where they lay in a dry niche. Taking one up and holding it to the flame until it caught sputtering life of its own, he followed a trail of footprints in the dust of the floor, moving ever deeper into the heart of the cliff. And always ahead a coil of blue smoke hanging in the musty air, by which he was doubly sure that Dyzm had passed this way.

Now the passage grew narrow, then wider; here it was high-ceilinged, there low; but as the light of the flambeau behind him grew fainter and fainter with distance, until a bend shut it off entirely, and as Tarra burrowed deeper and deeper, so he became aware of more than the work of nature here, where ever increasingly the walls were carved with gods and demons, with stalactites cut in the likenesses of kings and queens seated upon dripstone thrones. A gallery of the gods, this place—of an entire

mythology long-forgotten, or almost forgotten—and of
them that worshipped, or used to worship, the Beings of
that paleogaean pantheon.

Tarra gave an involuntary shudder as he crept silently
twixt grinning gargoyles and doomful demons, past looming, tentacled krakens and pschent-crowned, widemouthed
things not so much men as long-headed lizards; and it was
here, coming round a second bend in the passage and suddenly into a great terminal chamber, that he reached the
very heart of this secret, once-sacred place.

Or was it the heart?

For here—where the ceiling reached up beyond the limits
of torchlight, from which unsighted dome massy, morbidly
carven daggers of rock depended, and where the stalagmites
formed flattened pedestals now for teratological grotesques
beyond the Hrossak's staggered imagination—here the footprints in the dust led directly to a central area where blazed
another faggot, this one thrust callously into talon of a staring stone man-lizard. And at this idol's clawed feet more
bound bundles of dry wood, their knobs all pitched over.

Tarra lit a second torch and followed Dyzm's trail a few
paces more, to the exact centre of the chamber. Which was
where the trail ended—or rather, descended!

Between twin stalagmite thrones of winged, tentacled
krakens, (images of loathly Lord Cthulhu, Tarra knew from
olden legends of his homeland) steps cut from the very rock
commenced what seemed a dizzy spiral dive into unknown
bowels of earth. And up from that yawning pit came the
reek of Dyzm's torch, and from vaults unguessed came clatter of pebbles inadvertently dislodged.

Now Tarra knew at this stage that he had come far

enough. He felt it in his water: commonsense advising that he now retrace his steps. But to what end? No use now to plead ignorance of the oldster's secret, for certainly Dyzm would note the absence or use of two of his tarry torches. And anyway, 'twas curiosity had led the Hrossak on, not greed for more than he'd been offered. In no way did he wish any harm upon the other, (not at this stage of the adventure, anyway) but by the same token he saw no good reason why he should remain, as it were, in the dark in respect of the subterranean treasure vaults. Also he desired to know why, in the dead of night, any man should require to venture down into this place. What was it that lured the oldster? More treasure? But surely there would be time enough for that later? Alas, Tarra failed to take into account the greed of some men, which is limitless. To them those fabulous regions "Beyond the Dreams of Avarice" do not exist!

And so he set foot upon the first step, then the second, and by yellow light of flaring brand descended—but not very far. At the end of a single steep twist the corkscrew ended in a smaller chamber, where once again two stony sons of Cthulhu sat facing each other—this time across a circular shaft whose sides fell smooth and sheer into darkness. And here, too, some curious machinery: a drum of rope with pulleys, a winding handle and large copper bucket, all made fast to the weighty pedestal of one of the Cthulhu images. And tied to the other pedestal, a rope ladder whose rungs went down into gloom. Tarra peered over the rim and saw down there at some indeterminate depth the flickering light of Hadj Dyzm's torch.

Now the Hrossak examined the rope ladder more carefully, and satisfied himself that it was made of pretty stout stuff. Seating himself on the rim of the shaft, he leaned his weight on the ladder's rungs—and they supported him effortlessly. He began to lower himself—and paused.

Again that niggling mini-Tarra, the one that dwelled in the back of his mind, was whispering cautionary things to him. But cautioning of what? If an old man dared venture here at this hour, surely there could be little of any real danger? Tarra silenced the frantic whisperer in his head and peered about.

Seated there at pit's rim, he aimed his torch in all directions. There were unexplored niches and recesses in the walls here, true, and also he had this sensation of hooded eyes, of someone watching. But how possibly? By whom, watched? These stony idols, perhaps! And Tarra snorted his abrupt dismissal of the idea. At any rate, Hadj Dyzm was below, as witness the flare of his torch. Ah, well, only one thing for it—

And clenching the thin end of the faggot between his teeth, he once more set feet to rope rungs and began to descend. Up until which time, Tarra had not erred . . .

The flue swiftly widened out, like the neck of a jar, and at a count of only thirty rungs Tarra touched floor. There was the torch he had seen from above, guttering now on this cavern's floor, but of Hadj Dyzm—

The Hrossak stood with one hand on the ladder and turned in a slow circle, holding high his torch. Over there . . . more statues of Cthulhu and others of his pantheon. And over here . . . an open box carved from solid rock, its heaped contents spilling over on to the floor. But *such* contents!

Tarra stepped as in a dream toward that fabulous hoard,

and reaching it heard Dyzm's hoarse, echoing chuckle—*from above!*

He fell into a crouch, spun on his heel, leaped back toward the ladder—in time to see it whisked up, out of sight. And more important far, out of reach. So that now Tarra knew how sorely he'd been fooled, and how surely he was trapped.

"Hrossak?" came Dyzm's guttural query from overhead. "You, Tarra Khash—do you hear me?"

"Loud and clear, trustworthy one!" Tarra almost choked on the words.

"Then hearken a while," the other chortled, "and I'll tell you *all* the tale, for I've seen what a curious lad you are and I'm sure you'll be enthralled."

"By all means," Tarra growled. "Why, you might say I'm a captive audience!" And he too laughed, but a trifle bitterly.

"In all truth," said Dyzm, "I really did come out of Eyphra with a caravan—but of sheerest necessity, I assure you. Mayhap you've heard of the sulphur pits twixt Eyphra and Chill Sea?"

Tarra had: effluvium of extinct blowholes, the pits were worked by a penal colony under the watchful, cruel eyes of guards little better than criminals themselves. It was said that men aged ten years for every one spent in those hellholes, and that their skins rapidly grew withered and yellow from . . . the . . . work!

Withered and yellow, aye. Which was a fair description of the way Tarra's brain felt right now.

He sighed, shook his head in dismay, sat down in the dust. He looked up. "You escaped, hey?"

"Not so fast, Hrossak! Oh, you're right, I was there, indeed

I was—for three long years! And all that time spent planning my escape, which is all anyone does in that place, until finally it became imperative. You see, there was a ragged bone of a man in that place with me, and before he died he spoke to me of this place. His directions couldn't be simpler: come around the southern tip of the Mountains of Lohmi until you find a waterfall and pool, and so on. He had been here, you see, coming upon this place (quite genuinely) by accident. Later, weighed down with treasure, he'd fallen into the hands of mountain men. They were so awed by what he had with him that they let him live, even let him keep a bauble or two before cuffing him about a bit and pointing him in the direction of Eyphra. Aye, and weeks later he'd stumbled into that suspicious city a ragged starveling, filthy and verminous, so that when the people saw his few paltry nuggets and gems . . . Why! What else could he be but a thief? And so they'd taken away the last of his trove and sent him to dig in the sulphur pits, which was where I met him when they sent me there for murder. Ah!—but he'd already been there for four years, and it was something of a legend how long Death had fruitlessly stalked him. However that may be, all men must die in the end. And he was no exception . . .

"Now then: oft and again he'd told me the tale of these treasure vaults, but never how to get here until the very end, with the last gasp of his dying. And by then I knew he told the truth, for dying, what use would he have for lies? He knew he was finished, you see, and so had nothing to lose.

"For that matter, neither had I much to lose; which was why, at first opportunity, I ran off. No easy task, Tarra Khash, flight from the sulphur pits. I left three guards dead in my wake, and a fourth crippled, but at last I was free and running. Aye, and now I had somewhere to run.

"Bits of jewelry I'd taken from the dead guards bought me third-class passage on a caravan I met with where it entered the pass through Lohmi's peaks, following which I spent a deal of my time with a pair of guides, converting them from their loyalty to the caravan's master to my own cause. Ah!—but it's a powerful lure, treasure, as you've discovered."

Here Tarra gruffly interrupted. "What? *Hah!* You can have all your much-vaunted tomb-loot, Hadj Dyzm. Keep it and good luck to you. Nothing more than cursed curiosity caused me to follow you, and more fool me for that!"

Again Dyzm's chuckle, but darker now. "Well, and doubtless you've heard what curiosity did for the cat?"

Tarra nodded, almost groaning in his frustration. But then he took a deep breath, clenched his fists until the muscles of his arms bulged, and said: "But I've also heard how cats have nine lives. Be sure, Hadj Dyzm, that in one of them, this mouser will catch up with a certain rat!"

"Come now, Hrossak!" gurgled the other. "What's this I detect in your tone? Do you dare, in your unenviable position, to threaten? It bodes not well for our future dealings, I think! Be careful what you say. Better let me finish before you drop yourself even deeper in the mire. You see, I'm not an unreasonable man, and for all your treachery, I—"

"*My* treachery!" Tarra once more cut in, unable to believe his ears.

"Certainly. Didn't you follow me when I tended my camels in the dusk, spying on me all the way? I had thought you might discover the cave behind the falls there and then.

But no, you needed more encouragement. And so I gave you it—tonight! Aye, and haven't you admitted following me here, as I'd known you would? Curiosity, you say. But should I believe that? Am I as great a fool as you, then?"

"Amazing!" Tarra gasped. "And I'm talking to a self-confessed murderer!"

"Several times over!" Dyzm emphatically agreed. "And they needed killing all—but in any case, that's quite another matter, part of an entirely separate set of circumstances. Now hear me out:

"Where was I? Ah, yes—

"—So, there I was journeying with the caravan, putting a deal of distance twixt myself and sulphur pits, and along the way recruiting for my treasure hunt. And half-way down Lohmi's eastern flank, lo! the mountain men struck. In great numbers, too. Now, perhaps on another occasion my converted guides might have stayed and fought and died for their rightful master, but now they had a new master and he had promised them riches. Once more the old principle surfaces, Tarra Khash. Namely: a poor man will risk his all for very little gain, but a rich man's lust for life is that much stronger. Hasn't he more to live for? So it was with the guides: my whispers had set deepest desires in motion, creating a conflict of loyalties. The choice was this: stay and remain poor and perhaps die—or flee and live and grow fat and rich. Need I say more? I doubt it . . ."

"You lured the traitors here," Tarra nodded, "leaving caravan and all to tender mercy of mountain-bred barbarians. Very well, and where are your disciples now?"

"Alas, I know not," said Dyzm, and the Hrossak sensed his shrug. "Except that you are closer to them than I am."

"What?" Tarra gave a start, peering all about at the flickering shadows cast by his dying torch. (Hadj's upon the floor, had long since expired.) "Are you saying that they're down here?"

"Aye, somewhere. More than that I can't say; I've not seen them for a bit . . ." And this time Dyzm's chuckle was deep and doomful indeed.

"You mean some harm's befallen them, and you've made no effort to find and save them?"

"What? Lower myself down there?" the other feigned shock at the very suggestion. "Haven't I explained? You speak to a man who toiled three long years in the sulphur pits, remember? And you think I would willingly incarcerate myself in another of Earth's dark holes? For be sure such would be prison to me and surely drive me mad! No, not I, Tarra Khash."

And now the Hrossak, for all that he was a hard man, felt genuinely sickened to his stomach. "You let them starve down here!" he accused, spitting out the sour bile of his mouth into the dust.

"I did not!" Dyzm denied. "Indeed I would have fed them well. Meat and fishes aplenty—water, too, if they'd needed it. My promise was this: a meal each time they half-filled this bucket here with gold and jewels. Any more than that and the rope might break, d'you see? And given a stouter rope they'd doubtless swarm up it. Anyway, starve they did not and my promise was, after all, redundant . . ."

"And that was their only incentive, that so long as they worked you would feed them?" Tarra shook his head in disgust. " 'Young bucks,' you called them. Frightened pups, it seems to me!"

"Ah, no," answered Dyzm. "More than hunger goaded them, that has to be admitted."

His words—the way he spoke them, low and phlegmy, almost lingeringly—set Tarra's skin to tingling. After a while, in as steady a voice as he could muster, he said: "Well, then, say on, old fox: what other incentives goaded them? Or better still get straight to the point and tell me how they died."

"Two things I'll tell you—" Dyzm's voice was light again, however throaty, "—about incentives. And one other thing about my age, for this fox is in no way old. 'Aged' I am, aye—by dint of sulphur steam in my throat and lungs, and my skin all yellowed from its sting—but not aged, if you see the distinction. And my belly puffed and misshapen from years of hunger, and likewise my limbs gnarly from hard labour. But my true years can't number a great many more than your own, Tarra Khash, and that's a bitter fact."

"I'd marked all that for myself," said Tarra, "but—"

"But let me speak!" Dyzm's turn to interrupt. And: "Incentives, you wanted. Very well. One: I would take four half-buckets of treasure—only four—and then lower the ladder and let them up, and all three of us would get our share. Two: the quicker they got to work and began filling the bucket, the better for them, for their time would likely be . . . limited."

Limited? Tarra liked not the word. "By the amount of food you could provide?"

"No, game is plentiful in and around the lake, as you've seen. Guess again."

"By the number of torches you could readily prepare, whose light the two would need in order to do your bidding?"

"No, the preparation of torches proved in no way inconvenient."

Tarra frowned. "Then in what way limited?"

He heard Dyzm's gurgly, self-satisfied sigh. "I cannot be

sure," he finally said. "It was only . . . something that my friend in the sulphur pits warned me about."

"Oh?"

"Aye, for I also had it from him—in his dying breath, mind you, which was a deep one—that the ancient race of kings whose tombs and treasures these were, had set certain guardians over their sepulchres and sarcophagi, and that even now the protective spells of long-dead wizards were morbidly extant and active. Which is to say that the place is cursed, Tarra Khash, and that the longer you stay down there—in what you will shortly discover to be a veritable labyrinth of tombs—the more immediate the horror!"

IV

HORROR? AND THE Hrossak cared for *that* word not at all! Nor on this occasion did he doubt the veracity of what Dyzm had said: it would explain why the pool and country around had not been settled. Nomads and hill men alike were wary of such places, as well they might be. Finally he found voice: "And the nature of this doom?"

"Who can say" Dyzm replied. "Not I, for the two who went before you did not live to tell me. But they did tell me this: that in a certain tomb are twin statues of solid gold, fashioned in the likeness of winged krakens not unlike the dripstone idols of these cavern antechambers. And having loaded three half-buckets of treasure for me, they went off together to fetch me one of these statues; their last trip, as would have been. Alas, they returned not . . . But you need a fresh torch, Hrossak, for that one dies." He let fall a fat faggot and Tarra quickly fired it.

"Now then," Dyzm continued in a little while, "this is what I propose. Find for me that tomb and fetch me a kraken of gold, and that will suffice."

"Suffice?"

"I shall then be satisfied that you are a sincere man and worthy to be my partner in future ventures. And when I have the statue, then shall I lower the ladder and we'll be off to Chlangi together, and so on to Klühn."

Tarra could not keep from laughing, albeit a mite hysterically. "Am I to believe this? Fool I am, Hadj Dyzm—great fool, as you've well proved—but *such* a fool?"

"Hmm!" Dyzm gruffly mused. He dropped more torches. "Well, think it over. I can wait a while. How long the demon guardians will wait is a different matter. Meanwhile: 'ware below!—I lower the bucket." And down came the bucket on the end of its rope.

Tarra at once tugged at the rope, testing it, and as the bucket came to rest upon the floor he swung himself aloft, climbing by strength of his arms alone. Man-high he got— and not an inch higher. With soft, twangy report rope parted, and down crashed Hrossak atop bucket and all. "*Ow!*" he complained, getting up on his feet.

Above, Dyzm chuckled. "Ow, is it?" he said. "Worse than that, Tarra Khash, if the rope had held! Did you think I'd sit here and do nothing until you popped up out of the hole? I've a knife here you could shave with, to cut you, or rope, or both. Oh, I know, 'twas desperation made you try it. Well, you've tried and failed, so an end to tomfooleries, eh? Now I'll lower the rope some and you can make a knot; after which you can get off and find me my kraken statue. But a warning: any more heroics and I'll make you fetch both!"

"Very well," Tarra answered, breathing heavily, "but first tell me something. Right here, a pace or two away, lies a great stone box of treasure. Doubtless your two dragged it here for you. Now tell me: why were its contents never hauled aloft?"

"Ah!" said Dyzm. "That would be their fourth haul, when they told me about the statues. I had forgotten."

"So," said the Hrossak, nodding, "returning with this box—their *fourth* haul and not the third, as you first alleged—these idiots told you about the golden, winged kraken idols, so that you spurned this latest haul in favour of the greater marvel they described. Is that it?"

"Something like that, aye. I'm glad you reminded me. Perhaps before you get off searching you'd like to—"

"I would *not* like to!" answered Hrossak hotly. "It's either contents of this box *or* one of these damned idols—if I can find 'em—but not both. Which, I rather fancy, is what they told you, too."

Hadj Dyzm was peeved. "Hmm!" he grumbled. "Perhaps you're not so daft after all, Hrossak. But . . . I've set my heart on an idol, and so you'd better be off, find and fetch it."

"Not so fast," said Tarra. "Your word before I go: you *will* fetch me up, when I return with statue?" (Even though he knew very well that Hadj Dyzm would not.)

"My word," said the other, very gravely.

"So be it," said the Hrossak. "Now, which way do I go?"

"I was right after all," said Dyzm, sighing. "You are daft— and deaf to boot! How should I know which way you must go? I would suggest you follow prints on dusty floor, as so recently you followed mine . . ."

———

V

A LITTLE WHILE later Tarra knew exactly what the fox had meant by a labyrinth. Following sandal prints in the dust, he moved from cavern to cavern, and all of them alike as cells in a comb of honey. A veritable necropolis, this place, where bones were piled about the walls in terrible profusion, and skulls heaped high as a man's waist. Not all dead kings, these ossified remains; no, for most wore fetters about their ankles, or heaps of rust where ages had eaten the metal away. And about their shoulders small wooden yokes turned almost to stone; and each skeleton's right hand with its little finger missing, to mark him (or her) as property of the king.

Tarra wrinkled his nose. They had been savages in those days, he thought, for all their trappings of civilization, their carving and metal-moulding, their love of jewelry, their long-forgotten death-rituals, of which these bones formed the merest crumbling relics. Still, no time to ponder the ways of men whose race was old when the desert was young; there was much to be done, and not all of Hrossak's searching concerned with golden idols, either!

Tarra Khash remembered all too clearly the years he'd spent trapped in Nud Annoxin's well-cell in Thinhla. Hah!— he'd never thought to be in just such predicament again. And yet now . . . ? Well, life is short enough; it was not Tarra's intention to spend the rest of his down here. Ideas were slowly dawning, taking shape in his brain like wraiths of mist over fertile soil as he pondered the problem.

Shuddering a little (from the cold of the place, he told himself, for he had not brought his blanket with him) he passed through more of the domed caves, always following the print tracks where they were most dense—but to one side of them, so that his own trail would be clear and fresh—and knowing that these ways had been explored before. At least he had something of an advantage in that; but they, his predecessors, had had each other's company. Company?—in this place of death Tarra would be satisfied right now by sight of rat, let alone fellow man!

His predecessors . . . He wondered what fate had overtaken them. Aye, and perhaps he'd soon enough find that out, too.

But for now—if he could only find something to use as grapple. And something else as rope. For the fox couldn't sit up there for ever. He too must eat and drink. Grapple and rope, aye—but what to use? A long golden chain, perhaps? No, too soft and much too heavy, and all other metal doubtless rotten or rusted utterly away. And Tarra aware with every passing moment, as ideas were first considered, then discarded, that the "guardians" of this place—*if* they weren't merely frighteners conjured out of Hadj Dyzm's own imagination—might even now be waking!

Such were his thoughts as he came by light of flaring faggot into a central chamber large by comparison as that of a queen at the centre of her hive. A queen, or a king, or many such. For here the walls had been cut into deep niches, and each niche containing massy sarcophagus carved from solid rock, and all about these centuried coffins the floor strewn with wealth untold!

But in the middle of this circular, high-domed cavern, there reposed the mightiest tomb of all: a veritable mausoleum, with high marble ceiling of its own held up by fluted marble columns, and an entrance guarded by—

Guarded? The word was too close to "guardian" to do a

lot for Tarra's nerves. But like it or not the tomb *was* guarded—by a pair of golden krakens, wings and all, seated atop onyx pedestals, one on each side of the leering portal. Somewhat awed (for this must surely be the last resting place of the greatest of all these ancient monarchs) the Hrossak moved forward and stuck his torch in the rib-cage of a skeleton where it lay at the foot of the pedestal on the left . . . stuck it there and slowly straightened up, felt goose-flesh crawl on naked arms and thighs and back—and leapt backward as if fanged by viper!

Long moments Tarra stood there then, in torchlight flickering, with heart pounding, longing to flee full tilt but nailed to the spot as if his feet had taken root in solid rock. And all the while his gaze rapt upon that cadaver whose ribs supported hissing brand, *that skeleton which even now wore ragged robe, upon whose bony feet were leather sandals of the sort had made those recent prints in dust of ages!*

The Hrossak took a breath—and another—and forced his hammering heart to a slower pace and the trembling of his limbs to marble stillness. And breathing deeply a third time, he slowly crouched and leaned forward, studying morbid remains more closely. The bones were burned as from some mordant acid. In places their pitted surfaces were sticky and shiny-black with tarry traces, possibly burnt and liquefied marrow. Tatters of skin still attached, but so sere and withered as to be parchment patches, and the skull . . . that was worst of all.

Yawning jaws gaped impossibly wide in frozen scream, and torch-flung shadows shifted in empty sockets like frightened ghosts of eyes. Still crouching, shuddering, Tarra took up his torch and held it out at arm's length toward the other pedestal. As he had suspected (without, as yet, knowing *why* he suspected) a second skeleton, in much the same condition, sprawled beneath the other kraken. And again the word "guardians" seemed to echo in Hrossak's head.

But the images were only of gold, not loathsome flesh and alien ichor, and even were they alive—if they were, indeed, *the* guardians—their size would hardly make them a threat. Why, they were little more than octopuses, for all the goldsmith's loathsome skill!

Tarra gazed into sightless golden eyes, glanced at wings folded back, laid his hands upon tentacles half-lifted, apparently in groping query. Cold gold, in no wise threatening. And yet it seemed to the Hrossak there was a film of moisture, of some nameless tomb-slime, on the surface of the metal, making it almost slippery to the touch. That wouldn't be much help when it came to carrying the thing. And if he could not find means to manufacture grapnel and rope, then for certain he must put his faith in Hadj Dyzm— initially, anyway.

He moved round behind the pedestal, closed his arms about the belly of the idol until his hands clasped his elbows, lifted. Heavy, aye, but he thought it would fit into the bucket. Only . . . would the rope be strong enough?

Rope! And again a picture of rope and grapple burned on the surface of his mind's eye. Tarra eased the idol back on to its pedestal, bent down and tore at the tatters which clothed the mysteriously slain cadaver. At his touch they crumbled away. Whatever it was seared the bones—seared the flesh *from* those bones—it had also worked on the coarse cloth. No, he could hardly make a rope out of this rotten stuff; but now he had a better idea. Dyzm himself would furnish the rope!

First, however—

He checked his torch, which was beginning to burn a trifle low, then turned toward the open door of the sepulchre. This was sheer curiosity, he knew—and he minded what Hadj Dyzm had said of curiosity—but still he had to know what sort of king it was whose incarceration in some dim bygone age had warranted mass slaughter in and about these tomb-caves.

Pausing before the high, dark portal, he thrust out torch before him and saw within—

No carven coffin here but a massive throne, and seated thereon a shrivelled mummy all of shiny bone and leather, upright and proud and fused to marble seat by nameless ages. Indeed, the very fossil of a thing. A *thing*, aye, for the huge creature was not and had never been human . . .

Entering, Tarra approached a throne whose platform was knee-high, staring up at what in its day must have been a fearsome sight. Even now the thing was terrifying. But . . . it was dead, and dead things can hurt no one. Can they?

He held his torch high.

The mummy was that of a lizard-man, tall, thin and long-headed; with fangs curving down from fleshless jaws, and leathery chin still sprouting a goatlike beard of coarse hair; and upon its head a jewelled pschent, and in its talon of a hand a sceptre or knobby wand of ebony set with precious stones.

So this had been the living creature whose likeness Tarra had seen carved from the dripstone of the upper caves. Also, it had been a king of kings, and crueller far than any merely human king. He looked again at the wand. A fascinating thing, the Hrossak reached up his hand to jewelled, ebony rod, giving it a tug. But it was now one with dry claw, welded there by time. He tugged harder—and heard from behind him a low rumble!

In the next split second several things. First: Tarra remembered again his dream of a great slab door slamming shut. Then: he saw that in fact the wand was not held fast in claw but attached by golden link to a lever in the arm of the throne. Finally: even thinking these thoughts he was hurling himself backward, diving, slithering out of tomb on his belly as the door, falling in an arc from the inner ceiling, came thundering down. Then Tarra feeling that monstrous counterbalanced slab brushing his heels, and its gongy reverberations exactly as he had dreamed them!

His torch had gone flying, skittering across the floor in a straight line; but now, its impetus spent, it rolled a little in the dust. This had the effect of damping the flame. Still rolling, it flickered lower, came to rest smoking hugely from a dull red knob. The darkness at once crept in . . .

Ignoring his fear (snarling like a great hound at his back) Hrossak leapt to the near-extinguished brand, gathered it up, spun with it in a rushing, dizzy circle. This had the double effect of creating a protective ring about himself in the sudden, gibbering darkness, and of aerating the hot heart of the faggot, which answered by bursting into bright light. The shadows slunk back, defeated.

Panting, fighting to control mind and flesh alike, for this last close call had near unmanned him, the Hrossak suddenly found himself angry. Now berserker he was not—not in the way of the blood-crazy Northmen of the fjords—but when Tarra Khash was roused he really *was* roused. Right now he was mad at himself for ignoring his own instincts in the first place, mad at whichever ancient architect had designed this place as death-trap, mad at his predicament (which might yet prove permanent,) but most of all mad at the miserable and much loathed Hadj Dyzm, who must now be made to pay for all. Nor was Hrossak temper improved much by the fact that the skin of his hands, arms and chest had now commenced to itch and burn terribly, an affliction for which he could find no good cause or reason unless—

—Unless nothing!—for these were precisely the areas of his person which he had pressed against the golden kraken idol!

Was that vile metallic sweat he had noticed upon the thing some sort of stinging acid, then? Some poison? If so, patently the centuries had detracted from its potency. Before striding from the main chamber and following his own trail back toward the entrance shaft, Tarra stooped, scooped up dust, layered it upon the stinging areas. Also, he glanced once more at the golden idols.

They crouched, gleaming, upon their pedestals exactly as before . . . and yet somehow—different? Were they not, perhaps, more upright? Did their eyes not seem about to pop open? Had their tentacles not stretched outward fractionally, perhaps threateningly, and was not the sheen of slime upon their metal surfaces that much thicker and slimier?

The Hrossak snorted. So much for a wild imagination! But enough of that, now he must put his plan into action without delay. This place was dangerous; something hideous had happened to the men who came here before him; time was wasting and there could well be other horrors down here which as yet Tarra knew nothing about. He returned quickly to where the bucket lay upon the floor at the end of its rope.

"Ho!" came Hadj Dyzm's harsh greeting as Tarra fired a fresh torch. "And where's my idol, Hrossak?"

Tarra looked up. Dyzm's evil face peered down from ceiling hole, but anxiously, Tarra thought. "Oh, I've found your damned idols, foxy one," he called up, "and nearly came to grief doing it! This place is booby-trapped, and I was very nearly the booby!"

"But the idol," Dyzm pressed. "Where is it?"

Tarra thought fast. "Three things," he said. "First: the kraken idols lie on a lower level. Not deep, but impossible to scale carrying idol. Second: I have a solution for first. Third: as you've seen, I had to return for fresh torch."

"Clown!" snapped Dyzm. "Waster of time! Why did you not take spare faggot with you?"

"An oversight," Tarra agreed. "Do you want to hear my solution?"

"Get on with it."

"I need hauling gear—namely, a rope."

"What's this?" Dyzm was suspicious.

"To hoist idol up from below," Tarra lied again. "Also, 'twere a good test: a chance to see if the rope is strong enough."

"Explain."

"Easy: if the rope breaks from weight of kraken alone, certainly it will break with bucket and idol both."

"Ah!" Dyzm's suspicion seemed confirmed. "You want me to toss down the bucket rope in order to make yourself a grappling hook."

Tarra feigned exasperation. "What? Have I not already tried to climb, and did not the rope break? The idol, however, is fairly small, not quite the weight of a man."

"Hmm! How much rope do you need?"

Enough to hang you! Tarra thought, but out loud he said: "Oh, about ten man-lengths."

"What?" Dyzm spluttered. "You're surely mad, Hrossak! Am I then to give you a length *twice* as long as distance between us? Now surely you plan to make a grapnel!"

"Of what?" Tarra sighed. "Crumbling bones for hook, or soft gold, perhaps? Now who's wasting time? Even if it were possible, how could I climb with you up there to cut me or rope or both with your sharp knife? 'Twas you pointed that out in the first place, remember? And anyway, I have your promise to let down the ladder—or had you forgotten that too?"

"Now, now, lad—don't go jumping to hasty conclusions." Tarra could hear him shuffling about a little; a thin trickle of dust drifted down from above; finally:

"Very well, assume I give you the length of rope you say you need. What then?"

"First I fetch the idol. Then you lower what rope you have left, and I tie mine to it. Ah!—and to be certain it won't break, we use a double length. You then haul up idol in bucket. And if you're worried about me swarming up the rope, well, you still have your knife, right? *Then*—you toss down rope ladder for me. And the last quickly, for already I've had enough of this place!"

Dyzm considered it again, said: "Done!"

A moment later and the rope began coiling in bottom of bucket, and as it coiled so Tarra gazed avidly at the heavy *handle* of that container, which he knew he could bend into a perfect hook for hurling! Finally Dyzm cut the rope, let its end fall.

"There!" he called down. "Ten man-lengths."

Tarra loosened the rope from bucket handle, coiled it in

loops over one shoulder. He must now play out the game to its full. Obviously he could neither make nor use grapple with Dyzm still up there, and so must first ensure his departure.

"Incidentally," he said, in manner casual. "Those booby-traps I mentioned. It wasn't one such which killed your last two partners."

And, "Eh?" from above, in voice startled. "How do you mean? Did you find them?"

"Aye, what's left of them. Obviously the work of your unknown 'guardians,' Hadj. But these caves are extensive, possibly reaching out for many miles under the desert. The guardians—whatever they are—must be elsewhere. If they were here . . . then were we both dead in a trice!"

"Then were *you* dead in a trice, you mean," the other corrected.

But Tarra only shook his head. "Both of us," he insisted. "I found one of your lads on a high, narrow ledge near-inaccessible. He was all broken in parts and the flesh slurped off him. The other, in like condition, lay in narrow niche no more than a crack in the wall—but the horrors had found him there, for sure. And would the funnel of this well stop them? I doubt it."

The other was silent.

Tarra started away, keeping his head down and grinning grimly to himself; but Dyzm at once called him to a halt. "Hrossak—do you have any idea of the true nature of these guardians?"

"Who can say?" Tarra was mysterious. "Perhaps they slither, or flop. Likely, they fly! One thing for sure: they suck flesh from bones easy as leeches draw blood!" And off he went.

Now this was the Hrossak's plan: that he wait a while, then cause a loud commotion of screaming and such, and shrieking, "The guardians! The guardians!" and gurgling most horribly until Hadj Dyzm must surely believe him dead. All of which to be performed, of course, right out of sight of him above. Then utter silence (in which Tarra hoped to detect sounds of fox's frenzied flight), and back to break handle from bucket, form grapnel, attach double length of rope, and so escape. Then to track villain down and break his scrawny neck!

That had been his first plan . . .

But now, considering it again, Tarra had second thoughts. Since he must wait down here for at least a little while, why not turn the interval to his own advantage? For even now, if things went wrong—if for instance, the real guardians came on the scene—he might still have to rely on Hadj Dyzm to get him out of here quickly. His chance of the latter happening, especially now, after putting the fears up the fox, were slim, he knew; but any port in a storm. Better slim chance than no chance at all. And so it were best if he *appeared* to be following Hadj's instructions right up to the very end. Anyway, the thought of stealing one of the idols was somehow appealing.

With these thoughts on his mind, he rapidly retraced his steps to the cave of the golden krakens where they waited on their pedestals before the tomb of the lizard-king, and—

By light of flaring torch the Hrossak gaped at transformation taken place in the idols. For they did *not* wait atop their pedestal—not exactly. And now, truth slowly dawning, Tarra began to discern the real nature of the curse attaching to these subterranean tombs. Doubtless the alien monarchs of this long-extinct race had been great wizards, whose spells and maledictions had reached down through dim and terrible centuries. But in the end even the most powerful spells lose their potency, including this one. What must in its primordial origin have been a swift metamorphosis indeed were turned now to tortuously slow thing—but deadly thing for all that, as witness the pair of charred cadavers.

With creep impossibly slow—so slow the eye could scarce note it—the kraken idols were moving. And doubtless the process was gradually speeding up even as the spell persisted. For they had commenced to slither down the length of their pedestals, sucker arms clinging to the tops as they imperceptibly lowered themselves. Their eyes were half-open now, and gemstone orbs gleamed blackly and evilly beneath lids of beaten gold. Moreover, the acid ooze which their bodies seemed to exude had thickened visibly, smoking a little where it contacted the onyx of the pedestals.

Tarra's first thought was of flight, but where to flee? Go back and tell Hadj Dyzm and the fiend would doubtless leave him here till krakens were fully transformed. And would there be sufficient time remaining to make and use grapnel? Doubtful . . .

Doom descended on the Hrossak's shoulders like an icy cloak; he felt weighed down by it. Was this to be the end then? Must he, too, succumb to kraken kiss, be turned to bag of scorched and tarry bones?

Aye, possibly—but not alone!

Filled now with dreams of red revenge, which stengthened him, Tarra ran forward and fastened a double loop of rope about the belly of the kraken on the left, yanking until its tentacle tips slipped free from rim of pedestal. And back through shadow-flickered caves he dragged the morbid, scarcely mobile thing, while acrid smoke curled up from rope, where an as yet sluggish acid ate into it. But the rope held and at last sweaty Hrossak emerged beneath the spot where Hadj Dyzm waited.

"Have you got it?" the fox eagerly, breathlessly called down.

"Aye," panted Tarra, "at the end of my rope. Now send down your end and prepare to wind away." And he rolled the bucket out of sight, as if in preparation.

Down came Hadj's rope without delay, and Tarra knotting it to the middle of *his* length, and Hadj taking up the slack. Then the Hrossak hauled kraken into view, and fox's gasp from above. "Beautiful!" he croaked, for he saw only the gold and not the monstrous mutation, the constantly accelerating mobility of the thing.

The rope where it coiled kraken's belly was near burned through now, so Tarra made fresh loops under reaching tentacles and back of wings. Once he inadvertently touched golden flesh of monster—and had to bite his lip to keep from shouting his agony, as the skin of his knuckles blackened and cracked!

But at last, "Haul away!" he cried; and chortling greatly the fox took the strain and commenced turning the handle of his gear. And such was his greed that the bucket was now forgotten. But Tarra had not forgotten it.

And so, as mass of transmuting gold-flesh slowly ascended in short jerks, turning like a plumb bob on its line, Hrossak stepped into shadow and tore handle from bucket, quickly bending it into a hook. Stepping back, he thrust hook through loop of rope before it was drawn up too high, and standing beneath suspended idol cried: "Now let down the ladder, Hadj Dyzm, as agreed, lest I impede your progress with my own weight. For it's a fact you can't lift idol and me both!"

"One thing at a time," the other answered. "First the idol."

"Damn you, Hadj!" cried Tarra, hanging something of his weight on the hook to let the other see he was in earnest—only to have the hook straighten out at once and slip from loop, leaving Tarra to fall to his knees. And by the time he was back on his feet, rope and idol and all had been dragged up well beyond his reach, and Hadj's chuckle echoing horribly from on high—for a little while.

Then, while Hrossak stood clenching and unclenching his fists and scowling, Hadj's voice in something of a query: "Hrossak—what's this nasty reek I smell?" (And idol slowly turning on its line, disappearing up the flue.)

"The reek of my sweat," answered Tarra, "mingled with smoke of torch's dying—aye, and in all likelihood my dying, too!" He stepped out of harm's way as droplets hissed down from above, smoking where they struck the floor. And now the idol almost as high as the rim, and droplets of acid slime falling faster in a hissing rain.

Tarra kept well back, listening to fox's grunting as he worked the gear—his grunting, then his squawk of surprise, and at last his shriek of sheerest horror!

In his mind's eye Tarra could picture it all in great detail:

The gear turning, winding up the rope, a ratchet holding it while Hadj Dyzm rested his muscles before making the next turn. And the kraken coming into view, a thing of massy, gleamy gold. Another turn, and eyes no longer glazed glaring into Hadj's—and tentacles no longer leaden reaching—and acid no longer dilute squirting and hissing!

Then—

Still screaming to burst his heart—fat bundle of rags entwined in golden nightmare of living, lethal tentacles—Hadj and kraken and all came plummeting down the shaft. Even the rope ladder, though that fell only part way, hanging there tantalizingly beyond Hrossak's reach.

And Hadj's body broken but not yet dead, flopping on the floor in terrible grip, his flesh melting and steaming away, as Tarra bent the bucket's handle back into a hook and snatched up a length of good rope. And horror of horrors, now the *other* kraken slithering into view from out the dark, reaching to aid its evil twin!

Now the Hrossak cast for dear life; cast his hook up to where the lower rungs of the ladder dangled. Missed!—and another cast.

Hideous, hissing tentacles reaching for his ankles; vile vapour boiling up from no longer screaming fox; the entire chamber filled with loathsome reek—and the hook catching at last, dragging ladder with it to slime-puddled floor.

Then Tarra was aloft, and later he would not remember his hands on rungs at all. Only the blind panic and shrieking terror that seemed to hurl him up and out of the hole—and up the spiral steps—and down the long tunnel of carven sta-lactites to the waterfall—and so out into the night. And no pause even to negotiate the ledge behind the fall, but a mighty dive which took him through that curtain of falling water, out and down under the stars to strike the lake with hardly a splash; and then the exhausted swim back to shore against the whirlpool's pull, to where a fire's embers smoul-dered and guttered still.

After that—

Morning found a rich, rich man following the foothills east with his camels. And never a backward glance from Tarra Khash . . .

Kiss of the Lamia

BULLY BOYS OUT of Chlangi they were, desperadoes riding
forth from that shunned city of yeggs and sharpers, on the
lookout for quick profits in the narrow strip twixt Lohmi's
peaks and the Desert of Sheb. And the lone Hrossak with his
team of camels easy meat where they caught him in ambush, by the light of blind old Gleeth, god of the moon. Or at
least, he *should* have been easy meat.

But the master and sole member of that tiniest of caravans was Tarra Khash, and meat were rarely so tough. For
all his prowess, however (which one day would be legended
in all of Theem'hdra), the brawny bronze steppeman was,
on this occasion, caught short. With only the stump of a
jewelled, ceremonial scimitar to defend himself, and nodding in the saddle as he let his mount pick out the way
through badland rockpiles and gulleys, Tarra was hardly
prepared for the three where they saw him coming and set
their snare for him.

Indeed the first he knew of it was when a sighing arrow
plunked through the polished leather of the scabbard across
his back, sank an inch into his shoulder and near knocked
him out of his saddle. Then, as a second feathered shaft

whistled by his ear, he was off the camel and tumbling in dust and grit, his hand automatically grasping the jewelled hilt of his useless sword. In the darkness all was a chaos of shock and spurting blood and adrenalin; where wide awake now Tarra heard the terrified snorting and coughing of his beasts, huddled to avoid their kicking hooves as they ran off; where the moonlight silvered the stony bones of some ruined, long-deserted pile, and where the dust of Hrossak's fall was still settling as stealthy shadows crept in upon him.

Out of the leering dark they came, eyes greenly ablaze in greed and blood-lust, darting in the shadows, and fleet as the moonbeams themselves where the way was lit by Gleeth's cold light and by the blue sheen of far stars. Men of the night they were, as all such are, as one with the darkness and silhouetted dunes.

Tarra lay still, his head down, eyes slitted and peering; and in a little while a booted foot appeared silently before his face, and he heard a hoarse voice calling: "Ho! He's finished—feathered, too! 'Twas my arrow nailed him! Come on, you two!"

Your arrow, hey, dog? Tarra silently snarled, coming from huddle to crouch, straightening and striking all in the same movement. The stump of his not-so-useless sword was a silver blur where it arced under a bearded jackal's chin, tearing out his taut throat even as he screamed: "He's al—*ach-ach-ach!*"

Close behind the Hrossak, someone cursed and gripped the arrow in his back, twisting it sharply. He cried out his agony—cut off as a mountain crashed down on the back of his skull—and without further protest crumpled to the earth.

Tarra was not dead, not even unconscious, though very

nearly so. Stunned he lay there, aware only of motion about him in the night, and of voices gruff as grit, coming it seemed from far, far away:

"Gumbat Chud was ever a great fool. 'My arrow!' he yells, 'my arrow!' And this fellow meanwhile slitting his throat nice as that!"

And a different voice: "Is he dead?"

"Gumbat? Aye. See, he now has two mouths—and one of 'em scarlet!"

"Not him, no—the stranger."

"Him too, I fancy, I gave him such a clout. I think it almost a shame, since he's done us such a favour. Why, with Gumbat gone there's just the two of us now to share the spoils! So waste no time on this one. If arrow and clout both haven't done for him, the badlands surely will. Come on, let's get after his beasts and see what goods he hauled."

The other voice was harder, colder: "Best finish him, Hylar. Why spoil a good night's work by leaving this one, perchance to tell the tale?"

"To whom? But . . . I suppose you're right, Thull. We have had a good night, haven't we? First that girl, alone in the desert, wandering under the stars. Can you believe it?"

A coarse chuckle. "Oh, I believe it, all right. I was first with her, remember?"

"You were last with her, too—pig!" spat the first voice. And: "Well, get on with it, then. If you want this fellow dead, get it done. We've beasts to chase and miles to cover back to Chlangi. Pull out the arrow, that'll do for him. His life—if any's left—will leak out red as wine!"

Thull did as Hylar suggested, and shuddering as fresh waves of agony dragged him under, the Hrossak's mind shrank down into pits of the very blackest jet . . .

———

TARRA KHASH THE Hrossak, inveterate wanderer and adventurer, had a lust for life which drove him ever on where other men would fail. And it was that bright spark, that tenacious insistence upon life, which now roused him up before he could bleed to death. That and the wet, frothy ministrations of his camel, kneeling beside him in starlit ruins, where it washed his face and grunted its camel queries. This was the animal Tarra had used as mount, which, over the two hundred miles now lying in their wake, had grown inordinately fond of him. Eluding its pursuers, it had returned to its master much as a dog might do, and for the past half-hour had licked his face, kneed him in the ribs, and generally done whatever a camel might for a man.

Finally coming awake, Tarra gave its nose an admonitory slap and propped himself up into a seated position. He was cold but his back felt warm, stiff and sticky; aye, and he could feel a trickle of fresh blood where his movements had cracked open a half-formed scab. In the dirt close at hand lay the man he'd killed, Gumbat Chud, and between them a bloody arrow where it had been wrenched from his back and thrown down. Tarra's scabbard lay within reach, empty of its broken sword. They'd taken it for its jewels, of course.

Staring at the arrow, his blood dry on its point, Tarra remembered the conversation he'd heard before he blacked out. He especially remembered the names of the two who had stood over him: Hylar and Thull, Gumbat Chud's bandit brothers. Rogues out of Chlangi, aye—and dead ones when he caught up with them!

But for now . . . the Hrossak was fortunate and he knew it. Only a most unlikely set of circumstances had spared him. The ambushers might easily have slit his throat, but they hadn't wanted to waste time. Indeed, Chud's arrow might have missed the scabbard and hit his heart, which would have ended things at once! Also, the reavers could have caught instead his camel—this one, which carried food, water, blankets, all those things necessary for the maintenance of life—and probably had caught the three pack animals, which were far more heavily laden.

Heavily laden indeed!

Tarra thought about all the gold and jewels those animals carried: twelve full saddle bags! And wouldn't those badland marauders lose their eyeballs when they turned them on that lot! What a haul! Tarra almost wished he was one of his ambushers—except that wasn't his line of work. Ah, well: easy come, easy go—for now. Until he caught up with those two. Anyway, it was his own fault. Only a damn fool would have tried to take a king's ransom through a den of thieves and out the other side. And he'd known well enough Chlangi's reputation.

Tomb-loot—*hah!* Ill-gotten gains. And hadn't his father always warned him that anything you didn't work hard for wasn't worth having? Trouble was, he'd never heeded his father anyway. Also, he *had* worked hard for it. Damned hard! He thought of the subterranean sarcophagi of ancient, alien kings whose tombs were source of loot—and of his narrow escape from that place—and shuddered. And again: tomb-loot, *hah!*

Tarra's head argued with his back as to which of them hurt worst. Climbing groggily to his feet, he gently shrugged his blanket robe from his shoulders, wincing a little where it had adhered to drying scab of blood, then washed the wound as best he could with clean water from a skin in the camel's packs. The arrow had not gone deep; his broken sword's leather scabbard had saved him. Now he wrapped that scabbard in a soft cloth and re-strapped it tight in former position across his back, thus staunching the flow of blood. Then . . . a kerchief soaked in water round his head, and a bite of dried meat and gulp of sour wine, and Tarra was ready to take up the chase. It wasn't a wise pursuit, he knew—indeed it might well be the last thing he ever did—but that's the way it was with Tarra Khash. Hylar and Thull, whoever they were, had hurt him deliberately and for no good reason, and now he would hurt them. Or die trying . . .

The night was still young, not long past the midnight hour, when he struggled up into his mount's ridgy saddle and goaded the beast once more in the direction of Chlangi, cursing low under his breath as each smallest jolt set his head to ringing and his back to dull, angry throbbing. And so, at a pace only a little faster than walking, Tarra Khash the Hrossak journeyed again under moon and stars.

He went wary now, his eyes tuned to the night, but for a mile or two there was nothing. Then—

Tarra was not aware what it was *exactly* which drew his eyes to the cross lying silvered on the side of a dune; in other circumstances (were his senses not so alert for strange smells, sights or sounds) then he might have passed it by. It could have been a figure of white stone, or a scattering of bones, or simply the bleached roots of an olive or carob tree long drowned in the desert's ergs and sandpapered to a reflective whiteness; but whichever, he turned his camel's head that way.

And as he drew closer . . . what he saw then brought him down from the back of his beast in a blur of painful motion, tossing his blanket over the naked, ravaged figure of a girl pegged down on the gentle slope of the dune. A moment more and he pressed water-soaked kerchief to cracked, puffed lips, then breathed a sigh of relief as the girl's throat convulsed in a choke, and breathed more deeply as she first shook her head and finally sucked at the cloth where he held it to her mouth. Then she gazed at Tarra through eyes bruised as fallen fruit and dusted with fine sand, wriggled a little way back from him, affrightedly, and tried to ask:

"Who—?"

But he cut her off with, "*Shh!* Be still. I'll not harm you."

Even as she continued to cringe from him, he tore up the long pegs and ties which bound her to the earth and broke them, then wiped her fevered face with damp rag and wrapped her in the blanket. A moment later and she lay across the camel's saddle, face down, while he swiftly led the beast from this brutal place in search of some rude shelter.

In a little while he found low, broken walls with sand drifted against them, and to one of these pegged a sheet of tentage to form a refuge. Therein he lay the unprotesting girl and propped up her head so that she could watch him while he built a fire in the lee of the wall just outside the tent. Over the fire he boiled up soup from a pouch of herbs and dried vegetables, and likewise fried several near-rancid strips of bacon in their own fat on a flat stone until they were crisp and sweet. These he offered to the girl, but having merely tasted the soup and sniffed at the bacon she then refused both, offering a little shake of her head.

"Well, I'm sorry, lass," Tarra told her, squatting down and satisfying his own hunger, "but this is the best I can do. If you're used to finer fare I'm sure I don't know where I'll find it for you in these parts!" He went to the camel and brought her the last of his wine, and this she accepted, draining the skin to the last drop. Then, while Tarra finished his food she watched him closely, so that he was ever aware of her eyes upon him. For his own part, however obliquely, he watched her, too.

He little doubted that this was the girl those curs out of Chlangi had laughed about, which in itself would form a bond between them, who had both suffered at the hands of those dogs; but just as the bandits had done before him, he too marvelled at the mystery of it: a girl like this, wandering alone beneath the stars in so desolate a place. She seemed to read his thoughts, said:

"I make . . . a pilgrimage. It is a requirement of my . . . order, that once in a five-year I go to a secret place in the Nameless Desert, there to renew my . . . vows."

Tarra nodded. "Who is your god?" he asked, thinking: *for he's let you down sorely this night, and no mistake!*

"His name is . . . secret," she answered in a moment. "I may not divulge it."

"Myself," said Tarra, "I'm partial to Old Gleeth, blind god of the moon. He's out tonight in all his glory—do you see?" And he lifted up the skirt of the tent, so that moonbeams fell within. The girl shrank back into shadow.

"The light," she said. "So silvery . . . bright."

Tarra let fall the flap, sat staring at her through eyes narrowed just a fraction. "Also," he said, "I'll not have anything said against Ahorra Izz, god of—"

"—Scarlet scorpions," she finished it for him, the hint of a hiss in her voice.

Slowly Tarra nodded. "He's a rare one," he said, "Ahorra Izz. I wouldn't have thought many would know of him. Least of all a young sister of—"

"In my studies," she whispered, cutting him off, "I have concerned myself with all the gods, ancient and modern, of all the peoples of Theem'hdra. A god is a god, black or white—or scarlet. For how may one conceive of Good if one has no knowledge of Evil?"

And vice versa, thought Tarra, but he answered: "How indeed? Truth to tell, I didn't find Ahorra Izz at all evil. In fact I'm in his debt!"

Before he could say more or frame another question, she asked: "Who are you?"

"Tarra Khash," he answered at once, in manner typically open. "A Hrossak. I was set upon by the same pack of hairies who . . . happened your way. They robbed me. Aye, and they put an arrow in my back, too. Hence my stiffness. I was tracking them back to Chlangi when I found you. Which makes for a complication. Now I have your skin to consider as well as my own. Mine's not worth a lot to anyone, but yours . . . ?" He shrugged.

She sat up, more stiffly than Tarra, and the blanket fell away from her. Under the bruises she was incredibly lovely. Her beauty was . . . unearthly. "Come," she held out a marble arm. "Let me see your back."

"What can you do?" he asked. "It's a hole, that's all." But he went to her anyway. On hands and knees he looked at her, close up, then turned his back and sat down. He unfastened the straps holding his empty scabbard in place, and her hands were so gentle he didn't even feel her take the scabbard away.

And anyway—what *could* she do? She had no unguents or salves, not even a vinegar-soaked pad.

And yet . . . Tarra relaxed, sighed, felt the pain going out of his shoulder as easy as the air went out of his lungs. Well, now he knew what she could do. Ointments, balms?—*hah!* She had fingers, didn't she? And now Tarra believed he knew her order: she was a healer, a very special sort of physician, a layer on of hands. He'd heard of such but never seen one at work, never really believed. But seeing—or rather, feeling—was believing!

"A pity you can't do this for yourself," he told her.

"Oh, I shall heal, Tarra Khash," she answered, her voice sibilant. "Out there in the desert, under the full moon, I was helpless, taken by surprise no less than you. Now I grow stronger. Your strength has become mine. For this I thank you."

Tarra's voice was gruff now. "Huh! If you'd take some food you'd grow stronger faster!"

"There is food and food, Tarra Khash," she answered, her voice hypnotic in its caress. "For all you have offered, I am grateful."

Tarra's senses were suddenly awash in warm, languid currents. Her hands had moved from his shoulder to his neck, where now they drew out every last trace of tension. Her head on his shoulder, she cradled his back with her naked breasts. He slumped—and at once jerked his head erect, or tried to. What had she been saying? Grateful for what he'd offered? "You're welcome to whatever I have," he mumbled, scarcely aware of her sharp intake of breath. "Not that there's much . . ."

"Oh, but there is! There is!" she whispered. "Much more than I need, and though I'm hungry I shall take very little. Sleep now, sleep little mortal, and when you wake seek out those men and take your vengeance—while yet you may. For if I find them first there'll be precious little left for you!"

Sweet sister of mercy? A healer? Layer on of hands? Nay,

none of these. Even sinking into uneasy slumbers, Tarra tried to turn his drowsy head and look at her, and failed. But he did force out one final question: *"Who . . . are you?"*

She lifted her mouth from his neck and his blood was fresh on her pale lips. "My name is Orbiquita!" she said—which was the last thing he heard before the darkness rolled over him. The last thing he *felt* was her hot, salty kiss . . .

"LAMIA!" SNAPPED ARENITH Han, seer and runecaster to the robber-king Fregg, of doomed Chlangi. "She was a lamia, a man-lusting demon of the desert. You two are lucky to be alive!"

It was Fregg's dawn court, held in the open courtyard of his "palace," once a splendid place but now a sagging pile in keeping with most of Chlangi's buildings. Only the massive outer walls of the city itself were undecayed, for Fregg insisted that they at least be kept in good order. To this end he used "felons" from his court sessions, on those rare occasions when such escaped his "justice" with their lives intact.

Chlangi's monarch was one Fregg Unst, a failed con man long, long ago hounded out of Klühn on the coast for his frauds and fakeries. His subjects—in no wise nicer persons than Fregg himself—were a rabble of yeggs, sharpers, scabby whores and their pimps, unscrupulous taverners and other degenerates and riff-raff blown here on the winds of chance, or else fled from justice to Chlangi's doubtful refuge. And doubtful it was.

Chlangi the Doomed—or the Shunned City, as it is elsewhere known—well deserved these doleful titles. For of all places of ill-repute, this were perhaps the most notorious in all the Primal Land. And yet it had not always been this way.

In its heyday the city had been opulent, its streets and markets bustling with merchants, its honest taverners selling vintages renowned throughout the land for their clean sweetness. With lofty domes and spires all gilded over, walls high and white, and roofs red with tiles baked in the ovens of Chlangi's busy builders, the city had been the veriest jewel of Theem'hdra's cities. Aye, and its magistrates had had little time for members of the limited criminal element.

Now . . . all good and honest men shunned the place, had done so since first the lamia Orbiquita built her castle in the Desert of Sheb. Now the gold had been stripped from all the rich roofs, the grapevines had returned to the wild, producing only small, sour grapes and flattening their rotten trellises, arches and walls had toppled into disrepair, and the scummy water of a many-fractured acqueduct was suspect indeed. Only the rabble horde and their robber-king now lived here, and outside the walls a handful of hungry, outcast beggars.

Now, too, Fregg kept the land around well scouted, where day and night men of his were out patrolling in the badlands and along the fringe of the desert, intent upon thievery and murder. Occasionally there were caravans out of Eyphra or Klühn; or more rarely parties of prospectors out of Klühn headed for the Mountains of Lohmi, or returning therefrom; and exceeding rare indeed lone wanderers and adventurers who had simply strayed this way. Which must surely elevate the occurrences of last night almost to the fabulous. Fabulous in Fregg's eyes, anyway, which was one of the reasons he had brought his scouts of yestereve to morning court.

Their tale had been so full of fantastic incident that Fregg could only consider it a fabrication, and the tale wasn't all he found suspect . . .

Now the court was packed; battle-scarred brigands rubbed shoulders with nimble thieves and cutthroats, and Fregg's own lieutenants formed a surly jury whose only concern was to "get the thing over, the accused hanged, and on with the day's gaming, scheming and back-stabbing." Which did not bode well for transgressors against Fregg's laws!

Actually, those laws were simple in the extreme:

Monies and goods within the city would circulate according to barter and business, with each man taking his risks and living, subsisting or existing in accordance with his acumen. Monies and etc. from without would be divided half to Fregg and his heirs, one third to the reaver or reavers clever enough to capture and bring it in, and the remaining one sixth part to the city in general, to circulate as it might. More a code than a written law proper. There was only one real law and it was this: Fregg's subjects could rob, cheat, even kill each other; they could sell their swords, souls or bodies; they could bully, booze and brawl all they liked and then some . . . *except* where it would be to annoy, inconvenience, preempt or otherwise interfere with, or displease, Fregg. Simple . . .

Which meant that on this occasion, in some way as yet unexplained, last night's far-scavenging scouts had indeed displeased Fregg; a very strange circumstance, considering the fantastic haul they'd brought back for him!

Now they were here, dragged before Fregg's "courtiers" and "council" and "jury" for whatever form of inquisition he had in mind, and Arenith Han—a half-breed wizard of doubtful dexterity, one time necromancer and failed alchemist in black Yhem, now Fregg's right-hand man—had opened the proceedings with his startling revelation.

"What say you?" Burly, bearded Fregg turned a little on his wooden stool of office behind a squat wooden table, to peer at his wizard with raised eyebrows. "Lamia? This girl they ravaged was a lamia? Where's your evidence?"

Central in the courtyard, where they were obliged to stand facing into a sun not long risen, Hylar Arf and Thull Drinnis shuffled and grimaced, surly at Fregg's treatment of them. But no use to protest, not at this stage; they were here and so must face up to whatever charge Fregg brought against them. The fallen wizard's examination of their spoils, and his deductions concerning the same and the nature of at least one of their previous owners, that was simply for openers, all part of the game.

Sharing space in the central area were two camels, a pair of white yaks and, upon the ground, blankets bearing various items. Upon one: tatters of sorely dishevelled female apparel; upon the other, eight saddle bags, their contents emptied out in a pile of gleam and glitter and golden, glancing fire. Treasure enough to satisfy even the most avaricious heart—almost. Probably. Possibly.

"Observe!" Arenith Han, a spidery, shrivelled person in a worn, rune-embellished cloak scuttled about, prodding the yaks and examining their gear. "Observe the rig of these beasts—especially this one. Have you ever seen the like? A houdah fixed upon the back of a yak? A *houdah*? Now, some tiny princess of sophisticate kingdom might well ride such gentle, canopied beast through the gardens of her father's palace—for her pleasure, under close scrutiny of eunuchs and guards—and the tasselled shade to protect her precious skin from sun's bright ray. But here, in the desert, the badlands, the merest trajectory of a good hard spit away from Chlangi's walls? Unlikely! And yet so it would appear to be . . ."

He turned and squinted at the uncomfortable ruffians. "Just such a princess, our friends here avow, was out riding in the desert last night. She rode upon this yak, beneath this shade, while the other beast carried her toiletries and trinkets, her prettiest things, which is in the nature of princesses when they go abroad: frivolously to take small items of comfort with them. Ah!—but I have *examined* the beasts' packs. Behold!"

He scattered what was contained in the packs on to the dust and cracked flags of the courtyard—contents proving to be, with one exception, ample handfuls of loamy soil—stooped to pick up the single extraneous item, and held it up. "A book," he said. "A leather-bound runebook. A book of spells!"

Oohs! and *Aahs!* went up from the assemblage, but Han held up a finger for silence. "And *such* spells!" he continued. "They are runes of transformation, whose purpose I recognize e'en though I cannot read the glyphs in which they're couched—for of course they're writ in the lamia tongue! As to their function: they permit the user to alter her form at will, becoming a bat, a dragon, a serpent, a hag, a wolf, a toad—even a beautiful girl!"

Hylar Arf, a hulking Northman with mane of blue-black hair bristling the length of his spine, had heard enough. Usually jovial—especially when in a killing mood—his laughter now welled up in a great booming eruption of sound. One-handed, he picked the skinny sorcerer up by the neck and dangled him before the court. "This old twig's a charlatan!" he derided. "Can't you all see that? Why!—

here's Thull Drinnis and me alive and kicking, no harm befallen us—and this fool says the girl was lamia? *Bah!* We
took her yaks and we took *her,* too—all three of us, before
Gumbat Chud, great fool, got himself slain—and you can
believe me when I tell you it was *girl*-flesh we had, sweet
and juicy. Indeed, because he's a pig, Thull here had her
twice! He was both first and last with her; and does he look
any the worse for wear?"

"We're not pleased!" Fregg came to his feet, huge and
round as a boulder. "Put down our trusted sorcerer at once!"
Hylar Arf spat in the dust but did as Fregg commanded, setting Arenith Han upon his feet to stagger to and fro, clutch-
ing at his throat.

"Continue," Fregg nodded his approval.

The wizard got well away from the two accused and
found the fluted stone stump of an old column to sit on. Still
massaging his throat, he once more took up the thread—or
attempted to:

"About . . . lamias," he choked. And: "Wine, wine!" A
court attendant took him a skin, from which he drank
deeply. And in a little while, but hurriedly now and eager to
be done with it:

"About lamias. They are desert demons, female, daughters of the pit. Spawned of unnatural union betwixt, *ahem,*
say a sorcerer and a succubus—or perhaps a witch and
incubus—the lamia is half-caste. Well, I myself am a 'breed'
and see little harm in that; but in the case of a lamia things
are very much different. The woman in her lusts after men
for satisfaction, the demon part for other reasons. Men who
have bedded lamias and survived are singularly rare—but
not fabulous, not unheard of! Mylakhrion himself is said to
have had several."

Fregg was fascinated. Having seated himself again following Hylar Arf's outburst, he now leaned forward. "All very interesting," he said. "We would know more. We would know, for example, just exactly *how* these two escaped with their lives from lamia's clutches. For whereas the near-immortal Mylakhrion was—some might say 'is'—a legended magician, these men are merely—" (he sniffed) "—*men*. And pretty scabby specimens of men at that!"

"Majesty," said Arenith Han, "I am in complete agreement with your assessment of this pair. Aye, and Gumbat Chud was cut, I fear, of much the same cloth. But first let me say a little more on the nature of lamias, when all should become quite clear."

"Say on," Fregg nodded.

"Very well." Han stood up from column seat, commenced to pace, kept well away from the hulking barbarian and his thin, grim-faced colleague. "Even lamias, monstrous creatures that they are, have their weaknesses; one of which, as stated, is that they lust after men. Another is this: that once in a five-year their powers wane, when they must needs take them off to a secret place deep in the desert, *genius loci* of lamias, and there perform rites of renewal. During such periods, being *un*-natural creatures, all things of nature are a bane, a veritable poison to them. At the very best of times they cannot abide the sun's clean light—in which abhorrence they are akin to ghouls and vampires—but at the height of the five-year cycle the sun is not merely loathed but lethal in the extreme! Hence they must needs travel by night. And because the moon is also a thing of nature, Old Gleeth in his full is likewise a torment to them, whose cold silvery light will scorch and blister them even as the sun burns men!"

"Ah!" Fregg came once more erect in his seat. He leaned forward, great knuckles supporting him where he planted them firmly on the table before him. "The houdah on the yak!" And he nodded, "Yes, yes—I see!"

"Certainly," Arenith Han smiled. "It is a shade against the moon—which was full last night, as you know well enow."

Fregg sat down with a thump, banged upon the table with heavy hand, said: "Good, Han, good! And what else do you divine?"

"Two more things, Majesty," answered the mage, his voice low now. "First, observe the contents of her saddle bags: largely soil! And does not the lamia, like the vampire, carry her native earth with her for bed? Aye, for she likes to lie down in the same charnel earth which her own vileness has cursed . . ."

"And finally?" Fregg grunted.

"Finally—observe the *motif* graven in the leather of the saddle bags, and embroidered into the canopy of yon houdah, and blazoned upon binding of runebook. *And*—" Han narrowed his eyes, "—carved in the jade inset which Thull Drinnis even now wears in the ring of gold on the smallest finger of his left hand! *Is it not indeed the skull and serpent crest of the Lamia Orbiquita herself?*"

Thull Drinnis, a weaselish ex-Klühnite, at once thrust his left hand deep into the pocket of his baggy breeks, but not before everyone had seen the ring of which the wizard made mention. In the stony silence which ensued, Drinnis realized his error—his admittance of guilt of sorts—and knew that was not the way to go. So now he drew his hand into view and held it up so that the sun flashed from burnished gold.

"A trinket!" he cried. "I took it from her and I claim it as a portion of my share. What's wrong with that? Now enough of this folly. Why are we here, Hylar and me? Last night we brought more wealth into this place than was ever dreamed of. Chlangi's share alone will make each man and dog of you rich!"

"He's right!" Hylar Arf took up the cry. "All of you rich— or else—" he turned accusingly to Fregg, "—or else our noble king would take it all for himself!"

And again the stony silence, but this time directed at Fregg where he sat upon his stool of office at his table of judgement. But Fregg was wily, more than a match for two such as Arf and Drinnis, and he was playing this game with loaded dice. Now he decided the time was ripe to let those dice roll. He once again came to his feet.

"People of Chlangi," he said. "Loyal subjects. It appears to me that there are three things here to be taken into consideration. Three, er—shall we say 'discrepancies?'—upon which, when they are resolved, Hylar and Thull's guilt or innocence shall be seen to hang. Now, since my own interest in these matters has been brought into question, I shall merely present the facts as we know them, and you—*all* of you—shall decide the outcome. A strange day indeed, but nevertheless I now put aside my jury, my wizard, even my own perhaps self-serving opinions in this matter, and let *you* make the decision." He paused.

"Very well, these are the facts:

"For long and long the laws of Chlangi have stood, and they have served us moderately well. One of these laws states that all—I repeat *all*—goods of value stolen without and fetched within these walls are to be divided in predetermined fashion: half to me, Chlangi's rightful king, one third to them responsible for the catch, the remainder to the city.

And so to the first discrepancy. Thull Drinnis here has seen fit to apportion himself a little more than his proper share, namely the ring upon his finger."

"A trinket, as he himself pointed out!" someone at the back of the crowd cried.

"But a trinket of value," answered Fregg, "whose worth would feed a man for a six-month! Let me say on:

"The second 'discrepancy'—and one upon which the livelihoods and likely the very lives of each and every one of us depends—is this: that if what we have heard is true, good Hylar and clever Thull here have rid these parts forever of a terrible bane, namely the Lamia Orbiquita."

"Well done, lads!" the cry went up. And: "What's that for a discrepancy?" While someone else shouted, "The monster's dead at last!"

"*Hold!*" Fregg bellowed. "We do not know that she is dead—and it were better for all if she is not! Wizard," he turned to Arenith Han, "what say you? They beat her, ravished her, pegged her out under the moon. Would she survive all that?"

"The beating and raping, aye," answered Han. "Very likely she would. The staking out 'neath a full bright Gleeth: that would be sore painful, would surely weaken her nigh unto death. And by now—" he squinted at the sun riding up out of the east. "Now in the searing rays of the sun—now she is surely dead!"

"Hoorah!" several in the crowd shouted.

When there was silence Fregg stared all around. And sadly he shook his head. "Hoorah, is it? And how long before word of this reaches the outside world, eh? How long before the tale finds its way to Klühn and Eyphra, Yhem and Khrissa and all the villages and settlements between?

Have you forgotten? Chlangi the Shunned—this very Chlangi the Doomed—was once Chlangi the bright, Chlangi the beautiful! Oh, all very well to let a handful of outcast criminals run the place now, where no right-minded decent citizen would be found dead; but with Orbiquita gone, her sphere of evil ensorcelment removed forever, how long before some great monarch and his generals decide it were time to bring back Chlangi within the fold, to make her an honest city again? Not long, you may rely upon it! And what of *your* livelihoods then? And what of *your* lives? Why, there's a price on the head of every last one of you!"

No cries of "bravo" now from the spectators but only the hushed whispers of dawning realization, and at last a sullen silence which acknowledged the ring of truth in Fregg's words.

And in the midst of this silence:

"We killed a lamia!" Hylar Arf blustered. "Why, all of Theem'hdra stands in our debt!"

"Theem'hdra, aye," answered Fregg, his voice doomful. "But not Chlangi, and certainly not her present citizens."

"But—" Thull Drinnis would have taken up the argument.

"—But we come now to the third and perhaps greatest discrepancy," Fregg cut him off. "Good Thull and Hylar returned last night with vast treasure, all loaded on these camels here and now displayed upon the blanket for all to see. And then they took themselves off to Dilquay Noth's brothel and drank and whored the night away, and talked of how, with their share, they'd get off to Thandopolis and set up in legitimate business, and live out their lives in luxury undreamed . . .

"But being a suspicious man, and having had news of this fine scheme of theirs brought back to me, I thought: "What?

And are they so displeased with Chlangi, then, that they must be off at once and gone from us? Or is there something I do not yet know? And I sent out trackers into the badlands to find what they could find."

(Thull and Hylar, until this moment showing only a little disquietude, now became greatly agitated, fingering their swords and peering this way and that. Fregg saw this and smiled, however grimly, before continuing.)

"And lo!—at a small oasis known only to a few of us, what should my trackers find there but a *third* beast, the very brother of these two here—and four more saddle bags packed with choicest items!" He clapped his great hands and the crowd gave way to let through a pair of dusty mountain men, leading into view the beast in question.

"We are all rich, all of us!" cried Fregg over the crowd's rising hum of excitement and outrage. "Aye, and after the share has been made, now we can *all* leave Chlangi for lands of our choice. That is to say, all save these two . . ."

Thull Drinnis and Hylar Arf waited no longer. The game was up. They were done for. They knew it.

As a man, they went for Fregg, swords singing from scabbards, lips drawn back in snarls from clenched teeth. And up on to his table they leaped, their blades raised on high—but before they could strike there came a great sighing of arrows which stopped them dead in their tracks. From above and behind Fregg on the courtyard walls, a party of crossbowmen had opened up, and their massed bolts not only transfixed the cheating pair but knocked them down from the table like swatted flies. They were dead before they hit the ground.

And again there was silence, broken at last by Fregg's

voice shouting: "So let all treacherous dogs die; so let them all pay the price!"

And someone in the crowd: "The fools! Why did they come back at all?"

"Good question!" answered Fregg. "But they had to come back. They knew that I am a caring king, and that if they failed to return I would worry about them and send out others to discover their fate. And they knew also that with beasts so loaded down with gold and gems, their pace would be slow and my riders would surely catch them. Moreover, they would need provisions for their long trek overland, and extra beasts, and how to purchase such without displaying at least a portion of their loot? And finally they knew that my intelligence is good, that I am rarely lacking in advance knowledge in respect of travellers and caravans in these parts. What if I *expected* them to return with loot galore? And so they brought two-thirds of it back, and left the rest in the desert, to be collected later on their way to Thandopolis . . .

As he fell smugly silent a new voice arose, a voice hitherto unknown in Chlangi, which said: "Bravo, lord Fregg! Bravo! An object lesson in deduction. How well you understand the criminal mind, sir."

All eyes turned to Tarra Khash where he now threw off his blanket robe and draped it over the back of the camel he led; to him, and to the beast itself, which trotted straight to other three and greeted them with great affection. Plainly the four were or had been a team; and since this burly bronze clout-clad Hrossak was their master . . . what did that make him but previous owner of treasure and all? Possibly.

Tarra was flanked by a pair of hulking thugs from the

guardroom in the west gate, who seemed uncertain exactly what to do with him. Fregg could have told them; but now that he'd met the Hrossak, so to speak, he found himself somewhat curious. "You're a bold one," he told Tarra, coming forward to look him up and down.

"Bold as brass!" one of the guards ventured. "He came right up to the gate and hailed us, and said he sought audience with the king or chief or whoever was boss here."

"I'm boss here," said Fregg, thumbing his chest. "King Fregg Unst the First—and likely the last. Who are you?"

"Tarra Khash," said Tarra. "Adventurer by profession, wanderer by inclination . . ." And he paused to look at the dead men where their bodies lay sprawled in the dust of the courtyard. "Excuse me, but would these two be called, er, Hylar and Thull?"

"Those were their names, aye," Fregg nodded. "Did you have business with them?"

"Some," said Tarra, "but it appears I'm too late."

The session was breaking up now and the crowd thinning as people went off about their business. A half-dozen of Fregg's men, his personal bodyguards, stayed back, keeping a sharp eye on Tarra Khash. Others began to bundle up the treasure in the blankets.

"Walk with me a little way," said Fregg, "and tell me more. I like your cut, Tarra Khash. We seldom have visitors here; at least, not of their own free will!" He chuckled, paused, turned and said to his men: "That ring on Drinnis' finger—I want it. Make sure it's with the rest of the stuff and bring it to me in the tower."

"Hold!" said Tarra. "A moment, King Fregg." He stepped to blanket and stooped, came erect holding the jewelled hilt of his scimitar. "I've a special affection for this piece," he said. "It belongs in the scabbard across my back. I hope you don't mind."

Fregg gently took it from him. "But I *do* mind, Tarra Khash!"

"But—"

"Wait, lad, hear me out. See, I've nothing against you, but you simply don't understand our laws. You see, upon the instant loot is brought into the city, said loot belongs to me, its finders, and to the city itself. And no law at all, I'm afraid, to cover its retrieval by rightful owner. Not even the smallest part of it. Also, I perceive these stones set in the hilt to be valuable, a small treasure in themselves." He shrugged almost apologetically, adding: "No, I'm sorry, lad, but at least three men—and likely a good many more—have died for this little lot. And so—" And he tossed the jewelled hilt back with the other gems.

"Actually," Tarra chewed his lip, eyed the swords and crossbows of Fregg's bodyguards, "actually it's the hilt I treasure more than the stones. Before it was broken there were times that sword saved my miserable life!"

"Ah!" said Fregg. "It has sentimental value, has it? Why didn't you say so? You shall have it back, of course! Only come to me tonight, in my counting room atop the tower, and after I've prised out the stones, then the broken blade is yours. It seems the least I can do. And my thanks, for in your way you've already answered a riddle I'd have asked of you."

"Oh?" Tarra raised an eyebrow.

"Indeed. For if you were rightful owner of this hoard in the first place, why surely you'd agonize more over the bulk of the stuff than the mere stump of a sword, not so?"

Tarra shrugged, grinned, winked, and tapped the side of

his nose with forefinger. "No wonder you're king here, Fregg. Aye, and again you've gauged your man aright, I fear."

Fregg roared with laughter. "Good, good!" he chortled. "Very good. So you're a reaver, too, eh? Well, and what's a reaver if not an adventurer, which is what you said you were? You took this lot from a caravan, I suppose? No mean feat for a lone wanderer, even a brave and brawny Hrossak."

"You flatter me," Tarra protested, and lied: "No, there were ten of us. The men of the caravan fought hard and died well, and I was left with treasure."

"Well then," said Fregg. "In that case you'll not take it so badly. It seems you're better off to the extent of one camel. As for the treasure: it was someone else's, became yours, and now has become mine—er, Chlangi's."

Tarra sucked his teeth. "So it would seem," he said.

"Aye," Fregg nodded. "So count your blessings and go on your way. Chlangi welcomes you if you choose to stay, will not detain you should you decide to move on. The choice is yours."

"Your hospitality overwhelms me," said Tarra. "If I had the change I'd celebrate our meeting with a meal and a drink."

"Pauper, are you?" said Fregg, seeming surprised. And: "What, penniless, an enterprising lad like you? Anyway, I'd warn you off Chlangi's taverns. Me, I kill my own meat and brew my own wine! But if you're desperately short you can always sell your blanket. Your camel will keep you warm nights . . ." And off he strode, laughing.

Which seemed to be an end to that.

Almost . . .

TARRA WAS ONE of the last to pass out through the courtyard's gates, which were closed at once on his heels. On his
way he'd given the place a narrow-eyed once-over, especially the tumbledown main building and its central tower.
So that standing there outside the iron-banded gates, staring
up thoughtfully at the high walls, he was startled when a
voice barked in his ear:

"Hrossak, I overheard your conversation with Fregg.
Quickly now, tell me, d'you want a meal and a wineskin?
And then maybe a safe place to rest your head until tonight? For if your're thinking of leaving, it would be sheerest folly to try it in broad daylight, despite what Fregg says!"

The speaker was a tiny man, old and gnarly, with an eye-
patch over his left eye and a stump for right hand. The latter
told a tale in itself: he was a failed thief, probably turned con
man. But . . . Tarra shrugged. "Any port in a storm," he said.
"Lead on."

And when they were away from Fregg's sorry palace
and into the old streets of the city proper: "Now what's all
this about not leaving in daylight? I came in daylight, after
all."

"I'm Stumpy Adz," the old-timer told him. "And if it's to
be known, Stumpy knows it. Odds are you're watched even
now. You're a defenceless stranger and you own blanket,
saddle, camel and gear, and leather scabbard. That's quite a
bit of property for a lad with no friends here, save me."

"I wear loincloth and sandals, too," Tarra pointed out.
"Are they also lusted after?"

"Likely," Stumpy Adz nodded. "This is Chlangi, lad, not
Klühn. Anyway, I've pillow for your head, cabbage tops and
shade for the beast, food and drink for your belly. Deal?"

"What'll I pay?"

"Blanket'll do. It's cold here nights. And as Fregg pointed out: you've your camel to keep you warm."

Tarra sighed but nodded. "Deal. Anyway, I wasn't planning on leaving till tonight. Fregg's invited me to call on him in his tower counting house. I have to get my sword back—what's left of it."

"Heard that, too," said Stumpy. *"Huh!"*

He led the way into a shady alley and from there through a heavy oak door into a tiny high-walled yard, planked over for roof with a vine bearing grapes and casting cool shade. "Tether your beast there," said Stumpy. "Will he do his business?"

"Likely," said Tarra. "He doesn't much care where he does it."

"Good! A treat for the grapevine . . ."

Tarra looked about. Half-way up one wall was a wooden platform, doubtless Stumpy's bed (Tarra's for the rest of the day), and behind the yard a low, tiled hovel built between the walls as if on afterthought. It might one time have been a smithy; cooking smells now drifted out of open door.

"Gulla," Stumpy called. "A meal for two—and a skin, if you please. Quick, lass, we've a visitor."

Tarra's ears pricked up. "Lass?" If not the old lad's wife, then surely his daughter. The latter proved to be the case, but Tarra's interest rapidly waned. Gulla Adz was comely enough about the face but built like a fortress. Tarra could feel his ribs creaking just looking at her. Looking at *him,* as she dished out steamy stew in cracked plates atop a tiny table, she made eyes and licked her lips in a manner that made him glad his bed was high off the ground.

Stumpy chased her off, however, and as they ate Tarra asked:

"Why the '*huh!*,' eh? Don't you think Fregg'll give me back my sword, then?"

"His own, more likely—between your ribs! No, lad, when Fregg takes something it stays took. Also, I fancy he makes his own plans for leaving, and sooner rather than later. I'd make book we're kingless within a week. And there'll be no share out, that's for sure! No, this is just what Fregg's been waiting for. Him and his bullies'll take the lot—and then he'll find a way to ditch them, too."

"Why should he want to leave?" asked Tarra Khash, innocently. "It seems to me he's well set up here."

"He was, he was," said Stumpy. "But—" and he told Tarra about the Lamia Orbiquita and her assumed demise. Hearing all, Tarra said nothing—but he fingered twin sores on his neck, like the tiny weeping craters of mosquito bites. Aye, and if what this old lad said about lamias were true, then he must consider himself one very fortunate Hrossak. Fortunate indeed!

"That treasure," he said when Stumpy was done, "was mine. I'll not leave without a handful at least. And I want that sword-hilt, with or without its jewels! Can I buy your help, Stumpy, for a nugget of gold? Or perhaps a ruby big enough to fit the socket behind your eye-patch?"

"Depends what you want," said Stumpy carefully.

"Not much," Tarra answered. "A good thin rope and grapple, knowledge of the weakest part of the city's wall, details of Fregg's palace guards—how many of them, and so forth—and a plan of quickest route from palace, through city, to outer wall. Well?"

"Sounds reasonable," the oldster nodded, his good eye twinkling.

"Lastly," said Tarra, "I'll want a sharp knife, six-inch blade and well balanced."

"Ah! That'll cost you an extra nugget."

"Done!—if I make it. If not . . . you can keep the camel." They shook on it left-handed, and each felt he'd met a man to be trusted—within limits.

Following which the Hrossak climbed rickety ladder to shady platform, tossed awhile making his plans, and finally fell asleep . . .

TARRA SLEPT UNTIL dusk, during which time Stumpy Adz was busy. When the Hrossak awoke Stumpy gave him a throwing knife and sat down with him, by light of oil lamp and floating wick, to study several parchment sketches. There was meat sizzling over charcoal, too, and a little weak wine in a stone jar beaded with cold moisture. Stumpy lived pretty well, Tarra decided.

As for the Hrossak: he was clear-headed; the stiffness was still in his shoulder but fading fast; the two-pronged bite on his neck had scabbed over and lost its sting. What had been taken out of him was replacing itself, and all seemed in working order.

He took leave of Stumpy's place at the hour when all cats turn grey and headed for the south gate. At about which time, some three hundred and more miles away in the heart of the Nameless Desert . . .

Deep, deep below the furnace sands, cooling now that the sun was caught once more in Cthon's net and drawn down, and while the last kites of evening fanned the air on high—in a crimson cavern with a lava lake, where red imps danced nimbly from island to island in the reek and splash of molten rock—there the Lamia Orbiquita came awake at last and stretched her leathery wings and breathed gratefully of the hot brimstone atmosphere.

She lay cradled in smoking ashes in the middle of a smouldering island which itself lay central in the lava lake; and over her warty, leathery, loathsome form hunched a mighty black lava lump glowing with a red internal life of its own and moulded in perfect likeness of—what else but another lamia? And seeing that infernally fossilized thing crouching over her she knew where she was and remembered how she got here.

The whole thing had been a folly, a farce. First: that she failed to make adequate preparation for her journey when she knew full well that the five-year cycle was nearing its peak, when her powers would wane even as the hated moon waxed. Next: that having allowed the time to creep too close, and most of her powers fled, still she had not used the last of them to call up those serfs of the desert, the djinn, to transport her here; for she scorned all imps—even bottle imps, and even the biggest of them—and hated the thought of being in their debt. Finally: that as her choice of guise under which to travel she had chosen that of beautiful human female, for once the change was made she'd been stuck with that shape and all the hazards that went with it. The choice, however, had not been completely arbitrary; she could take comfort in that, at least. The human female form was small and less cumbersome than that of a dragon; and where girls sometimes got molested and raped, dragons were usually slain! She could have been a lizard, but lizards making a beeline across the desert are easy prey for hawks and such, and anyway she hated crawling on her belly. Flying creature such as harpy or bat were out of the question; since they must needs flit, they could not shade themselves against sun and moon. Her true lamia form was likewise problematic: impossible to shade in flight and cumbersome afoot. And so she had chosen the shape of a beautiful human girl. Anyway, it was her favourite and had served her well for more than a century. The victims she had lured with it were without number. Moreover, yaks and camels did not shy from it.

Ah, well, a lesson learned—but learned so expensively. A veritable string of errors never to be repeated. The ravishment had been bad enough and the beating worse, but the loss of her runebook and ring were disasters of the first magnitude. Orbiquita's memory was not the best and the runes of metamorphosis were anything but easy. As for the ring: that had been gifted to her by her father, Mylakhrion of Tharamoon. She could not bear to be without it. Indeed, of the entire episode the one thing she did not regret was the Hrossak. Odd, that . . .

Stretching again and yawning hideously, she might perhaps have lingered longer over thoughts of Tarra Khash, but that was a luxury not to be permitted. No, for she was in serious trouble and she knew it, and now must prepare whatever excuses she could for her lateness and unseemly mode of arrival here in this unholy place.

Aye, for the eyes in the lava lamia's head had cracked open and now glared sulphurously, and from the smoking jaws came voice of inquisitor, demanding to be told all and truthfully:

"What have you to say for yourself, Orbiquita, borne here by djinn and weary nigh unto death, and late by a day so that all your sisters have come and gone, all making sport over the idleness or foolhardiness of the hated Orbiquita? You know, of course, the penalty?"

"I hate my sisters equally well!" answered Orbiquita unabashed. "Let them take solace from that. As to your charges, I cannot deny them. Idle and foolhardy I have been. And aye, I know well enow the price to pay." Then she told the whole, miserable tale.

When she reached the part concerning Tarra Khash, however, the lava lamia stopped her in something approaching astonishment: "What? And you took not this Hrossak's life? But this is without precedence!"

"I had my reasons!" Orbiquita protested.

"Then out with them at once," ordered the lava lamia, "or sit here in stony silence for five long years—which is, in any case, your fate. Of what 'reasons' do you speak?"

"One," said Orbiquita, "he saved me from Gleeth's scorching beams."

"What is that? He is a man!"

"My father was a man, and likely yours too."

"*Hah!* Do not remind me! Say on, Orbiquita."

"Two, though I suspect he guessed my nature—or at least that I was more than I appeared—still he offered no offence, no harm, but would have fed and protected me."

"Greater fool he!" the lava lamia answered.

"And three," (Orbiquita would not be browbeaten) "I sensed, by precognition, that in fact I would meet this one again, and that he would be of further service to me."

And, *"Hah!"* said lava lamia more vehemently yet. "Be sure it will not happen for a five-year at least, Orbiquita! 'Precognition,' indeed! You should have gorged on him, and wrapped yourself in his skin to protect your own from the moon, and so proceeded here without let and indebted to no one. Instead you chose merely to sip, summoning only sufficient strength to call up detested desert djinn to your aid. All in all, most foolish. And are you ready now to take my place, waiting out your five years until some equally silly sister's deed release you?"

"No," said Orbiquita.

"It is the law!" the other howled. "Apart from which, I'm impatient of this place."

"And the law shall be obeyed—and you released, as is only right—eventually . . . But first a boon."

"What? You presume to—"

"Mylakhrion's ring!" cried Orbiquita. "Stolen from me. My runebook, too. Would you deny me time to right this great wrong? Must I wait a five-year to wipe clean this smear on *all* lamias? Would you suffer the scorn of *all* your sisters—and not least mine—for the sake of a few hours, you who have centuries before you?"

After long moments, calmer now but yet bubbling lava from every pore, the keeper of this place asked, "What is it you wish?"

"My powers returned to me—fully!" said Orbiquita at once. "And I'll laugh in Gleeth's face and fly to Chlangi, and find Mylakhrion's ring and take back my runebook. Following which—"

"You'll return here?"

"Or be outcast forever from the sisterhood, aye," Orbiquita bowed her warty head. "And is it likely I'll renege, to live only five more years instead of five thousand?"

"So be it," said the lava lamia, her voice a hiss of escaping steam. "You are renewed, Orbiquita. Now get you hence and remember your vow, and return to me here before Cthon releases the sun to rise again over Theem'hdra. On behalf of all lamias, I have spoken."

The sulphur pits which were her eyes lidded themselves with lava crusts, but Orbiquita did not see. She was no longer there . . .

TARRA KHASH LEFT Chlangi by the south gate two hours after the sun's setting. By then, dull lights glowed in the city's streets in spasmodic pattern, flickering smokily in the taverns, brothels, and a few of the larger houses and dens—and (importantly) in Fregg's palace, particularly his apartments in the tower. It was a good time to be away, before night's thieves and cutthroats crawled out of their holes and began to work up an interest in a man.

Out of the gate the Hrossak turned east for Klühn, heading for the pass through the Great Eastern Peaks more than two hundred miles away. Beyond the pass and fording the Lohr, he would cross a hundred more miles of grassland before the spires and turrets of coastal Klühn came into view. Except that first, of course, he'd be returning—however briefly, and hopefully painlessly—to Chlangi.

Jogging comfortably east for a mile or more, the Hrossak never once looked back—despite the fact that he knew he was followed. Two of them, on ponies (rare beasts in Theem'hdra), and keeping their distance for the nonce. Tarra could well imagine what was on their minds: they wondered about the contents of his saddle bags, and of course the camel itself was not without value. Also they knew—or thought they knew—that he was without weapon. Well, as long as he kept more than arrow or bolt's flight distance between he was safe, but it made his back itch for all that.

Then he spied ahead the tumbled ruins of some ghost town or other on the plain, and urged his mount to a trot. It was quite dark now, for Gleeth sailed low as yet, so it might be some little time before his pursuers twigged that he'd quickened his pace. That was all to the good. He passed along the ghost town's single skeletal street, dismounted and tethered his beast by a heap of stones, then fleet-footed it back to the other end and flattened himself to the treacherous bricks of an arch where it spanned the narrow street. And waited.

And waited . . .

Could they have guessed his next move? Did they suspect his ambush? The plan had been simple: hurl knife into the back of one as they passed beneath, and leap on the back of the other; but what now?

Ah!—no sooner the question than an answer. Faint sounds in the night growing louder. Noise of their coming at last. But hoofbeats, a beast at gallop? What was this? No muffled, furtive approach this but frenzied flight! A pony, snorting its fear, fleeing riderless across the plain; and over there, silhouetted against crest of low hill, another. Now what in—?

Tarra slid down from the arch, held his breath, stared back hard the way he had come, toward Chlangi, and listened. But nothing, only the fading sounds of drumming hooves and a faint whinny in the dark.

Now instinct told the Hrossak he should count his blessings, forget whatever had happened here, return at once to his camel and so back to Chlangi by circuitous route as previously planned; but his personal demon, named Curiosity, deemed it otherwise. On foot, moving like a shadow among shadows, his bronze skin aiding him considerably in the dark, he loped easily back along his own route until—

It was the smell stopped him, a smell he knew at once from its too familiar reek. Fresh blood!

More cautiously now, nerves taut as a bowstring, almost in a crouch, Tarra moved forward again; and his grip on the haft of his knife never so tight, and his eyes never so large where they strained to penetrate night's canopy of dark. Then he was almost stumbling over them, and just as smartly drawing back, his breath hissing out through clenched teeth.

Dead, and not merely dead but gutted! Chlangi riff-raff by their looks, unpretty as the end they'd met. Aye, and a butcher couldn't have done a better job. Their entrails still steamed in the cool night air.

The biters bit: Tarra's trackers snared in advance of his own planned ambush; and what of the unseen, unheard killers themselves? Once more the Hrossak melted into shadow, froze, listened, stared. Perhaps they had gone in pursuit of the ponies. Well, Tarra wouldn't wait to find out. But as he turned to speed back to his camel—

Another smell in the night air? A sulphur reek, strangely laced with cloying musk? And where had he smelled that dubious perfume before? A nerve jumped in his neck, and twin scabs throbbed dully as if in mute answer.

To hell with it! They were all questions that could wait . . .

HALF A MILE from Chlangi Tarra dismounted and tethered his camel out of sight in a shallow gulley, then proceeded on foot and as fast as he could go to where the east wall was cracked as by some mighty tremor of the earth. Here boulders and stones had been tumbled uncemented into the gap, so that where the rest of the wall was smooth, offering little of handholds and making for a difficult climb, here it was rough and easily scaleable. Fregg knew this too, of course, for which reason there was normally a guard positioned atop the wall somewhere in this area. Since Chlangi was hardly a place people would want to break *into*, however, chances were the guard would have his belly wrapped around the contents of a wineskin by now, snoring in some secret niche.

The wall was high at this point, maybe ten man-lengths, but Old Gleeth was kind enough to cast his rays from a different angle, leaving the east wall in shadow. All should be well. Nevertheless—

Before commencing his climb Tarra peered right and left, stared long and hard back into the night toward the east, listened carefully to see if he could detect the slightest sound. But . . . nothing. There were bats about tonight, though— and big ones, whole roosts of them—judging from the frequent flappings he'd heard overhead.

Satisfied at last that there were no prying eyes, finally the Hrossak set fingers and toes to wall and scaled it like a lizard, speeding his ascent where the crack widened and the boulders were less tightly packed. Two-thirds of the way up he rested briefly, where a boulder had long since settled and left a man-sized gap, taking time to get his breath and peer out and down all along the wall and over the scraggy plain, and generally checking that all was well.

And again the stirring of unseen wings and a whipping of the air as something passed briefly across the starry vault.

Bats, yes, but a veritable cloud of them! Tarra shivered his disgust: he had little time for night creatures of any sort. He levered himself out of his hole, began to climb again—and paused.

A sound from on high, atop the wall? The scrape of heel against stone? The snuffle of bored or disconsolate feet? It came again, this time accompanied by wheezy grunt!

Tarra flattened himself to wall, clung tight, was suddenly aware of his vulnerability. At which precise moment he felt the coil of rope over his shoulder slip a little and heard his hook clang against the wall down by his waist. Quickly he trapped the thing, froze once more. Had it been heard?

"Huh?" came gruff inquiry from above. And: "Huh?" Then, in the next moment, a cough, a whirring sound diminishing, a gurgle—and at last silence once more.

For five long minutes Tarra waited, his nerves jumping and the feeling going out of his fingers and toes, before he dared continue his upward creep. By then he believed he had it figured out—or hoped so, anyway. The guard was, as he had suspected might be the case, asleep. The grapple's clang had merely caused him to start and snort into the night, before settling himself down again more comfortably. And perhaps the incident had been for the best at that; at least Tarra knew now that he was there.

With infinite care the Hrossak proceeded, and at last his fingertips went up over the sill of an embrasure. Now, more slow and silent yet, he drew up his body until—

Seated in the deep embrasure with his back to one wall and his knees against the other, a bearded guardsman grinned down on Tarra's upturned face and aimed a crossbow direct into the astonished "O" of his gaping mouth!

Tarra might simply have recoiled, released his grip upon

the rim and fallen. He might have (as some men doubtless would) fainted. He might have closed his eyes tight shut and pleaded loud and desperate, promising anything. He did none of these but gulped, grinned and said:

"Ho! No fool you, friend! Fregg chooses his guards well. He sent me here to catch you asleep—to test the city's security, d'you see?—but here you are wide awake and watchful, obviously a man who knows his duty. So be it; help me up from here and I'll go straight to our good king and make report how all's . . . well?"

For now the Hrossak saw that all was indeed well—for him if not for the guard. That smell was back, of fresh blood, and a dark pool of it was forming and sliming the stone where Tarra's fingers clung. It dripped from beneath the guard's chin—where his throat was slit from ear to ear!

Aye, for the gleam in his eyes was merely glaze, and his fixed grin was a rictus of horror! Also, the crossbow's groove was empty, its bolt shot; and now Tarra remembered the whirring sound, the cough, the gurgle . . .

Adrenalin flooded the Hrossak's veins as a flash flood fills dry river beds. He was up and into the embrasure and across the sprawling corpse in a trice, his flesh ice as he stared all about, panting in the darkness. He had a friend here for sure, but who or what he dared not think. And now, coming to him across the reek of spilled blood . . . *again* that sulphurous musk, that fascinating yet strangely fearful perfume.

Then, from the deeper shadows of a shattered turret:

"Have you forgotten me then, Tarra Khash, whose life you saved in the badlands? And is not the debt I owed you repaid?"

And oh the Hrossak knew that sibilant, whispering voice,

knew only too well whose hand—or claw—had kept him safe this night. Aye, and he further knew now that Chlangi's bats were no bigger than the bats of any other city; knew *exactly* why those ponies had fled like the wind across the plain; knew, shockingly, how close he must have come last night to death's sharp edge! The wonder was that he was still alive to know these things, and now he must ensure no rapid deterioration of that happy circumstance.

"I've not forgotten," he forced the words from throat dry as the desert itself. "Your perfume gives you away, Orbiquita—and your kiss shall burn on my neck and in my memory forever!" He took a step toward the turret.

"Hold!" she hissed from the shadows, where now a greater darkness moved uncertainly, its agitation accompanied by scraping as of many knives on stone. "Come no closer, Hrossak. It's no clean-limbed, soft-breasted girl stands here now."

"I know that well enow," Tarra croaked. "What do you want with me?"

"With you—nothing. But with that pair who put me to such trial in the desert—"

"They are dead," Tarra stopped her.

"What?" (Again the clashing of knives.) "Dead? That were a pleasure I had promised myself!"

"Then blame your disappointment on some other, Orbiquita," Tarra spoke into darkness. "Though certainly I would have killed them, if Fregg hadn't beaten me to it."

"Fregg, is it?" she hissed. "Scum murders scum. Well, King Fregg has robbed me, it seems."

"Both of us," Tarra told her. "You of your revenge, me of more worldly pleasures—a good many of them. Right now I'm on my way to take a few back."

The blackness in the turret stirred, moved closer to the door. Her voice was harsher now, the words coming more quickly, causing Tarra to draw back from brimstone breath. "What of my runebook?"

"Arenith Han, Fregg's sorcerer, will have that," the Hrossak answered.

"And where is he?"

"He lives in Fregg's palace, beneath his master's tower."

"Good! Show me this place." She inched forward again and for a moment the moonlight gleamed on something unbearable. Gasping, Tarra averted his eyes, pointed a trembling hand out over the city.

"There," he said, his voice breaking a little. "That high tower there with the light. That's where Fregg and his mage dwell, well guarded and central within the palace walls."

"What are guards and walls to me?" she said, and he heard the scrape of her clawed feet and felt the heat of her breath on the back of his neck. "What say you we visit this pair together?"

Rooted to the spot, not daring to look back, Tarra answered: "I'm all for companionship, Orbiquita, but—"

"So be it!" she was closer still. "And since you can't bear to look at me, close your eyes. Also, put away that knife—it would not scratch my scales."

Gritting his teeth, Tarra did both things—and at once felt himself grasped, lifted up, crushed to hot, stinking, scaly body. Wings of leather creaked open in the night; wind rushed all about; all was dizzy, soaring, whirling motion. Then—

Tarra felt his feet touch down and was released. He staggered, sprawled, opened his eyes and sprang erect. Again he stood upon a parapet; on one hand a low balcony wall,

overlooking the city, and on the other an arabesqued archway issuing warm, yellow light. Behind him, stone steps
winding down, where even now something dark descended
on scythe feet! Orbiquita, going in search of her runebook.

"Who's there?" came sharp voice of inquiry from beyond
the arched entrance. "Is that you, Arenith? And didn't I say
not to disturb me at my sorting and counting?"

It was Fregg—Fregg all alone, with no bully boys to protect him now—which would make for a meeting much
more to Tarra's liking. And after all, he'd been invited,
hadn't he?

Invited or not, the shock on Fregg's face as Tarra entered
showed all too clearly how the robber-king had thought
never to see him again. Indeed, it was as if Fregg gazed
upon a ghost, which might say something about the errand
of the two who'd followed Tarra across the plain; an errand
unfulfilled, as Fregg now saw. He half came to his feet, then
slumped down again with hands atop the huge oak table
that stood between.

"Good evening, Majesty," said Tarra Khash, no hint of
malice in his voice. "I've come for my broken sword, remember?" He looked all about the circular, dome-ceilinged
room, where lamps on shelves gave plenty of light. And
now the Hrossak saw what a magpie this jowly bandit really
was. Why, 'twere a wonder the many shelves had room for
Fregg's lamps at all—for they were each and every one
stacked high with stolen valuables of every sort and description! Here were jade idols and goblets, and more jade in
chunks unworked. Here were silver statuettes, plates,
chains and trinkets galore. Here were sacklets of very precious gems, and larger sacks of semi-precious stones. Here
was gold and scrolls of gold-leaf, bangles of the stuff hanging

from nails like so many hoops on pegs, and brooches, and medallions on golden chains, and trays of rings all burning yellow. But inches deep on the great table, and as yet unsorted, there lay Fregg's greatest treasure—which oh so recently had belonged to Tarra Khash.

"Your sword?" Fregg forced a smile more a grimace on to his face, fingered his beard, continued to stare at his visitor as if hypnotized. But at last animation: he stood up, slapped his thigh, roared with laughter and said, "Why of course, your broken sword!" Then he sobered. "It's here somewhere, I'm sure. But alas, I've not yet had time to remove the gems." His eyes rapidly swept the table, narrowing as they more slowly returned to the Hrossak's face.

Tarra came closer, watching the other as a cat watches a mouse, attuned to every breath, to each slightest movement. "Nor will there be time, I fancy," he said.

"Eh?" said Fregg; and then, in imitation of Tarra's doomful tone: "Is that to be the way of it? Well, before we decide upon all that—first tell me, Hrossak, how it is you've managed to come here, to this one place in all Chlangi which I had thought impregnable?"

Before Tarra could answer there came from below a shrill, wavering cry borne first of shock, then disbelief, finally terror—cut off most definitely at zenith. Skin prickling, knowing that indeed Orbiquita had found Arenith Han, Tarra commenced an involuntary turn—and knew his mistake on the instant. Already he had noted, upon a shelf close to where Fregg sat a small silver crossbow, with silver bolt loaded in groove and string ready-nocked. Turning back to robber-king he fell to one knee, his right hand and arm a blur of motion. Tarra's knife thrummed like a harp where its blade was fixed inches deep in shelf's soft wood, pinning

Fregg's fat hand there even as it reached for weapon. And upon that pinned hand, glinting on the smallest finger, a ring of gold inset with jade cut in a skull and serpent crest.

Blood spurted and Fregg slumped against the shelves—but not so heavily that his weight put stress on the knife. "M-mercy!" he croaked, but saw little of mercy in the hulking steppeman's eyes. Gasping his pain, he reached trembling free hand toward the knife transfixing the other.

In a scattering of gems and baubles Tarra vaulted the table, his heels slamming into Fregg's face. The bandit was hurled aside, his hand split neatly between second and third fingers by the keen blade! Screaming Fregg fell, all thought of fighting back relinquished now to agony most intense from riven paw. Gibbering he sprawled upon the floor amidst scattering gems and nuggets, while Tarra stood spread-legged and filled the scabbard at his back, then topped his loot with hilt of shattered sword.

Until, "Enough!" he said. "I've got what I came for."

"But *I* have not!" came Orbiquita's monstrous hiss from the archway.

Tarra turned, saw her, went weak at the knees. Now he looked full upon a lamia, and knew all the horror of countless others gone before him. And yet he found the strength to answer her as were she his sister: "You did not find your runebook?"

"The book, aye," her breath was sulphur. "Mylakhrion's ring, no. Have you seen it, Tarra Khash? A ring of gold with skull and serpent crest?"

Edging past her, Tarra gulped and nodded in Fregg's direction where he sat, eyes bugging, his quivering back to laden shelves. "Of that matter, best speak to miserable monarch there," he told her.

Orbiquita's claws flexed and sank deep into the stone floor as she hunched toward the now drooling, keening robber-king.

"Farewell," said Tarra, leaping out under the archway and to the parapet wall, and fixing his grapnel there.

From below came hoarse shouts, cries of outrage, the clatter of many feet ascending the tower's corkscrew stairs. "Farewell," came Orbiquita's hiss as Tarra swung himself out and down into the night. "Go swiftly, Hrossak, and fear no hand at your back. I shall attend to that."

After that—

All was a chaos of flight, of hideous screams fading into distance behind, of climbing, falling, of running and riding, until Chlangi was a blot, then less than a blot, then vanished altogether into distance behind him. Somewhere along the way Stumpy Adz dragged him to a gasping, breathless halt, however brief, gawped at a handful of gems, disappeared dancing into shadows; and somewhere else Tarra cracked a head when unknown assailant leaped on him from hiding; other than which he remembered very little.

And through all of that wild panic flight, only once did Tarra Khash look back—of which he wished he likewise had no recall.

For then . . . he had thought to see against the face of the moon a dark shape flying, whose outlines he knew well. And dangling beneath, a fat flopping shape whose silhouette seemed likewise familiar. And he thought the dangling thing screamed faintly in the thin, chill air of higher space, and he thought he saw its fitful kicking. Which made him pray it was only his imagination, or a dark cloud fleeing west.

And after that he put it firmly out of his mind.

As for Orbiquita:

She hated being in anyone's debt. This should square the matter. Fregg would make hearty breakfast for a hungry sister waking up from five long years of stony vigil . . .

In the Temple of Terror

I

Den of Thieves

WEIRD ENERGIES FORMED flickering green and blue traceries in the black clouds boiling over Klühn, patterned like webs of giant, lightning-spawned spiders, with central strands going down in a coil and lending the dome of a certain temple a cold and eerie foxfire all its own.

This was the first of three nights at the full of the moon, and the alien aurora was a thing familiar now to the inhabitants of Klühn where the city stood, a jewel of civilization and sophistication, at the mouth of the Lohr on the shore of the Eastern Ocean. Each month, when the moon was full, for three nights the sky would boil, while filaments of fire wove sentient skeins all funnelled down to the Temple of Secret Gods. And the aurora was the reason why Klühn's peoples—those of less adventurous or fool-hardy inclinations, at least; those unwilling to tempt whatever supernatural forces were at work here—were now abed, shivering in their sheets, leaving the streets to the handful of yeggs and sharpers and vagabonds who wandered there, whose souls were already sold.

Less than novel in the eyes of common residents (the aerial phenomenon had first occurred a year ago, and every month since), the manifestation was a thing of wonder to Tarra Khash; a wonder and a pestilence, for it threatened to ruin his sleep. Sleep was unsatisfactory at best of times—on bed of hard planks with one tattered blanket, and every smallest wind a freezing hurricane howling in through the iron bars of his cage, or causing it to sway at the end of its chain, suspended from the high, overhanging parapet wall of the Square of Justice—but with the night flickering green and blue like this it were impossible! And so, sitting there in the fabulous dark (or what should be dark), his blanket wrapped tight about him like the feathers of some strange, gaunt bird, Tarra stared and wondered, and pondered the wretchedness of his position and the path of fate which had led him to it . . .

Two weeks gone, having forded the Lohr some miles west of the fork, the Hrossak had entered Klühn through the West Gate; in dusk of evening had headed straight for the market area, sold his camel, bought clothes more fitting to city life and discarded his much-worn and now highly disreputable loin-cloth. Then, fitted out in silken shirt (with sleeves rolled up to show the width of his forearms), bell-bottomed, piratical trousers of a coarse weave, and leather calf-boots folded down near the top—with his scabbard slung across his back, jewelled hilt of ceremonial scimitar protruding, but iron-pinned to thwart would-be thieves—he had swaggered forth to find himself lodge down by the wharves. After hiring a luxurious turret room overlooking the bay on the one hand and Lohr's wide mouth on the other, and having bathed and filled his belly with meat and wine, and further having slept for an hour or two, then he had been ready for come-what-may.

Now, Hrossaks are a breed who believe in living, and Tarra was no exception. He could take it hard without complaint when necessary, but liked it soft on occasion, certainly. Recently, indeed for quite some little while, it had been the former, and in Tarra's eyes latter were long overdue. Which was why he had decided to let his hair down. The plan was simple: find an eatery and put away something rare and spicy—to supplement the not insubstantial meal already consumed, but not enjoyed in haste of chomping—drink a bottle or two of the rarest wine, then hie him to a bawdy-house and bed some luscious whore. Morning would be soon enough to worry about his wealth: what to do with it, how to spend it (for what was money for if not the spending?) and how best the fortune might be employed in furtherance of his future and pursuance of his career. Ah!—but there had lain the rub, there the roots of his dilemma . . .

For Tarra Khash was a wanderer, an adventurer, and wealth tends to moor a man much as an anchor holds fast the fleetest ship. He could buy himself a property, he supposed, high-walled and secluded, to serve as his base; but then he must look for a caretaker, too, servants to tend the place when he was away. All very difficult. But . . . such are the problems of rich men. Anyway, tomorrow would be time enough for all that; doubtless there'd be businessmen in the city to advise him this way or that—for a fee, of course.

These had been his thoughts on his first night in Klühn . . .

And on the second—

—The third, and etc.

Then, a week ago, he had stumbled somewhat intoxicated upon Ellern Thark's gambling den, and as easily as that his problems had all been solved.

Gambling hadn't been new to the Hrossak: he'd seen dice and cards of various sorts used in Hrossa for the amusement of steppemen, had even gamed himself on rare occasion; but there on the steppes the stakes had been so small as to be insignificant, while in Ellern Thark's place they were . . . something else! Why, a man could lose an entire fortune here in less than a week—or three days, if he tried hard enough and if crafty proprietor kept him topped up with booze!

That's all it had taken, three days; with Tarra staggering back to his turret room before dawn, sleeping it off, then back to Thark's place to send good money chasing after bad, and not once catch it; and Tarra never quite sober enough to realize that the dice were loaded and the cards marked, and always sufficiently optimistic to believe he'd get his money back. It had all become hazy in his head: a continuous clatter of dice, a dizzy blur of brightly daubed cards, an unending gurgle of fiery liqueurs and anaesthetic ales. Until finally—

Broke!

Neither nugget nor gemstone, jade- nor silver-piece, bauble nor button. Only the bejewelled hilt of his ceremonial sword, and a pinch or two of gold dust shaken out of now utterly vacant scabbard to satisfy his landlord's needs. Then and only then had the Hrossak started to put two and two together, and the sum always coming out five; and only *then* recalling certain things hitherto meaningless, which now took on aspect of vast import.

Clinching it, finally he overheard from where he sat, head in hands in a secluded tavern booth, how "that big dumb Hrossak" had been robbed of king's ransom at Ellern Thark's, and that had set a pot boiling in his belly whose steam could only find release in volcanic violence. While the pot boiled, however, building up pressure, Tarra had fuelled its fire with thoughts of all he'd gone through to win his fortune in the first place:

He'd thought of the desert-hidden treasure vaults of alien kings he'd robbed—or been sent to rob—and of the vengeance of the golden guardians of those subterrene sepulchres, which he'd only just escaped with skin intact; of his subsequent flight to Chlangi the Doomed, where lamia's kiss had seared his neck and possibly his soul, and where he'd had to steal back a portion of his tomb-loot from robber-king Fregg, now a pile of bones somewhere in Nameless Desert's heart. He'd thought of arduous camel-trek to Klühn, weighed down by scabbard full of gold and gems strapped firmly to his back, and of all he'd dreamed to do with that hard-earned fortune, dreams now turned to dust—by Ellern Thark, a sharper lower than a lizard's gut, boss of a fleapit den of thieves.

And then other vague memories had come, rapidly growing clearer, finally overlapping the mindless kaleidoscope of cards and dice and drink. Tarra had remembered how, on occasion, he'd seen Thark watching while he gamed, and how that fjord-born snake had winked at his dealers at certain times, or introduced fresh, cool dice into the game. Aye, too cool by far!

Hah! Tarra's luck had always seemed to run low where Northmen were concerned—at cards or at anything else, whether the dice were loaded or not—and now it seemed the pattern continued to run true. Well, he couldn't prove a thing and he knew it, but it wasn't only his pocket that was hurting and he must do something. Mayhem seemed the only answer, and yet—

Perhaps there was another way . . .

He still had the jewelled hilt of his sword, after all—for the moment, anyway—and that was surely worth a small fortune in itself. Why not roll the dice one last time at Ellern's place? One last shot—for all or nothing!

And so that night Tarra had ventured yet again to the gambling den, and a sorry, sodden sight he must have been on arrival. The wonder was he was let in at all, but when he showed the thugs on the door the gems where they gleamed in the hilt of his shattered sword . . .

Inside it had been business as usual. The sigh and flutter of cards and the skittering of ivory and jade dice; the *oohs!* and *aahs!* of spectators; curses or guffaws of gamers; the lamps suspended from high-beamed ceiling, lending the scene glints of a coppery colour; and the half-clad Yhemni slave-girls, moving sinuously among patrons with trays of spicy sweetmeats and clinking goblets of wine, their dusky skins agleam with oils and their filed teeth flashing white in dark faces.

But in the crush of bodies about the tables, Tarra had spotted Ellern Thark at once—and Thark had spotted him.

The proprietor of the den was as big a northern barbarian as any Tarra had ever come across in all his wanderings, and big in *all* directions. Not yet thirty, Thark's aspect was truly awesome. A young, full-blooded Northman, his mane of hair was blue-black to match his eyes; and they in turn were set in the face of a hawk, scarred from knife and fist fights and weathered by northern winters. His arms and legs were trunks of muscle, likewise scarred in places, and his chest and back formed a wedge of meat rising up from a waist narrow as Tarra's own. Strong as an ox, devious and deadly formidable; that was Ellern Thark. The soft silks of his clothing couldn't hide it, and the wicked gleam in his slitted eyes where they gazed on Tarra Khash made no slightest attempt.

A moment earlier Thark had been deep in heated conversation with a yellow-robed, bald-pated priest of the Temple of Secret Gods, and Tarra had remembered how he had seen such in here on several previous occasions. This had caused him to revisit what little he had learned of their obscure and cryptic sect:

The first disciples of the order (he had been given to understand in casual conversation) had appeared in the city some five years earlier, arriving from Thinhla, Eyphra, even from as far away as Thandopolis, bringing with them the entirely conjectural ikons and instruments of their faith. Not far from Klühn's central plazas, they had procured land and commenced construction of their mighty ziggurat temple with its lesser outer domes and massive central dome of hammered copper, a project which had paid most of the city's builders and craftsmen well indeed and had kept them in work for all of four years—which had been good not only for them but Klühn in general. For Klühn was a commercial city and lived by its commercialism. Also, the peoples of Klühn were not opposed to a multitude of gods, even secretive ones, if such brought them wealth. And however cryptogenic the gods of these yellow-robed priests, they did not appear inimical; indeed the sect members kept well to themselves and bothered no one. At least, not at first. Later things had been different . . .

Now Klühn had various playboy princelings of mixed origins—socialites who dwelled here for the climate and good living in the main, rather than by laying claim to the lands around—but no real king, else the doings of the Secret Gods Sect came perhaps under closer scrutiny. But . . . after the temple was builded and its high outer walls erected fortress-like, then the changes had gradually come about and things were finally seen to be more complicated—and perhaps more sinister—than had at first seemed likely.

Even then the ordinary, normally industrious citizenry was not affected, not at first; only dealers in land, property, jewelry, gold and silver merchants, whoremasters, vice-lords and such felt the sting; and felt it where it most hurt: in their pockets. For it now appeared that the priests of the sect held within their temple an oracle of great power, all-knowing, all-seeing, and that the special function of this oracle was to advise the priests of any and all shady transactions taking place in the arenas of those aforementioned businesses and concerns, so that soon Klühn's over- and under-world barons alike found themselves in the grip of temple-spawned blackmail! And in a trice the priests had their fingers in every pie, and all concerned paid tribute to the Temple of Secret Gods, lest *their* most precious secrets be shouted abroad.

Then it had been the turn of Klühn's simpler folk, when they too had started to feel the pinch. For now they found themselves levied of a tax, which they must pay in respect of the protection they received from the yellow-robed priests. But protection from what? The answer to that was simple: against dark forces which even now strove to destroy Klühn and her citizens, whose periodic attacks only the presence of the temple itself staved off! (The temple, its oracle, and its priests, of course.)

The monthly manifestations of weird energies, aye! The boiling clouds and strange lightnings, the doomful darkness and flickering corpse-fires swirling over the city, whose forces seemed drained by temple's copper dome, and doubtless by efforts of droning priests and sphinxy oracle within! And what to do but pay, or else go unprotected from all this strangeness? For Klühn in her opulence and arrogance had sinned, and now sinners and innocents alike were taken to task, and the Secret Gods' Sect had come in their mercy to pave the city's way back to righteousness and sanctity in the eyes of their unknown gods.

So that the question now asked was this: had those strange and furtive priests really come to stave off a doom, or had the doom simply followed them here? And if so, what to do about it?

The answer to which was this: nothing!

For the original handful of yellow-robes was now an hundred, and the sellswords they'd hired an hundred more, so that only a fool or madman would say or go against them. And him who did—why, he simply vanished, or was ruined!—object lesson to more cautious men.

And Klühn, which had no king and hence no army, must suffer in silence.

It was just such a yellow-robe Tarra Khash had seen in heated conversation with Ellern Thark that night he had chosen to take his revenge, and he remembered now how both had seemed to glare at him across that thronging den of thieves and fools. Or maybe they glared because of their argument, which had perhaps spared Tarra from closer scrutiny. Aye, and just as well, that.

Anyway, Thark's acknowledgement of his presence had been merely cursory; what else should it be, in light of the fact that the Hrossak was obviously drunk and had doubt-less rolled in the gutter on his way here? Well, his visit wouldn't last long. What little he'd brought with him could be robbed in a trice, just as his vaster fortune had been robbed. The man deserved no better; obviously he was even greater clown than Thark had first taken him for!

But as Thark's interest in him had waned, so Tarra had wormed his way closer to barbarian and yellow-robe, so that soon he was able to overhear something of their conversation. Ostensibly they watched a dice game while they talked, but that was just for show. In fact, it seemed the priest was giving Ellern Thark a hard time, at least from the harsh tone of Thark's agitated voice as Tarra heard him answer:

"Yes, yes, I've agreed all that—though all the gods know 'twere near impossible! Doesn't Gorgos know he's bleeding us dry? Why, if not for the fact that I've had a good week I'd not be *able* to pay! Easy as that. Unwilling is one thing—indeed something to be expected—but unable something else again. Blackmail all you will, you so-called 'priests,' but what weight will your threats carry when there's nothing left, eh? You'll bring the entire city down on your heads if you're not careful; aye, and your soldiers will surely be called upon to earn their keep then, by Yibb!"

"Calm yourself!" the other had answered sharply. "And waste not your ire on me, Ellern Thark. I am merely Gorgos' messenger. He tends the oracle, and he determines the toll. You *have* done well this week, beyond a doubt, else were your dues lighter. You have not always paid so high."

"High?" Thark burst out, his voice louder now than harsh whisper. "High? I call it *extortion*!"

" 'Ware, Northman!" the yellow-robe's hiss was ice. "You live well here, would you jeopardize your position?"

At which junction there had come a roar of rage from the gaming table close at hand, where a burly merchant with fat hands dripping rings had grabbed the table's dice-caster by his skinny neck and was now shaking him like a rat. "Cheat!" the merchant roared, shaking away. "I can lose as fast as any man without help from you!" Finally he hurled the dealer to the floor—which was where Ellern Thark stepped in.

"Sir," he pushed through the crush, "that man's in my employ. If he's a cheat I'll break all his fingers and toss him in the street—refund your losses, too—but if he's innocent you've a problem on your hands. I'll not have my house impugned without chance to answer back. Neither beggar nor rich man calls Ellern Thark a cheat!"

"You?" the merchant had turned to him red-faced, taken in his massive size and the angry glint in his blue-black barbarian eyes. "*Huh!* I don't know about you," he said, "but this one—" he pointed at the choking, coughing dealer where he clawed at the floorboards, "—this one's a thief! Him and his dice both!" And he slammed down a pair of dice on the table. Thark, nimble-fingered, snatched them up at once.

"Are these the dice?" he snapped. "Did he cheat you with these?" He held the dice out—but Tarra saw his other hand now placed jauntily on hip, close to a silken pocket.

"Aye, with them," said the merchant. "Toss 'em and see for yourself. Sixes every time. They're weighted, obviously."

Thark grinned—but it was the grin of a crocodile. "These are house dice," he said, "and innocent of trickery. As am I, and as is he whose throat you've sorely crushed. Lady Luck's the villain, sir—or villainess if you like. And no wonder, for I've heard she only runs with gentlemen . . ."

"*What?*" the other had been furious. He snatched back

the dice (the ones Thark offered him), shook them, let them roll. A one and a three. Purple with rage, he stared, then turned on Thark. "You must've swapped 'em!" he roared. "Why you're a bigger—"

The Northman hit him once, stiff-fingered, his hand vanishing in the other's gut up to his wrist, propelling him off his feet and through the crush of people, all air expelled in one gigantic *whoosh* of breath, and accusation gone with it. "*Out!*" Thark bellowed, pointing, his men closing in on the merchant even as he caromed from a support pillar and fell. "Into the gutter with him—and don't let me see him in here again. What? Is this a brothel and are we whores, we should suffer insults from such as him? What were his losses, that so enraged him? Two small pieces of silver, I'll wager!"

"A little more than that, Ellern Thark," said damaged dealer's assistant, a dark Yhemni maid with gleaming breasts, standing by the table. "I hold the stakes." She tipped them on to the table: two small pouches of gold dust, a chunk of raw silver big as a man's thumb, two large rings aglitter with precious stones.

"A pittance!" cried Thark. "And would I give my house a bad name for this? Why, I'd gamble it myself on a single throw, high score wins!"

"Done!" Tarra Khash had then drunkenly rumbled, stumbling forward to clasp Thark's hand where it had strayed back toward his silk pocket. "Shake on it. And here—you shoot first." He picked up the dice, passed them to Thark.

Thark glowered at the dice in the palm of his great hand; his dark glance went to the stakes. "Where's your money, Hrossak? Haven't you lost enough yet?" His voice was cold as the Chill Sea.

Never taking his eyes from Thark's huge yet overly agile hands, Tarra fished out a huge ruby freshly gouged from the hilt of his sword. It joined the other items in keeping of the Yhemni wench, putting the rest of the purse in the shade. "Well?"

"So be it," Thark grunted, his lips curling back in half-grin, half-snarl. He blew on the dice, tossed them . . . a three and a four.

"Seven!" cried Tarra. "My throw!" He took up the dice, gave them a shake, let them roll. Two fives. "Good!" said Tarra, reaching for his winnings.

As the crowd pushed closer Thark wiped the snarl from his face, said: "There! That's the sort of game I like: quick and clean." He made as if to pocket the dice, appeared to change his mind. "Since your luck's in, Hrossak, mayhap you'd care to try it again?"

"Aye, why not?" Tarra gestured expansively, reeling just a little and thinking: *and here's where I close you down, dog!* "What stakes, Ellern Thark?"

"Why, what you see," said the other, the smallest niggle of a doubt beginning to form at the back of his mind. The Hrossak seemed drunk, and yet—

"A pittance!" Tarra had cut Thark's thoughts short. "You said it yourself—and my ruby the choicest morsel!"

"Very well," Thark answered, his face darkening again. "Beat me one more time—fairly mind!—and I'll pay four times the odds. Nay, for you, who've suffered such grievous losses here, I'll even make it fives! Now who could say fairer than that?"

Tarra had expected no less; he knew that Thark believed he couldn't lose. "Your word on it?" he said. "A fair game and no grudge held—and you'll bet odds of five to one I can't beat you again?"

"My word on it," Thark answered, growing uncomfortable under the gaze of so many eyes.

"And you'll cover anything I put up?"

"Should I have a scribe carve it in runes, Tarra Khash?" Thark shouted. "Now what's the delay?"

"No delay," said Tarra. "Only cover this!" And he'd produced and slammed down on the table the gem-crusted hilt of his sword, which amounted to everything he owned in the entire world of Theem'hdra.

At that a concerted gasp had gone up—and none louder than the hissing sigh of yellow-robed priest—while the crush of bodies had tightened as patrons vied for better vantage points. And no more pretended drunkenness on Hrossak's part, whose eyes now glinted keen as barbarian's own; but perhaps the sudden blossoming of respect and maybe even a little fear in Thark's northern breast, where his heart began to beat a little faster as he made a sign across the room to his cashiers in cage of iron bars.

Then from the strongroom was brought all the Hrossak's previous wealth, his ingots, jewels, nuggets of gold. And, "Satisfied now, Hrossak?" rasped Ellern Thark. "Is this what you wanted to see?"

"I think that'll do," Tarra had answered.

While all of this was in action, the yellow-robe had ogled and twitched, his gaze seeming riveted to Tarra's broken blade. Then, as Thark had blown on the dice in his fashion and prepared to throw them down, Tarra had thought to hear, however indistinctly, the said priest's excited whisper:

"Win, Thark! Win me that broken sword and consider all your dues paid for a year—aye, and Gorgos and all the priests of the temple in *your* debt for a change!"

Then the dice were rattling on the table, bouncing, skittering to a halt. Sixes, both!

And the massive Northman laughing, his hand moving toward the dice, doubtless to catch them up in triumph. But Tarra Khash moving first, snatching up the hilt of his sundered sword and smashing it down shatteringly on one of the dice—which had at once broken into pieces, displaying a base filled with lead! Thark's laughter dying on his lips . . .

. . . And in the ensuing silence, Hrossak's voice like knell of doom, saying: "It seems you lose, Ellern Thark—unless these loaded dice are your idea of fair?"

Then—

Thark's hand blurring toward hilt of wicked knife in his belt—a mistake, for Tarra's weapon was already in his hand. And while its blade was a mere stump, a six-inch shard, no more, still its edge was razor sharp. And in under Thark's ribs that shattered blade had driven, and across in a tearing of silk, and down to make a door in fleshy wall. And then through that door Thark's guts pouring, while his hands shot into the air, knife flying uselessly from shuddering fingers to lodge thrumming in ceiling joist. And still the stunned silence, until with a final tremor the barbarian's body had crashed like felled oak, life all spilled out and wet upon the shaken boards.

Then a motion to Tarra's rear—and swirly flash of yellow glimpsed out the corner of his eye—followed by sharp report like *snap* of great whip . . . shattering concussion . . .

more flashes, all brightly hued, all rapidly turning dark . . .
spiralling down into whirlpools of blackest jet . . .

II

Last of the Suhm-yi

THE REST OF it was very clear in the Hrossak's memory.

He had regained consciousness in a cell; the morning had
seen him in a city court charged with Ellern Thark's sudden
demise; chief witness for the prosecution was the yellow-
robe of the previous night, his bald pate full of lies and
treachery. Tarra had been framed neat as an eye in its orbit;
it appeared that after the priest crowned him, two pairs of
loaded dice had been "discovered" in his pockets. A would-
be cheat turned murderer, the verdict had not been difficult
to gauge in advance:

Ten days in a cage—time enough to repent his wicked
ways and make his peace with the world, while the good
folk of Klühn could come in hours of daylight and *tut-tut*
and ogle at him where he dangled high overhead—and on
the eleventh day the cage hauled up to its highest point, and
securing pin knocked neatly out from the chain's last link.
Then downward rush, and cage and bed and Hrossak and all
dashed to pieces on the flags 'neath the frowning walls of
the Square of Justice. And Tarra now suspended here, with
only seven days left to him in all the world, pondering on all
the fables he'd heard which had it that the justice of Klühn
and the kindness of her citizens were finest and fairest in
Theem'hdra. Well, perhaps, in days gone by—but hardly
relevant now, and no comfort at all to Tarra Khash . . .

The clouds over Klühn were breaking up now, their boiling less frenzied, traceries of weird energy thinning out and growing fainter. In a little while it would all be over; the skies would grow clear again, Old Gleeth the god of the moon would blaze like a silver skull over the far horizon. A skull, aye, for Tarra's mood was grown very morbid; he could find nothing wholesome in anything he saw or thought of. His position seemed entirely hopeless. But—

"Not quite, Tarra Khash," said a voice quite close. "Not *entirely* hopeless."

Tarra started, causing his cage to rock a little, and sat up straighter on his plank bed. What? And had he been doing his thinking out loud, then? And skulking night-watch come to chuckle at him out of the shadow of the wall? He turned his sour gaze that way.

Inside the Square's massy walls ramps had been built and machines for the hauling of cages, and openings like arched windows had been cut through the walls themselves from which food could be passed on long poles to prisoners in their cages. During the day the Square was open to visitors, when citizens with grievances—relatives of murdered persons, perhaps, or victims of vile assaults, frauds and such, even simple curiosity seekers—could climb the inner ramps at will, pass through the walls and hurl rotten fruit, bad eggs and worse language at the criminals suspended there. Now, in one such arched niche, the one closest to Tarra, a shadow stirred half in feeble moonlight. Tarra stared hard, wondering who this could be, at this time of night, come to torment him.

"Who indeed?" came soft, silvery query out of darkness. "Who reads the misery of your thoughts in the night, Tarra Khash, and comes to discover you here, caged like a strange wild bird? Don't you know me? Have you so soon forgotten the Inner Isles, the isles of the Suhm-yi?"

"*Suhm-yi!*" Tarra's answer came out a gasp. "Forgotten? Of course not. Oh, I know you now, Amyr Arn, last of your race! But what do you here, so far from crater sea?"

"You've answered that already, Tarra," came answer like silver bells in the night. "Last of my race, you said—and once I thought so, too. But now—now I'm not so sure."

"You mean there's another, like you? Here in Klühn?"

"Another, *un*like me. A female, aye—a Suhm-yi maid!"

Tarra jumped up, pressed his body to the bars, spread his legs to brace himself against the cage's sway. He had so many questions in him that they all vied to be out together, so that for long moments nothing was said at all. And then, just when he might have spoken, his words were anticipated.

"I'll tell you all," said Amyr Arn, "—but after I've got you down from here."

"Got me down? *Hah!*" Tarra laughed, however bitterly. "A job on your hands there, my friend. And how about the night-watch? Six of 'em, at least, in their guardroom at the base of the stone tower at the corner of the wall. Don't you think they'll have something to say about it?"

"Very little," Amyr answered, his voice a-tinkle. "I sent them up a flagon of wine all of an hour ago, when the sky was dancing with alien fires. A very special wine, it was—all laced with a rare, rare drug. By now they're snoring their heads off!"

"Oh?" Tarra gawped, then laughed and slapped his thigh. "And tomorrow, if I'm found absent, they'll likely wish they *had* snored them off! At least that's a peaceful way to lose 'em! But tell me, how'll you get me down?"

"*Shh!*" Amyr had cautioned. "Be quiet now. You'll see

soon enough. Have patience—I'll be but a little while gone . . ." Tarra saw twin flashes of gold; then, where a shadow had stirred, the niche in the wall was empty of all but moonbeams and a swirl of fine dust . . .

FOR THE NEXT few minutes Tarra let his mind wander back a six-month to his adventures in the Inner Isles, that volcanic tumble of jewel islands lying central in the crater sea. He had gone there hot on the trail of a gang of murderous Northmen, Kon Athar and his bully-boys, after they'd butchered two prospector pals of his near the source of the River Thand high in the Great Circle Mountains. The bar-barians had quested for treasure, and they'd crossed moun-tains seeking the legended Inner Isles where dwelled a half-fabulous (and only half-human, or perhaps totally *un*-human) race of manlike beings known only as the Suhm-yi, the "Seldom Seen."

Sailing the great crater sea on raft of logs, all the barbar-ian reavers found was this: isles of the Suhm-yi all layered in a thick red dust, and the Suhm-yi themselves—four-fingered, four-toed, silvery-skinned and golden-eyed—but every one of them dead. Dead of the poison in the dust, which had been blown there from some far volcanic disas-ter, and rained from the skies to kill them all off. All except two. Amyr Arn had been one, his mate, Lula, the other.

Amyr had been fishing when the Northmen came, far out on placid crater sea when they found his tiny jewel island. Aye, and they'd found his lovely Lula, too . . .

When Tarra Khash had followed their tracks to her body it was much too late, and then only the strict Suhm-yi code—which did not permit of vengeance—kept him safe from Amyr's wrath, his grief, his passion. Afterwards—

—They had buried her, and next day in Amyr's canoe Tarra had once more taken up the chase, and finally Kon Athar and his bullies were tracked down and slain. Tarra did this on his own, for again Suhm-yi vows would not permit Amyr to go with him. But at the end—strangely, for Amyr was not there—still the Hrossak had sensed the last of the Suhm-yi's intervention in the final vengeance, his hand in the thing; and since it doubtless saved his life, he'd welcomed that weird diversion. For it was not Tarra who struck Kon Athar down in the final fight but an arrow, speeding seemingly from out the very moon—a Suhm-yi arrow, Amyr's own—and Amyr nowhere in sight, but miles away upon another isle!

That was the fight where Tarra had lost his sword, or rather where he'd been left with only stump of curving scimitar blade; and it was also the last time he'd seen the Inner Isles, like ingots of silver gleaming under Gleeth's bright ray . . .

Tarra's cage gave a sharp downward lurch, jerking him where he sat on the edge of his plank platform. He turned his eyes upward but could see little, only the wall on one side like canyon of stone, and above, the gibbet arm from which his cage was suspended. Then came the creak of a pulley, the rattle of a chain (cut short in a moment) and again his cage fell an inch or two before jigging a little on the air. The Hrossak gulped, hoping his strange friend knew what he was about!

Evidently Amyr did for, having got the hang of it, now without a sound the cage descended smoothly a good man-length, coming to a gentle halt. Then a period when nothing seemed to be happening, except Tarra Khash listening to the thudding of his own heart, until once again the shadows stirred in the niche and golden eyes looked out and down a little on Tarra in the cage.

"Your turn now, bronze one," came Amyr's silvery whisper. "I only pray you're as strong as you look!"

"What must I do?" Tarra whispered back, senses all alert.

By now the last of the alien, webby spiderfires had flickered out in the sky overhead and the clouds were drifting west. Stars were gleaming through, and from the far horizon Gleeth's light slanted full on the face of the wall. Klühn's citizens were all abed, true, but still the air seemed suddenly fraught with urgency, both Hrossak and Suhm-yi knowing there was little time to waste.

"I've a grapple here," Amyr called across. "Catch and fix it firmly to base of cage. I'll attend to this end."

Tarra saw his plan, said: "The bars are strong, and there's a lock on the door. Even if I can haul cage and all to your niche, what then?" But even speaking he caught and fixed the three-pronged hook.

"I've a way with locks," Amyr answered, "—if you can hold cage steady while I work. There, my end of the line is fixed. Now, I shall pull from my end, and wind the line as we go, and you must haul from your end—except you cannot rest or loose the rope."

"Fear not," Tarra gruffly answered. "It means my life!" And now arm over arm he commenced to haul on the rope, the cage shifting from the perpendicular and towards Amyr in his arched-over niche. Swiftly the Hrossak worked, knowing he could not rest till it was done; Amyr, too, hauling and winding, until the cage dangled but an arm's length away from the window in the wall.

"Now hold fast!" warned Amyr, and leaning out he swiftly fixed another grapple. "There!—now take your ease, Hrossak."

Tarra rested—and felt the sudden agony in his muscles! All had been swiftly accomplished, aye, but with such an effort he'd scarce realized; and now his arms like leaden lumps, but silently screaming as blood once more thundered through burning sinew. Groaning softly, he watched Amyr's four-fingered hands working at the lock on the door, saw it spring open. After that—

The work of a moment to swing the door wide, take Amyr's glittering arm and step from cage to niche—and lean there in shadow against the wall, limbs atremble in sudden reaction. But in another moment:

"What now, Amyr Arn?" asked Tarra. "Where does your plan take us from here?"

"To my lodgings," the other answered, "where we can talk. Here, put this on." And for the first time, as he leaned out of the shadows, Tarra saw how he was dressed: in the yellow robe of a priest of the Temple of Secret Gods! Not only that, but the hooded robe he handed Tarra was yellow, too!

"Now what in all the—?" Tarra hissed, only to be cut off short with:

"No, no—don't go jumping to conclusions, my friend. It's no easy thing for a silver, comb-headed man to make his way in pink- and brown- and black-skinned city. Believe me, it were far easier to become a nameless, cowled priest than stay Amyr Arn of the Suhm-yi—however temporary the change! Aye, and you'll be safer swathed in yellow, too."

Donning the cassock, Tarra couldn't resist a chuckle; then Amyr was leading the way through the wall, down the ramps, past the silent guardroom in base of corner tower and so out into the night. And all unchallenged the pair strode through Klühn's dark streets to the poorer side of town, where with wooden latchkey Amyr let them into a cobbled courtyard, and in the inky darkness led Tarra up steep exterior steps to a high attic aerie.

"Nice," grunted the Hrossak, admiring the hideaway when lamp was lit, "but not much good for a fast getaway, if such were needed."

Amyr at once showed him a window in a gable where it overhung a back-street; showed him also a coil of rope, its end made fast to a stout roof timber. "There's your bolthole, Hrossak," he said, repeating the other's: " 'if such were needed.' "

Tarra chuckled. "It seems you've learned a lot since leaving your Inner Isles and becoming a yellow-robed priest!" he joked. "And what would your Suhm-yi gods think of that, I wonder? Or do you perhaps worship the same Secret Gods?"

" 'Ware!" said Amyr, his voice more lead than silver now. "That were true blasphemy, Tarra Khash. Secret Gods, did you say?" He tossed back his hood, shook his combed head in denial. "Demons, my friend, drawn down from nameless places far out beyond the farthest stars! But come, let's doff these robes and eat a bite together, and I'll tell you all I've done and learned since that time we said farewell."

They seated themselves side by side on a low bench, and from a table scarce higher than the floor ate a meal of fish soup and hard bread washed down with a little sour wine. Not much of a repast, but gourmet's delight to Tarra Khash, after three days of slops and crusts eaten in a swaying cage.

And seeing his hunger, Amyr let him take the greater part; so that while the Hrossak munched, the silver-scaled Suhm-yi commenced his tale.

"After you had gone from the Inner Isles, Tarra Khash, for long and long I prayed to the gods of the Suhm-yi, especially Gleeth, who sits at the head of their table. And I asked Gleeth should I stay here now, in crater sea, friendless and forlorn, amidst the dust and bones and ghosts of the Suhm-yi, or should I climb the high peak named Na-dom, fling myself down on the rocks, and so put an end to it?

"Now Gleeth's a cold one and seldom answers, but perhaps he took pity on one who thought himself last of the Suhm-yi. One evening when the moon hung full and low, great golden orb in the eastern sky—even over Klühn as I judged it—it seemed to me the moonbeams formed a stream, all shining down on that distant city of men; and I found great portent in the slant and fall of Gleeth's rays that night. I knew the locations of all the cities of Theem'hdra from the maps of my fathers, do you see? Oh, they had been called 'the Seldom Seen,' my people of the Inner Isles, aye, but they themselves were far-seeing indeed! And it seemed I'd inherited the vision of my fathers. Anyway, that night I dreamed . . .

"I dreamed of my Lula, lost to me and gone forever from the world, and gone with her all the dreams of Suhm-yi who might have been—except this one dream, my dream. And then I saw that it was not my Lula but some other: Suhm-yi, certainly, but a stranger. And it seemed she called to me from afar, crying in her loneliness even as I cried in mine, and I felt her pain deep in my heart like a blunt blade turning there.

That morning, starting up from my bed, I remembered

my dream—but more than that I remembered a tale from my childhood. At first the memory was weak, but the harder I willed it to return the stronger it grew, until finally I remembered all.

"I had been a child when it happened: a visitation from the outside world, the arrival of a sorcerer from the lands of men beyond the crater sea, beyond the Great Circle Mountains, beyond the coastal forests of the east. Aye, for he hailed from Shadarabar, jungled isle of mystery beyond the Straits of Yhem, and his skin was as black as the magicks he practised on the tiny island he made his home, there in the Inner Isles of the crater sea. His name was Gorgos!"

Here Tarra Khash started, but remained silent.

Amyr paused and nodded his combed head. "The same, I'm sure. But he was old even then, and like many old men he feared Death's stealthy encroachment. As is the way with wizards, Gorgos sought immortality. He had studied all Mylakhrion's works in that vein—those which were available to him—and the runebooks and librams and tablets of many another mage gone that same way before. And his thaumaturgies were terrible on the island he made his lair; so that soon no blade of grass would grow there, no bird nest in withered tree, no lizard scuttle on the bare stone. Even the sea around that rock was barren of fish, for Gorgos worked his morbid magicks there.

"Now you may well wonder why, since Gorgos was but one man and the Suhm-yi were many, his presence was suffered at all in the Inner Isles. But remember, he had worked no evil among us, asked nothing of us, kept well to himself and went not abroad from his dark rock. And the Suhm-yi were not the enemies of men; we preferred our solitude, naturally, but Gorgos did nothing to interfere with that.

Moreover, it was known he was a fugitive, that certain Yhemni kings wanted him dead, not to mention many fellow wizards; so that it were most unlikely he would shout his whereabouts abroad, the fact that he had come to the Inner Isles and found the legended Suhm-yi there. And so Gorgos was left to his own devices, and he left the Suhm-yi to theirs—for a little while!

But just as there are magicians among men, so in olden times were there sorcerers among the Suhm-yi; and because our races are different, their studies were likewise diverse. Gorgos, making no progress toward immortality through endeavours of merely human research, eventually turned his inquiries toward the now extinct, esoteric explorations of the ancient Suhm-yi. To do this, he must study the librams of Na-dom, holy of holies of all the isles of the Suhm-yi, and to this end he came to our elders to ask permission to visit Na-dom—which permission was, of course, refused. Only the High Priests of our race had ever set foot on Na-dom, and then rarely, for the Isle of the Sacred Spire held not only the relics of olden Suhm-yi civilization but also its treasures. Moreover, Na-dom was favoured of the gods, who were known on occasion to rest from their labours upon the high and windswept peak.

"When Gorgos was told these things he appeared to understand, made apology for his lapse of etiquette—for his request had bordered upon insult—and took his departure back to bleak, forbidding isle of magick. But all a sham, a show, a ploy; for in the course of time he turned his dark eyes once more upon Na-dom, and this time went there without recourse to the elders, and studied there the librams of the ancients.

"Now, upon Na-dom, as I have said, were all the olden

treasures of the Suhm-yi, long ago put aside as worthless relics of barbaric ages. What is gold, after all, but a bright, heavy clod of earth; and pearls but the cancer of seashells; and what are jewels but glittery pebbles of the earth? And how may they compare with the sparkling air, the deep pure sea, the rich living soil of the earth itself? But amongst these centuried remains of times immemorial were three curved swords, like as peas in a pod, which had been the property of the greatest of all Suhm-yi sorcerers. And Gorgos read in the olden runebooks how, by use of these strange swords, a learned mage might call down from beyond the stars powers more potent than any mundane magicks! And this he determined to do, in his search for immortality.

"The rest of the tale tells itself: Gorgos stole the runebooks and Swords of Power and made off with them. Fleeing the Inner Isles he took hostage a young girl-child and killed her parents, then set off in a ship of black sails across the crater sea and disappeared. From which day until now his whereabouts has remained secret in all the lands of Theem'hdra, for if he had reappeared surely the elders of the Suhm-yi would know it, and perhaps even the code of all life itself could not have stayed their hands then.

"Aye, and now I find myself given to wonder: was the red dust of disaster which killed my people truly a thing of nature, unconscious of its scourge, or was it perchance sent by black-skinned, black-hearted, blackest of all black magicians, in order to forestall Suhm-yi vengeance? If so, then surely I know why I alone, of all the Suhm-yi, was spared.

"There, Tarra Khash. That is my tale—what do you make of it?"

Tarra sat for long moments without speaking, chewing over the story and the last morsels of food both. Finally:

"It seems to me," he said, "those streaming rays you saw at the full of the moon—that strange aurora over Klühn—was nothing but the same monthly manifestation self-evident in the clouds this very night, which would be there whether you'd prayed to your gods or not. That is not, of course, to belittle your gods, but—"

"I too have thought it," Amyr cut him short. "But who may fathom the designs of gods? I asked for guidance and received it; should we ponder the origin of a miracle or its result?"

Tarra nodded: "I take your meaning. However, it likewise seems to me that your feet are set upon a forked path. On the one hand you seek a mate, long stolen from the Inner Isles, and on the other you seek vengeance for your entire race. Now, this side of you is new and puzzling to me. One: would you now forsake the ways of your fathers, as you seem to have forsaken crater sea? And two, tell me this: how may a silver-skinned Suhm-yi female, full-grown by now, remain hidden in a city of dull-fleshed men? You said it yourself: no easy thing."

"Tarra," Amyr answered, "*you* said it seemed I'd learned a lot since leaving crater sea and venturing into the world of men. Well, never a truer word spoken. I have looked at men and learned to live like them—when it is at all bearable. I have even learned to kill like them, in protection of my own life. That which would have been unthinkable a year ago is now possible, tomorrow probable, the day after likely. We live and we learn. The ways of my fathers?—they were the ways of a race. And where is that race now? I am no longer naive, Tarra Khash; my quest has not been blind; I've more yet to tell you. But first your questions. You know of course the Suhm-yi talent of mind-reading? Certainly, for you remarked upon it at our first meeting. Well, and has not this Gorgos got himself an oracle in his Temple of Secret Gods?"

Tarra's jaw fell open. "Ah!" he gawped. "Your Suhm-yi she! A mentalist, of course!"

Amyr's smile was grim, golden-slitted. "And Gorgos uses her to blackmail Klühn's shady dealers. She picks their innermost secrets right out of their skulls; Gorgos threatens them with exposure; they pay and he uses ill-gotten gains to fund his sect of black magicians!"

"You're sure of all this?"

"I cannot be wrong," answered Amyr, but without pride. "I, too, am a mentalist, remember? And what thoughts would I read better than those of one of my own kind?"

The Hrossak slowly nodded. "Go on," he said. "Tell me what else you know. But first . . . tell me more about these three Swords of Power. For there's something strange here, I think—a peculiar coincidence, perhaps too peculiar—though as yet I'm not sure how it all comes together."

Now Amyr's smile was wide and open as he answered: "Ah! But I had hoped *you* could tell *me* something of that, bronze one . . . However, let me say a little more.

"Now when Gorgos fled the Inner Isles, taking with him the girl, runebooks, swords and all, the High Priests of the Suhm-yi worked a curse—a very ancient, very powerful curse—to follow after him. And because the Suhm-yi had lost things they treasured, the girl and relics both, the curse they invoked was this: that so long as the Suhm-yi dwelled in their secret place, on greeny-blue expanse of crater sea, Gorgos would never be able to keep unto himself anything he held dear. His most treasured possessions would be lost or stolen, his truest servants would sicken and die; worms would infest the very apples of his life, turning them bitter.

And all of this for as long as a single Suhm-yi priest re-mained to renew the curse at its time of waning. And this, too, leads me to wonder about the red dust. For certainly . . . it were no simple Earth magic which came out of the sky to destroy an entire people! Aye, and that is why, before setting out upon my quest, I went to Na-dom and prayed to all the gods for the renewal of the curse. I am no priest, no, but I am the son of the highest of them all; and perhaps the gods have hearkened to me, and perhaps the curse is potent still. I hope so . . ."

Again Tarra nodded. "Let me take up the tale," he said. "Having left the Inner Isles, while making for parts un-known, Gorgos felt the first sting of your Suhm-yi curse: he lost the Swords of Power. And yes, I see by your expression I'm right!"

"Conjecture, Tarra, guesswork," answered Amyr. "But good guesswork. I've made discreet inquiry; it seems that for many a year Gorgos' hirelings have wandered abroad, seeking just such swords. What else have you deduced?"

"*Huh!*" the steppeman growled. "Why, 'tis plain that my sword—my broken scimitar, its hilt all set with jewels—was one of the very three! Which is why that lying yellow-robe made me out a cheat and murderer, when all I was guilty of in killing Ellern Thark was of doing Klühn a mighty favour!"

Amyr Arn seconded that with a sharp nod of his combed head. "I've heard of it, and I know you killed the Northman fairly—or at least as fairly as you could. All Klühn knows it—but only we two know why you took the blame."

"To give back to Gorgos one of his runic swords, eh?"

"To give him back the *third* sword!" said Amyr. "And so complete the set. Listen:

"One sword was rescued from the gut of a whale killed by

whalers out of Khrissa. The ice-priests of that city would have kept it, but Gorgos went there and traded a few paltry spells for it. If they had not parted with it," Amyr shrugged in a very human way, "then perhaps had Gorgos offered more powerful magicks—but not by way of trade! At any rate, the ice-priests knew and feared him, and so he got the sword.

"The second scimitar was brought to Klühn by a madman who said he'd found it on a peak called the Mount of the Ancients. That's debatable, for it's said he came into the city naked, raving and filthy, and slew a dozen before the blade was wrested from him and he himself killed. A princeling bought the sword in auction and the money was spread between the kin of madman's victims. Shortly after that, members of the Sect of Secret Gods began drifting in, the princeling's apartments were ransacked and he disappeared without trace; likewise the sword from the Mount of the Ancients.

"As for your shattered sword—entire when last I saw it in the Inner Isles—this is what I have learned:

"That once upon a time in Thinhla there dwelled a fat and offensive jeweller—"

"Wait!" Tarra held up a hand. "Wait, Amyr, and hear the true story from me." He frowned a dark frown, sent his memory winging back. "Aye, a fat and offensive jeweller indeed. Nud Annoxin was his name, and when a certain Hrossak staggered out of steaming coastal jungles more dead than alive, what did Nud do but hurl him into dungeon cell! And who'd tell of it better than me, for I'm the Hrossak who rotted down there for four long years!"

Amyr drew breath sharply. "A lifetime!" he hissed. "What had you done to deserve such?"

"Oh?" said Tarra, raising an eyebrow. "And must it be that I'd 'done' something? I'll tell you: I had found the jungle-cursed catacombs of Ahorra Izz, god of scarlet scorpions. Aye, and I'd come out of that place with my pockets full of rubies. That was what I had 'done'—and Nud Annoxin a thief and torturer of no mean prowess, I can tell you. He starved and tormented me for what I knew of the scorpion temple, till at the end he knew it all—or most of it. But it earned him nothing—except perhaps the ire of the biggest, reddest, awfullest arachnid you could ever imagine, Amyr Arn! Ire and sting both, the hellish sting of Ahorra Izz!" Tarra gave a shudder.

"You did not kill Nud?"

Tarra shook his tousled head. "No, though it's true he died the night I made my escape. Oh, I *would* have killed him—indeed I stole a ceremonial sword from his wall so to do—but the scorpion-god beat me to it."

Amyr nodded. "And it seems you beat Gorgos' seekers to the sword; since when they've searched far afield, and never a word of it—until you were spied with shattered hilt in Ellern Thark's place. Queer twists of fate, eh?"

"Queer indeed! But say, what good's to them that busted blade, with razor curve all gone and many a jewel prised from hilt? Gorgos'll work no magick with that shattered stump, that's for sure."

"Oh?" said Amyr. "Try telling that to the swordsmith who the yellow-robes have picked up from his shop these last three nights, returning him each morning weary unto death after a night's work in the temple. Tell it to the jeweller similarly suborned.

Tarra's brows knitted darkly. "So, they make it whole again. What evil does this Gorgos work, Amyr?"

"Any evil," the other answered. "All evils, if they'll help achieve his one great ambition. He desires immortality, Tarra, as he has desired and searched for it for all of an hundred years! And if it means death and destruction for any—for many, for all—what is that to Gorgos? Which is why, tomorrow night, I go to kill him."

Tarra had expected something of the sort. "Also to write *finis* on Suhm-yi vengeance," he said.

Amyr nodded.

"Also to win yourself a bride, and so prolong your devastated race."

Again the nod.

"*Hmm!* Well, I wish you luck in all your endeavours. But tomorrow night? I shall probably be miles away by then."

"Go safely," said Amyr at once. "And always remember me."

"You do not seek my aid in this mad venture? To enter Gorgos' temple, his very lair, slay him, steal his silver-scaled oracle—get out with skin intact? It's instant death if you're caught—especially you, last of the Suhm-yi."

"I have not asked for your help. As for my life: what good is it, one alone against the world? If the gods would spare me, then am I already spared, but if my life is to be spent, what better cause, eh? As for *your* life, that is something else entirely."

"Is that why you saved it this night?"

"I rescued you because you are my one friend in all the lands of Theem'hdra. Also, you were innocent."

Tarra shuffled about on the bench. "And what are friends for if not to help their friends, eh?" He was growing exasperated; he stood in Amyr's debt and knew it. He *would* help if Amyr asked, certainly, but it came hard to actually volunteer his neck!

Amyr read his mind. "I owed you from that former time in the Inner Isles," he said. "Now all is square."

"Were all Suhm-yi so prideful?" Tarra rasped.

"All."

The Hrossak gritted his teeth, puffed himself up—then seemed to collapse into himself. He gave a great sigh. "Please," he said then, "my dear friend Amyr Arn—please allow me to assist you in your great act of revenge, in the killing of this evil Gorgos and the freeing of his oracle, the Suhm-yi maid you'd take back to crater sea. I would deem myself honoured."

At last Amyr smiled. "Very well," he said. "I will be glad of your help."

"Good." Tarra sat back—sat up straighter—smiled broadly for a while, then frowned. At last he said: "Anyway, I've my own reason for wanting to get into the Temple of Secret Gods."

"Oh?" said Amyr. "Can I guess it?"

"*Hah!*" Tarra answered, and: "Listen to him! You already know it, stealer of thoughts! I want my sword back, aye . . ." He slapped his thigh, grinned, gazed deep into the other's golden eyes. "Well, come on, out with it—what's the plan . . . ?"

III

In the Temple of Terror

ULLI EYS OF the Suhm-yi was beautiful. In Suhm-yi eyes (had there been such to see her) and by their standards—in human eyes—she would be beautiful in the eyes of *any* warm-blooded creature. Alas, Gorgos' blood was cold as ice, cold as his schemes of deathlessness, which alone concerned him.

Ulli's form was a woman's form, full and round and wondrous; her skin was silvery, with shimmering highlights; her eyes were liquid gold, her lashes silver-silk shutters. Her beauty was innocent and it was utter—and yet she was not aware of it. Indeed she believed—or had believed until recently—that she was ugly, an alien, unnatural, awful creature created of a sorcerer's spells. That was what Gorgos had told her, and over the years flown since her childhood in the Inner Isles, she had almost come to believe it.

Then, a year ago, out of the strange psychic mists of her dreams had come hope in the form of a voice calling to her in the night—to remind her of deep, warm oceans and jewel islands, and of her Suhm-yi heritage—telling her that she was not alone. Moreover, the voice had promised her freedom! It had promised a return to Inner Isles, a love to fill her life, a destiny great beyond measure. She would be the mother of a race, whose children would one day people the jewel isles just as she remembered them from her childhood. And no more wandering the parched deserts and strange cities of men, and no more stealing men's dark thoughts and secrets for her master, Gorgos. For he was *not* her master but a great thief, and Ulli herself the most precious thing he had ever stolen.

When first these night visions had come to her, in her innocence Ulli had spoken of them to Gorgos, who always set great store by everything she told him of her dreams and fancies. Indeed that was her purpose—the reason he kept and fed her, hiding her ugliness and strangeness from the prying eyes of other men—to perform her auguries and mind-readings for him who alone cared for her, however coldly, in all the world.

But when she had seen how her dreams affected him, the rages he would fly into at mention of this like mind which spoke to Ulli out of nowhere, then she grew more cautious. And later, when Gorgos pressed her with regard to suspected fresh incursions or mental revelations, she would simply shake her head and say no, the voice no longer came in the night to disturb her sleep. But in fact it did, ever stronger, making her nights happy and filling her days with longing.

And lately, for a three-month, why!—the dreams had been stronger far than ever before, until Ulli could no longer doubt but that they were real. Somewhere, somehow, *he* was. *He* existed despite all Gorgos' denials to the contrary, that in fact she was not unique of her kind. Amyr, his name, a good name—Amyr, last male of the olden Suhm-yi—and Ulli, the last female. And now he was coming, coming here, coming to steal her away!

And oh, how she longed to be stolen!

But such dangers here: Gorgos and his disciples, the temple's labyrinthine ways, the yellow-robes and their mad dedication to an obsessed, power-crazed master. And Ulli, because she remained innocent, half-feeling she betrayed the ancient black magician. And Gorgos on the very verge of fulfilling his life's ambition, in which she had played so important a—

"Are you listening to me, Ulli?" Gorgos' voice, harsh as a file on glass, grated in her ears, shattering her chaotic thoughts and daydreams, drawing her back to cruel reality. "I'll swear you haven't heard a word! Where were you just then? What thoughts were you thinking, Ulli?"

His eyes were on her, cold, black, unblinking; his mouth was a black, fanged slit in skin wrinkled as an ebon walnut. She gasped; her hand flew to her mouth, she cowered back from him on silken cushions.

"What? *What?*" Gorgos pressed. "What thoughts *were* you thinking, my precious oracle, my silver-skinned pet—and were they really yours at all or the thoughts of some other?"

And now Ulli must lie:

"No thoughts at all, Gorgos my master. I am tired, no more than that. It wearies me, searching in the minds of Klühn's men and merchants and elite. Their secrets are often ugly, as you well know, and they leave a taste in my mind like slow poisons. Would that I need no longer search them out in their iniquities."

Gorgos' eyes slitted a little and stayed that way for a while, but at last he seemed satisfied with her answer. "Well, and perhaps you've done your last of that," he finally said. "For tonight—this very night—I'll finally call down to my command all the power I need. Then, if all goes according to plan, I shall be immortal, all-powerful, indestructible! Except—why!—what use shall I find for you then, my little Ulli?" His eyes were shiny black marbles where they fixed upon her, and his voice turned sibilant as he continued: "It's long been a scheme of mine to breed me some familiar creatures. You yourself could be said to be a familiar of sorts, I suppose; but what would be the result, I wonder, if I mated you with ghoul or night-gaunt?"

She knew better than to shrink back again, for Gorgos fed on fear. His vampire soul battened upon it. Instead she looked him straight in the eye, gold against jet, and said, "I have served you well master. Have you not said so yourself—that without me your temple were never builded, your servitors and soldiers never hired into your service?"

"True," he answered, his whisper the scrape of a claw on rusted iron, "all true. Aye, but perhaps you've been a two-edged sword for all that, Ulli Eys."

"A sword, master?" she answered. "With two edges? Why, whatever do you mean? Nay, I am but flesh and blood, and your poor servant."

Dark beneath his cowl, Gorgos' black eyes were shiny peering into hers. "Those golden orbs you wear for eyes," he said. "Sometimes I think me: what goes on behind them? And I answer: perhaps too much. You've been my oracle, true, and successful to be sure—but could you not be better? It's a custom in Khrissa to pierce the eyes of the snow larks to make them sing the sweeter. Now there's a thought, Ulli, there's a thought . . ."

Still she did not shrink, but perhaps she trembled a little. "And I have heard it said," she answered in a little while, "that while their songs are sweeter, it is always the same song. For the joy is gone out of them, and the sweetness is tinged with sadness, and whoever hears the blind snow larks singing is brought to tears." And again she reminded him: "I am your poor servant, O Gorgos."

He turned away, perhaps disappointed. "Aye, my servant—my secret oracle—but daughter of the Inner Isles for all that." And nodding knowingly, Gorgos strode out on to her balcony, his yellow, rune-inscribed robe belling behind him.

Ulli's rooms were in one of the outer domes. She had a small pool, blue-tiled, for bathing; soft white carpets of snow leopard pelts, and drapes of woven down; onyx shelves for her small collection of poems and books of songs and childish bric-a-brac, mainly beautiful and intricately coiled cowries from the shores of the crater sea. Curving windows of translucent shell opened on to a high, walled balcony, which perched at a height level with the great temple's outer wall. Central in the main room, a circular divan which also served as bed was heaped with silk cushions where it lay beneath the uppermost panel of the dome's curve, a thick circular window which magnified all the stars of night.

From her divan, Ulli watched Gorgos where he paused with his back to her at the balcony wall, his long curved fingernails tapping inquiringly upon the coping stones while his eyes gazed west. He was looking at the full moon, she knew, whose light must even now pour down on crater sea and Inner Isles. What went on in his mind, she wondered, just as he had wondered of hers? She could look, of course, but dared not. Gorgos was a magician of no small prowess and could sense such intrusions. Ulli shuddered. Indeed, his senses and thoughts were too keen far for her liking—and blacker than the pit itself!

And as well she didn't look into Gorgos' mind, for this time she would have shrunk from his thoughts, most assuredly. He was thinking: *she is Suhm-yi, she is the plague-carrier. A two-edged sword indeed! While she lives, I suffer—just as I have suffered ever since that day I stole her from the jewel isles. My plans have been thwarted, my greatest treasures lost or stolen. And yet through her I have regained all. Ah!—but when will the sword turn again, perhaps to strike with its perverse edge? Dare I wait to find out? Even I, Gorgos—whose breath shall be a gale, whose merest thought a command irresistible—dare I wait? No, for a curse is a curse; and this Suhm-yi curse remains potent, I*

feel it in my bones. So be it: tonight the Great Calling—the Unifi-
cation of All the Dark Forces—and tomorrow . . . ? Tomorrow I
shall revel! After that, then time enough to be rid of her. First a
trial mating or two, for the breeding of familiar creatures; and
perhaps a blinding, to see if she will indeed sing the sweeter; but
after that death by fire! Only the searing flame may still such a
curse, and only when it is stilled will I, Gorgos, finally fear noth-
ing in all the worlds of space and time! So be it, so—

"—be it!" The last two words he spoke out loud.

"Master?"

Gorgos turned from the balcony, strode back into the
room. "I have great works to perform, Ulli, thaumaturgies
vast. Tonight is my night! The sword is forged, renewed,
and the forces unite. The clouds are gathering over Klühn
and the sorceries of far stars are seeded in the skies. Tonight
you will not leave these apartments but stay here with all
doors locked. For when I call the very Elementals of Evil
out from the spaces between the stars, then nothing will be
certain, nothing guaranteed, nothing entirely safe. The
temple shall tremble tonight, Ulli, with all the applause of
the Inhabitants of the Dark Worlds where they reel beyond
the rim!"

In Gorgos' madness a white foam flecked the corners of
his wide slit mouth, gaping in the shadow of his cowl; the
yellow cowl which he now threw back to reveal his monstrous, bloated black head like a gargoyle's misshapen skull.
And opening wide his great jaws he bayed with mad laughter for a little while, before striding from the room to a sudden peal of thunder and a pattering of large, unseasonal
raindrops where they fell on the balcony's marble flags.

Back over his shoulder as he went, baying still, he cast,
"As for you, Ulli Eys—well, we shall see. We shall see . . ."

TARRA AND AMYR had slept 'til noon, following which they had eaten a light meal in Amyr's garret hideaway and gone over again in what detail they could the elements of his plan. And the very barest elements they were, for Amyr believed that the simplest way was always the best, that any great and complicated scheme could only tangle them in its intricacies like flies in a web.

Of the Temple of Secret Gods, Amyr had learned a little from the mind of Ulli Eys. Labyrinthine the temple's ways, aye, but all halls and passageways following the same general pattern, so that Amyr believed he could confidently negotiate its corridors, stairways and chambers—*if* he and Tarra could get into the place. For gaining access might well prove the hardest part; if not, making an exit certainly would!

Amyr's intelligence, gathered from several sources in the city—namely, a handful of furtive informers he'd paid to keep their eyes and ears open—had alerted him that Gorgos and his priests would be busy this night, all of them engaged in secret rituals on the temple's fifth and topmost level, whose ceiling was the great copper dome itself. Because of this Gorgos' grey-clad soldiers would be much in evidence in the gardens and on the paths between the walls and the temple's outer domes, and atop the walls themselves and in the watchtowers and stone gatehouse-cum-guardroom. Unlike the Square of Justice, this Temple of Secret Gods would in no wise prove an easy nut to crack. (So Tarra had thought.) But crack it they must.

"How crack it?" he'd asked. "Shall we climb the walls, or don our yellow robes and simply walk in? Me, I'm a fair clamberer as Hrossaks go, but still I'd vote for walking. Those temple walls are high as the city's own, where a fall is certain death!"

"You shall walk in," Amyr had answered, "but I must climb."

"Why?" Tarra had wanted to know. "Why can't we go together, by whichever route?"

"The yellow-robes always go singly, that's why. It's the rule of the temple, for Gorgos fears conspiracy. He fears many things, not least of which the Suhm-yi curse. But two of us walking into that place together is plainly out of the question. And since I am demonstrably the better climber—"

"What?" Tarra cut him short. "How's that? I didn't say I *couldn't* climb! And what makes you so good at it? Climbing's for strong arms, Amyr, not spindly things like yours. Also, it requires fingers that grip and toes to match—aye, and preferably five to a member, not just four like you've got!"

At which Amyr had smiled, showing teeth like mother of pearl. And taking Tarra's hand in one of his, he'd said: "Shake me off, bronze one. Go on, show me how weak is my grip."

Tarra had tried, but to no avail; Amyr's hand struck fast to his as a fly to the seeping resin of mountain pines. Then the Suhm-yi had shown him his fingers: spatulate as a tree frog's and, when required, just as adhesive! "No, Tarra, I'll not fall but go up that wall sure as a lizard."

"Huh! So it appears." But now the Hrossak became concerned for himself. "And as for me, *I'm* to walk in bold as brass, eh? Simple as that!" And he gave his fingers a testy snap.

Amyr sighed. "Tarra, you're contrary. Isn't it what you said you wanted?"

"Wanted? I'm not sure now I wanted any of it! It's just the thought of me going afoot while you're lizarding it up the wall, that's all. And anyway, what do I do when I get in through the gate?"

"You go straight through the gardens to the temple, enter—all unchallenged, hopefully—then to innermost chamber, where finally you climb all the stairs to the top-most level. There you'll find me waiting, again hopefully, and there too we'll find Gorgos and slay him. Chaos will ensue. The yellow-robes will be in disarray. Many will flee, terrified that their master is dead; others will see an opportunity to loot; some may seek to kill us. There we have the advantage; we shall be armed, of course, but they bear no arms. Gorgos will not have them in the temple in case someone makes an attempt upon his life. Lastly we flee, collecting Ulli the oracle along the way. I shall know where to find her."

"Huh!" Tarra grunted again. "A good many of those false priests may very well be cowards and thieves just as you say, but I'm sure there'll be fighters among 'em, too. Very well, I'll face ten if I've a knife and they've none—but what of the soldiers? Are we to flee the temple pursued by howling pack of yellow-robes and hampered by girl, and rush straight into the arms of a small army?"

"Tarra," Amyr had answered, "I guarantee that if we get back to the gatehouse, then that the soldiers will not stop us." He grinned secretively.

"Are you going to let me in on it?" Tarra was suspicious.

"I'll only say this," said Amyr, "that the soldiers would as soon stop Gorgos himself as try to detain us! If all goes according to plan, of course . . ."

———

IT FAST APPROACHED the midnight hour as Tarra Khash hugged his yellow cassock about him, drew his head back into the heavy cowl and shufflingly approached the main gate in the great wall of the Temple of Secret Gods. At the same time and less than fifty yards away, where the wall stood in its own shadow, Amyr climbed with the speed and agility of a spider. He climbed . . . but at the same time kept his mind in contact with Tarra's. This was something of an effort—concentrating in two directions at one and the same time—and fine droplets of silvery-grey sweat beaded Amyr's face where they came through carefully applied blacking.

Close to the top of the wall he heard something, grew rigid, drew back his mental probe from Tarra's mind and sent all his senses ahead of him. Two soldiers, atop the wall, talking . . . They were nervous, and rightly so; the sky directly overhead was livid with weirdly silent, flickering lightnings, where black clouds boiled *locally* in a sky otherwise clear and bright with stars.

"This must be the worst I've yet seen it," one soldier whispered to his companion. "It's almost alive, that sky! What goes on tonight in the temple, I wonder?"

"No clean or entirely sane thing!" answered the other. "Bet your soul on that—if it's not already sold. Tomorrow when I collect my pay, that's the last this lot will see of me. He calls down demons from the stars, this Gorgos. At least, that's what I've heard. Now what sort of priestly activity is that, I ask? No, rumour has it that in fact he's a black magician, and his oracle's a female creature, silver as the belly of a fish! Ugh!"

"Aye," the voice of the first was hushed, "I've heard the same. And I think I'll join you tomorrow, when you quit. I'll become an assassin again, or go pirating in the Straits of Yhem. Either one'll be cleaner work than this. Better paid, too . . ."

While taking all of this in, Amyr had been on the move, ascending at an angle and coming up over the parapet some little distance away. Not for nothing had his race been named the Suhm-yi—the "seldom seen"—and now he became one with the shadows of the fortifications as he shrugged a bundle from his back, fixed belt and sword at his waist, draped himself in yellow robe. And silent as a breath of night air, he approached the two where they stood close together at the parapet in the glow of strange aerial energies.

"And I'll shun Klühn evermore," one was now saying, "even though I was born here." There was a shiver in his voice as he continued: "Or at least I'll stay clear as long as this nest of false priests worship their alien demon-gods here!"

"The both of us," said the other, nodding. "Aye, we're surely of a mind on that." He glanced nervously about, at the sky, at the drawn features of his companion. "The yellow-robes are all dupes, and Gorgos is a madman!"

Something moved close by, something sensed before it was seen. Then a stir of yellow, the swish of a cassock . . . and a third figure stood with the two. Beneath the cowl all was dark—except a pair of golden eyes, ferally ablaze. "What?" said Amyr Arn, his voice a venomous hiss. "Do my ears deceive me? Conspiracy, treason!"

And who could this be but Gorgos himself, flown here on the wings of magick, grown out of the very night to confront the two in their treachery. "Master, we—" they began to babble as one, then fell to their knees at his feet. As he in-stinctively stepped back, one of them clutched at the hem of his cassock. The robe came open, displayed his silvery body in the blue-green light of the eerie aurora. It further dis-played the slender sword gripped in four-fingered hand.

Gasping their double-dose of shock, coming to their feet, snatching at their own weapons, the two were given no time to cry out. Amyr had not wanted to kill them; he had simply thought to test out his disguise. Well, the latter had seemed to work well enough—barring the accident of the trapped cassock—and as for the former:

Even as they sprang erect his rapier sliced the air between—sliced air and throats both, so that cries un-voiced became bloody gurgles as their swords, half-drawn, made twin thumps falling back into their scabbards. Then the two were toppling, and Amyr catching one and doing his best to muffle the fall of the other. And finally the night still again, with only the hideously seething sky for wit-ness . . .

And dumping the bodies over the wall, Amyr sent his mind out again to discover Tarra Khash—

—Which was just as well.

Tarra stood between a pair of grey-clad soldiers just inside the gate. He deliberately kept himself in shadow, his cowl drawn well forward to hide his face. The soldiers held his arms, their sword points at his middle. "For the last time, priest," said one, "tell us the answer to the challenge. Say it now, or be taken before the Sergeant of the Guard."

"But haven't I already told you, my son," mumbled Tarra, "that I've forgotten the damned—er, I mean daft—thing? It's slipped my mind, that's all. Give me a clue."

"A clue?" the second soldier's voice showed his disgust. "I

never heard anything like it! Fifty of your lot in and out of here today, and all of them knew the password."

"What's more," the first was becoming suspicious, "I never before heard a priest of *this* temple call any man his 'son!' You're for the Sergeant of the Guard, my friend. Or should I call you 'father?'" They began to haul him toward the light from the guardroom.

"No, wait!" cried Tarra, and beneath his cassock his hand caressed the sword Amyr had given him. "Once more, I beg you—try me with the password one more time."

Now their suspicions really were aroused. "What's this?" said one. "Frightened of the Sergeant of the Guard, is it? But all he'll do is verify your—"

"Please, *please!*" said Tarra, gritting his teeth, his grip tightening on hilt of hidden sword. "I'm in a hurry. There's this special ceremony tonight, you see, and—"

"All right, all right!" snapped the second soldier. "One last time. "I say 'night,' and you say—?"

"Gaunt!" said Tarra, the word popping into his mouth from nowhere. It was Amyr, stealing the password from the minds of the guards, filling Tarra's mind with it and leaving no room for anything else. "Gaunt," Tarra said again, as the soldiers loosened their grip on his arms and stood back. And yet again: "Gaunt!" he cried as they put away their weapons. "Yes, yes—that's it. Night and gaunt, of course!"

"Of course," the disgusted one snorted. "Very well, in you go—'father.'"

"Thank you, my son," said Tarra, stepping between them and into the shadows of the courtyard beyond. "Have a good night . . ."

Not far away, the merest shadow seemed to flow silently down an inner wall and melt into the gardens toward the domed central buildings. Silent that is except for a single snort or barely suppressed chuckle. Though Amyr's ancestors would doubtless disagree, it seemed to him that there were men the Suhm-yi could befriend and learn to live with. Likeable, even worthy men. Aye, and Tarra Khash must surely be the very best example.

Part of the night, Amyr came along a path to one of the outer domes. Here he paused, crouching down in darkness. There wasn't much of the latter now; the aurora was building to a fiery crescendo and the undersides of the boiling clouds were ablaze. He gazed upward at the curve of the building. Down here, well-lit passageways and corridors; up there, dark balconies at every level. Darkness suited Amyr: "seldom seen" in daylight, in darkness he simply disappeared.

He began to climb the wall, casting his mental probe before him into the mazy hive of evil within . . .

ULLI EYS KNEW Amyr's mind immediately.

Alone and shuddering in her apartments—terrified by the bilious flow and flux of green and blue light beyond her windows, and by the incessant, pregnant heaving of the vilely illumined clouds where they tossed beyond the enlarging lens directly over her bed—she grasped at that mind as a frightened child fastens to its father. There was comfort in it, and there was something new, which had never been before: nearness!

"You!" she half-whispered, half-thought the word. "Here?"

Never before had Ulli sensed the presence—the close proximity—of one of her own; unless it were as a child in the Inner Isles and now forgotten. If she closed her eyes she was sure she might even reach out and touch him. But knowing he was here—actually *here,* somewhere in Gorgos' blasphemous temple—now she grew more frightened for him than she was for herself. "But you'll be caught!" she gasped, again half out loud.

" *'Ware, Ulli!"* came Amyr's answer. *"Speak with your mind, girl. Merely think it, and I shall hear you. But do not speak with your tongue, lest someone see you and inquire to whom you address yourself."*

His voice was so warm in her mind, so resolute, self-assured, that she took courage from it. Her hands fluttering a little, nervously, she began to pace the floor of her room; and when next she spoke, it was with her mind alone:

"What do you here? Can I make you understand that of all nights, this is possibly the most dangerous? Tonight Gorgos attains power inconceivable, and possibly immortality!"

"Tonight Gorgos dies!" came back the answer. *"And his death were not merely your saving, Ulli Eys, but the saving of a world, I fancy."*

Again she was afraid. *"But how will you kill him? He is a mighty magician whose—"*

"Die he must," Amyr's mind-voice interrupted, *"however mighty his magick. A curse is on him, the curse of the Suhm-yi, and I am its instrument. Now I must be about my business. Fear not, Ulli, but keep your mind fixed fast upon me. Then, when it's over, I'll find you as surely as a northstone points out the polar constellations. Prepare yourself, gather up what small things you would take with you, for tonight you go free at last!"*

"Wait!" she cried after him, but too late. Only a dim trace, an echo of his mind, remained. Amyr Arn was intent upon other things.

THE MIND OF Tarra Khash was likewise intent—intent upon his body and on keeping it intact!

In the lower corridors, working toward the central area and the spiralling stairs he'd find there to take him up under the dome, Tarra was in something of a panic. The temple's maze was a veritable echo chamber, where every slightest sound from regions however far found its way to the Hrossak as he prowled along, senses alert. And such was the complexity of the way, where every hall and passage and archway of the labyrinth looked exactly like the one last negotiated, that despite the directions Amyr had earlier given—which had seemed simple enough at the time—now Tarra feared he was not only losing the way but also himself! Indeed, he could well picture himself lost down here forever—or until Gorgos and his priests found him. But however terrible that last thought, it was not the source of his growing panic. That sprang from his awareness of the sure passage of time, that time was of the essence, and that even now Amyr Arn probably approached the rendezvous. Tarra must hie him there at once! But . . . which way to hie?

For now, pausing at the junction of five passages all exactly alike, Tarra turned his head this way and that, tossing a mental coin to decide which way to go. It seemed to him that the droning cacophony of a hundred yellow-robes all chanting their entirely incomprehensible incantations came from . . . *that* way—straight ahead! But how to be certain in such a cauldron of sound?

On the other hand, because of the weird acoustics of the place—the dinning effect of its magnifying small sounds from afar—one tended to overlook sounds or events of a closer proximity. Such as fast-padding footfalls from behind!

Tarra turned, agile as a cat, his sword drawn beneath his yellow robe of priesthood.

"What?" cried the priest bearing down upon him, who appeared in something of a hurry. "I thought I was alone in my tardiness. Well, small odds—there are more than sufficient voices raised in invocation 'neath the great dome this night. Myself, I attend out of curiosity; I wish to see the forms of these fabulous forces Gorgos calls down from the stars—and their effect upon him! Aye, for he's promised us a new god tonight. Will you join me, brother?"

The yellow-robe was upon him, catching his elbow, solving his problem of a moment earlier by leading him down a passage which angled slightly to the left—but at the same time presenting another problem of similar proportions. For in that final moment of confrontation and contact the two had dimly recognized each other, and in the space of only two or three paces both had remembered!

Now, gasping, they whirled face to face once more, the priest knowing Tarra for a near-barbarian, a Hrossak, and Tarra knowing him as the bald-pate who'd coshed him at Ellern Thark's and later blackguarded him in the city court. "*You!*" they hissed as a man.

Then the priest's hand was at Tarra's throat, his other hand raised high. Upon his wrist he wore a wide, heavy strap of leather, all dully aglint with metal studs. And right now it was swinging for Tarra's head.

"So that's what you bonked me with that night," he rasped, ducking and thrusting all in one movement. His sword point pushed out his cassock a little way, slipped through, entered the priest's body under his ribs and sliced into his heart. His hand flew away from Tarra's throat; he strained up and back, as if to extricate himself from skewer's point, his jaws snapped shut in a snarling grimace, flew open again at once in a scarlet cough. And he fell.

Tarra let his sword slide free, stooped, wiped his blade red against yellow, quickly tossed back his robe and sheathed the bright metal. He dragged the body into the shadow of an arched doorway, out of the light of flickering flambeaux, returned to the passageway.

The chanting had risen to a fever pitch now, and surely something gathered itself all unseen, bunching its alien muscles in preparation—for what?

His skin atingle in nameless anticipation, in something closely approaching dread, still Tarra commenced to lope along the corridor toward the swelling sound; but before he could gather full momentum he emerged into a great hall where massive columns held aloft a titan, circular ceiling. The base of the central dome, it could only be, and about its perimeter stone steps winding upward . . .

IV

Spawn of the Star-Spaces!

THE GREAT CIRCULAR room beneath the central dome was all of twenty man-lengths in diameter. From its fantastically rune-inscribed mosaic floor to the curving beams which held aloft the hammered copper plates of the dome itself, the vertical height was perhaps eight or nine man-lengths. Half-way up the inward curving walls, a narrow balcony circled the chamber, with four equidistant flights of stairs leading down to the cryptically inscribed floor. Back of the balcony, large oval windows looked out over the lesser domes, which clustered towards and seemed fused with the central body; like copper breasts growing from a larger breast, their nipples formed of the sky-scanning apex windows evident in all the lesser bubbles. The great chamber itself was lit by seven huge brass lamps suspended from ceiling beams, lending the place a brazen glow.

Tarra, coming headlong up the winding stairs between the lower walls of the central structure, slowed his speed barely in time as he emerged on to the narrow inner balcony through a demon-carved archway; and then it was all he could do to still a loud gasp of awe and astonishment at the tableau now spread before him. Slowing his hammering heart and bringing his breathing back under control, he took a careful pace forward and let his eyes absorb all.

Central on the floor of the chamber, some four man-lengths below the balcony, a raised marble altar-stone supported the spreadeagled, yellow-robed form of Gorgos. He lay on his back, arms and legs spread wide beneath his rune-embellished robe, his black eyes bulging in his black face, which was tilted back to gaze upon the circular window in the curving copper ceiling. Forming a broken circle about his upper torso, three curving ceremonial scimitars lay sinistrally arranged, hilts to points. The one on his left curved upwards from his ribs toward his outstretched left hand; above his head the second curved between his hands; the third arced down from his right hand toward his right side. Tarra knew immediately that one of these swords was his own familiar blade restored: even at a distance the jewelled hilts were unmistakeable. Which one was a different matter.

His gaze couldn't linger long there, however, for there was more to be taken in. The hundred priests of the temple, for instance (ninety-nine of them, anyway) where they formed a rhythmically swaying, frenziedly chanting circle right round the balcony, their arms held low, hands touching, all eyes upon Gorgos stretched upon his altar dais. Some of the yellow-robes were Yhemnis, Tarra saw, black-skinned and pouty-lipped. Aye, and there might even be a Hrossak or two among 'em, too. He stepped forward, broke the ring, thrust his hands down until they contacted others on both sides.

There: now he was just another priest—for the moment, anyway. Possibly Amyr was also here; certainly he was supposed to be.

"Oh, I'm here all right, bronze one," came a voice soft in his mind, and the "Yhemni" on his immediate left gave his smallest finger an even smaller tweak. Tarra's involuntary start went unnoticed in the clamour of chanting and swaying of cassocked bodies, but before he could do anything to betray himself:

"Don't speak!" Amyr's mental warning was sharp as a knife. *"Say nothing—don't even peep at me out the corner of your eye.*

The Hrossak's thoughts whirled chaotically—but only for a moment or two. Then: "What now?" he thought back.

"I haven't had time to think yet," came Amyr's answer. *"But we have to do something, anything, to stop what's happening here. Have you looked at the sky?"*

The urgency in the Suhm-yi's mind-voice got through to Tarra, making his hair tingle at its roots. And again that sensation of elemental muscles bunching to spring, of alien intelligences rushing invisibly to and fro, so that one could almost feel the wind from their membrane wings. The priests felt it, too, sensed the gibbering approach of . . . *something*—for their monotonously repetetive chanting now lost entirely what little coherency it had had, changing its pitch, rising even higher, becoming a raucous blare that set the jaws to aching even worse than rotten teeth. It made it hard to even think . . .

"The sky!" Amyr insisted. *"Look at it!"*

Tarra slowly cranked his head back until he looked up at a steep angle at the circular window on the heavens. He looked—stared—stood transfixed!

Beyond that window—more properly a portal, designed in five sectors which even now began to retract, drawn back by unseen machinery—the clouds were roiling and throbbing like a canopy of blue volcanic mud, alive with weird energies that scorched and sizzled soundlessly, focusing upon the dome. The window was fully open now, and in through the opening crept green and blue tendrils of hissing, crackling fire, at first exploratory, then insistent, finally pulsing in through the portal in a twisting, writhing column of cold luminosity that reached down to and fully enveloped Gorgos on his dais.

Simultaneous with the influx of these seemingly sentient energies, the priests commenced to circle widdershins, single-file, about the narrow balcony, their shrieking ceasing abruptly and replaced by deep, bass, mass explosions of a repeated *sound* or *word*, recognition of which brought a frantic mental response from Amyr Arn.

"Tarra, listen to that! Do you know what it is?"

"No," the Hrossak thought back. "But whatever it is, I don't like it!"

And, "Thromb . . . *Thromb* . . . THROMB!" sang the priests, their skipping paces growing shorter but gaining speed as they continued their mad, well-practised wheeling dance about the balcony.

"But I do know what it is!" said Amyr. *"The Thromb are the veriest demons of the deep dark spaces between the stars. They are part of Suhm-yi legend, most evil of all evil elementals, spawn of all the darkness and misery and horror of the blind, reeling worlds beyond the rim!"*

"Thanks," Tarra thought back, trying to shout with his mind over the throbbing din, for he couldn't understand how that was not necessary, "I'm glad you brought me! But if what you say is true, then Gorgos is done for. Surely he can't live in that torrent of twisting fires? It'll shrivel him like a moth in a candle's flame!"

"Shrivel him? Man, it's feeding *him! The Suhm-yi had long suspected that Gorgos was not of this world—and now that suspicion is fact. He, too, is of the Thromb—doubtless called down by some crazed, long dead sorcerer. Aye, and now in his turn he opens the gates to all the Thromb. But before he can do that, first he must grow strong. Look, see how he feeds! See the sorcery of the dark stars!*

The form of Gorgos was bloating upon the marble dais. Seen almost as if through a jet of shining, snaking water, his outline shimmered, blurred—enlarged! And now, too, another manifestation of the spawn from the star-spaces; or perhaps the final phase of this, Gorgos' most terrible thaumaturgy.

For even as Tarra stared, his eyes jouncing in his head as he was whirled in the mad circling rush of the yellow-robes, the three scimitars enclosing Gorgos' upper half rose up from the dais and in their turn commenced to spin in mid-air, also widdershins, chasing each other in an ever-widening circle of flashing steel and glittering gems as they climbed slowly along the length of the column of living energy from the stars.

Beneath the circling swords, down on the dais where Gorgos' body throbbed and convulsed in the blue-green tube of eerie lightnings, a monstrous transformation was taking place. The magician's rune-covered robe bulged, splitting under the pressure from within, flying into tatters; beneath it he was huge, black, bloating larger still, but worst of all—

—Amyr had been right: Gorgos was never born of good clean earth—nor of any sane world or place or time! His voluminous yellow robe had hidden well the many groping tentacles and *appendages* and pustules with which, from neck to loins, his nightmare body was covered like a living mat!

Tarra dragged his eyes away, returned them to the circling swords. The glimmering of an idea was shaping itself in his mind.

Now the flying scimitars had wound themselves up halfway to the level of the balcony, and now too Amyr's mental cry was a sharp bark of frustration, rage and hatred in the Hrossak's mind:

"Tarra, we must act now—though I fear we're already too late. But at least we must try. Perhaps if we break this circle it will help. Come on, let's see if these crazy men can dance and chant their way through cold steel!"

In the next moment the two threw off their cassocks, turned back to back and commenced their gory work. Such was the tension in Tarra that the orgy of death which followed was almost a relief, though he was not, and never had been, a killer born. They slew, and as they slew continued to move to the left, Amyr pursuing and cutting down them that danced away from him, Tarra meeting his prey head-on and piling them up in a mound.

Such slaughter could not go long unnoticed or unanswered. The yellow-robes directly across the sweep of the balcony saw all at once, came to a disbelieving halt, began pointing, mouths agape. Others, piling into Tarra's kill, were tripped or skidded in blood and were brought down, creating even more of a blockage. Now outraged priests came clambering, screaming at the Hrossak across the mound of their slain colleagues; and others made a concerted rush on Amyr, however hampered by the narrowness of the way, which would only permit of two abreast.

Dispatching one screaming yellow-robe and toppling him over the balcony's low wall, Tarra found himself confronted by two more, flying at him in unison. He rammed home his rapier in one, but the other—quick-thinking if totally uncaring—immediately slammed both his covered forearms down on the flat of the thin blade where it skewered his staggering colleague. The blade broke, leaving Tarra with only the useless hilt.

"A curse on all puny swords!" roared the Hrossak. "Come on then, you bald-pates—come taste the iron in a steppe-man's knuckles!"

A snarling pack of them perched on and behind the mound of their dead, tensed to spring. Amyr backed up to Tarra, his face and hands black, body and limbs a liquid red on silver. The yellow-robes crept inward, closing in on the pair like a pincer. And—

"*Hold!*" came a great, rumbling bass command from the centre of the chamber, a magnified blast of sound which drowned all else in its sheer volume and shuddering intensity. "Back from them, back! They are mine—especially the silver one. Hail, Suhm-yi! I had expected you—but not in the very hour of my triumph, to make it so much sweeter. Hail, creature of the Inner Isles—hail and farewell!"

Gorgos' hideous eyes, huge, black as night and bulging, had not once shifted from their vertical staring; but while his nightmare body continued to pulsate and expand, entirely covering the dais now, a yet more fearful metamorphosis commenced. Seeing it, Tarra no longer felt entirely in command of his own senses. The thing was so utterly—

"Is that . . . that . . . is it real?" he gasped.

"Oh, yes," Amyr answered out loud. "It's real, and I fear it's the end of us. The end of everything!" His voice was full of despair, full of horror.

Growing out of Gorgos' side, a black, hairy stalk had stretched itself out, snaking across the mosaic floor. As it approached the wall directly beneath the balcony where they stood, frozen in their dread, so the end bloated out like some loathsome fungus, forming the spindly-legged likeness of an enormous spider. And anchored to Gorgos by hairy stalk, up the wall the red-eyed nightmare crept, until the tips of its forelegs appeared, chitin-tipped and tapping on the top of the balcony wall.

Now Gorgos' head turned stiffly on its neck and his black eyes glared at the pair. And matching that glare, his slit of a mouth curved upward in monstrous smile. "The forces are unified!" his booming bass voice declared. "I am Gorgos—soon to be immortal—*soon to be Lord of all the Thromb!*"

It was now or never: Tarra's idea crystallized.

The swords where they flew: one of them flew out of true! Its jewelled hilt tilted a little and its blade vibrated as from some strange imbalance. Oh, the swordsmith's work was good, the jeweller's, too, and both had served their purposes; but they were only human and the original blade had been forged out beyond the stars.

"So be it!" Tarra shouted. "But if I'm to die it's with my once-true sword in my hand. And it's with fire, not fear, in my heart. So to hell with you, Gorgos!"

Amyr read it in Tarra's mind, came to his aid.

As Tarra leaped up on to the balcony wall and teetered there for a moment, getting his balance, so the Suhm-yi sliced at the Gorgos-spider-appendage as it hauled itself into sight. This served to distract its attention from the Hrossak, and in the next moment—

Tarra leaped, head-first, arms stretching before him.

His flight was meant to intercept that of the circling swords—one of them, anyway—but later he would give the success of that wild leap greater consideration, and wonder perhaps if he were not somehow assisted. Certainly the way his fingers met, firmly clamped upon and dragged the scimitar from orbit might hint of some divine aid or interference. But anyway, the connection *was* made; the familiar, brightly-jewelled hilt *was* grasped, the scimitar *was* snatched, however reluctantly, from its weird sorcerous circling. But having snatched it, instead of rushing down through four man-lengths of thin air to the marble floor, Tarra clung to the sword and almost felt himself lowered, as if some power futilely sought to hold that unruly blade in orbit; so that he came down feet-first and with scarce a jolt. And no sooner his feet upon the floor—lo!—the sword was his, all flightiness going out of it at once, its metal weighing heavy and deadly in his hand.

"Mine!" he snarled his satisfaction—and without pause brought the fresh-forged blade slicing down to sever Gorgos' hairy spider-stalk.

Such a howling and a gibbering then! Purplish pus spurted, and the bloated monstrosity on the dais writhed and bayed its torment in a bass, disbelieving, utterly astonished tone, different again from previous voice of ultimate triumph: "No, *no!* The forces must remain unified! I must let them in . . . I have promised . . . they will exact payment!"

The place was full of an awful stench now, and Tarra heard from behind him an abominable *squelching* and clashing. He turned, saw Amyr lizarding down the wall from the balcony—saw also the pseudo-spider where it had fallen to the floor and now collapsed in upon itself, visibly rotting, its legs clattering a terrible staccato rhythm of death upon the runic floor.

Overhead, the two remaining scimitars had gone into mad orbits all their own; they banged against the high beams, clanged on the copper of the dome, scythed among the dumbfounded, now terrified yellow-robes where they gawped and gasped all about the balcony. Also, there was anger in the unseen, alien energies now; their manifestation of flickering fire, forming the writhing column of blue-green light 'twixt ceiling-portal and dais, began to sway and bend and vibrate like small tornado, losing its coherency. It seemed the very air shrieked, whipping in small panic-ridden gusts all about.

Amyr bounded to Tarra's side. "I think we've won. Rather, I think *you've* won!"

Gorgos heard, or somehow knew what he had said. "Not yet!" came his bass croak like belch of thunder. Pseudopods sprouted, became hooks of chitin, bony claws and pincers, all lashing toward the two where they stood frozen in horror. But this time Amyr was quickest off the mark. *"You've done your bit, Hrossak,"* he said in Tarra's mind as he made a dive under the flailing, deadly barrier and on to the dais. *"Now it's my turn!"*

Then he was on his feet within the tossing, clashing wall of murderous armour, where now he seemed caught up in Gorgos' loathsome body tentacles. For a moment Tarra thought the horror had him—but then there came bright flash of rapier's razor edge and Gorgos's head leapt free, spurting, bounding from the dais to roll free on mosaic floor.

Tarra turned his face away then in disgust at the incredibly swift *katabolism* which took place atop the dais, and the indescribable stench that rose up—which must surely be poisonous—as Gorgos' pseudo-tissues turned to steaming slime and slopped over the altarstone's rim. And, "There!" cried Amyr Arn. "Suhm-yi curse fulfilled, Gorgos. And how will you unify the forces now, eh?"

After which . . . madness!

All hell seemed let loose beneath the great dome. The small, sentient winds gathered into one howling gust which roared out through the ceiling portal, extinguishing the fires in the hanging lamps as it went; the spiralling column of blue-green radiation whirled faster yet, swaying erratically as it commenced a withdrawal; the yellow-robed priests moaned and screamed their terror, divesting themselves of their cassocks as they fled from the chamber en masse, their crush entirely blocking the exit, so that their milling bodies came pouring over the balcony in a churning flood of terrified humanity.

Tarra and Amyr sprang away from the dais, and yet at the same time felt pulled by some awful suction toward it. Overhead the portal was closing, and still the frenziedly whirling blue-green tongue of flickering energies withdrew. Its tip cleared the portal as the edges of glass approached a closure;

and down through the final gap lashed sudden lightning in a prolonged burst, splitting the dais asunder and sending chunks of marble flying. Gorgos' body—what was left of it—seemed snatched up in lightning fork, dragged aloft, elongating and separating into vile lumps as it went. These . . . *portions* . . . of the magician, crashing against the sharp sectors of the closing window, burst portal and frame outwards into the night. Tarra and Amyr felt themselves lifted as by a great hand, dragged toward the gaping, broken portal. Up to the level of the balcony they were lifted, weightless as thistledown, and for one mind-searing moment it seemed they too must be drawn out into the spaces between the stars. But then—

—It was as if the chamber breathed in a great breath of air—a sort of cleansing psychic implosion—before expelling it in a mighty shout of denial. Gorgos should never have been, he was no more, the sane world was determined to be rid of him and every last trace of his works. And the same great hand which had picked Tarra and Amyr up, now hurled them sideways across the curving balcony, out through a shattering oval window and down toward Death in a shower of coarse glass fragments. Except Death was not expecting them, had made no arrangements to greet them, indeed did not yet want them.

Instead they whirled down, hugging together, through another window—this one thicker, circular, and laying along a horizontal plane—and finally plunged down upon a great round bed piled high with softest silk cushions. And there they lay, bruised and scratched and winded, but entirely intact, getting their breath as the world stopped whirling.

Amyr was first up, then Tarra, snatching up his jewelled sword from the tumbled bed. And when the Hrossak turned to stare about this lesser chamber beneath this lesser dome of copper—

What should he see but Amyr Arn, clasping to his bosom a sobbing creature, infinitely lovely and all of a silver sheen, even as he himself. Ulli Eys, certainly, oracle no more but glad prisoner now of a greater power far than any alien magick.

Then, all three, they fled the place—down into its mazy lower levels, through the empty, groaning corridors and halls, and out into the teeth of a suddenly raging storm— while behind them the temple tottered and was broken, and all the domes fell in upon the place, and the Temple of Secret Gods went the way of its monstrous master and became less than nothing.

And not a yellow-robe in sight, for all who lived had fled, the soldiers with them, so that all that remained of Gorgos' dream was an empty, high-walled square of ruins where not even the weeds would grow, and which from that day forward was shunned . . .

WITHIN THE HOUR the storm had blown itself out, the clouds had all raced madly away, clearing the sky, and the people of Klühn had come out to light their lamps and candles and dance in the streets. And all through the night they danced and feasted, and all the shops in the bazaars were thrown open, and everything was free to them who knew how precious was life and liberty. And all and all they had forgotten how sweet and clean the breeze off the sea could be, but would not forget again.

As for Tarra and Amyr and Ulli: they, too, would have stayed and revelled, but they had other things to do. All three, they travelled under the moon and stars, male and female Suhm-yi, commencing their long trek back to crater sea, and Tarra Khash the Hrossak—

Ah! But that's another story . . .